Kenneth Arant

A SNAKE'S RISE

A Snake's Life – Book 3

PROLOGUE

O N A PLANET FURTHER DOWN YGGDRASIL'S branches than any "civilized" world, Orochi found himself sitting at a marble round table with seven other gods and goddesses. Each god had a placard denoting their name and their domain on the table in front of them, which was useful since Orochi recognized few of them. He'd been sealed for the better part of the last five millennia, and most of the other guests were relatively young, so far as gods kept track of that kind of thing, so aside from Carlas: the time god who freed him, and Fieren: a god of forging and armor making, Orochi didn't recognize anyone.

Though that didn't mean much to a group of shapeshifters. Even Orochi had changed his appearance to one closely resembling that of a cobra-beastman to accommodate his host's wishes. He was still vastly oversized for his race, but he preferred it that way. It served as a reminder to those around him who he was and what he was capable of.

The—he hesitated to call it the sky, as the twitching and oozing mass of tentacles that surrounded the planet made that difficult. Aside from the nightmarish skyline, the rest of the scenery was quite beautiful: Waist high white flowers were as innumerable as blades of grass, trees of vibrant green produced succulent fruits by the hundreds, and the all-encompassing eye of the squid surrounding the planet cast a silver light down upon the planet's surface.

Eden: That was this place's original name. Once upon a time it was a paradise, unrivaled in beauty and security. It was the birthplace of dozens of races; however, all were eventually cast out for one reason or another. Now the planet belonged to the host of this little get together, and it was one of her prized possessions.

There was a flash of golden light off to Orochi's left, which prompted everyone, save him, to look. Orochi knew who it was, after all—there was only one empty seat left and no one would be stupid enough to show up without an invitation.

A woman even larger than Orochi himself stepped around the table and sat in the high-backed chair at one end. She was twice as wide as she was tall. Eight spindly tentacles served as legs and carried her to her seat. Her unnerving eyes were pitch black save for the silver pinprick in the center that served as her pupils. The pinpricks danced wildly as she absorbed everything about the group sitting before her.

Orochi amused himself with the idea of the chair exploding into splinters the moment she sat down but knew it wouldn't happen. Like the gods that occupied them, the table and chairs were divine in nature. It would take more than a little weight to break one.

The chair let out an ominous *creak* as soon as she sat down, and Orochi had to suppress a smile.

Fieren led the gods in standing and bowing to the newcomer. "Praise be to the mother." The other six copied his action almost immediately, while Orochi remained seated. He would sooner bow his head to that Torga whelp.

"**Orochi.**" Mother's voice was oily and slid over his ears like a vat of grease. Oh, how Orochi hated her voice. "**Have you no respect for your savior?**" she asked, her words ending in a gap-toothed smile that made Orochi wanna claw out his own eyes.

"I do. But I'll not bow to you," he responded flatly.

"You insolent—" Fieren began. Mother silenced him with a look and a smile that sent shivers down Orochi's spine, even though it hadn't been directed at him.

"**No matter. So long as you do your part, I shall graciously overlook this breach of decorum,**" she said grandly. "**Now, onto other business. Where are we on project Ragnarök?**"

"We're advancing at a steady pace," a young goddess replied immediately. She had raven colored hair, purple eyes with eleven concentric rings, and skin the color of gold. "Seven of the nine Origin seals have been deconstructed and the corresponding beasts have begun to move. However, we—uh—it would seem the Devourer has somehow escaped his prison. If we don't find a way to remove him from the equation, he could interfere with our plans."

"**Orochi will handle this matter.**"

"Of course." Orochi wished he could've left at that moment and do just that, but he knew the head cow wouldn't tolerate it. So, he was stuck counting the seconds until he could leave and never look back.

CHAPTER ONE

REINA, DONNA, AND LEON PASSED THROUGH THE market district on their way to the castle. While Leon and Donna were still in their adventuring gear, Reina had changed into something a bit more comfortable. Namely, a baggy gray tunic with a hood, a black skirt that hung down to just above her knees, and a pair of black leather shoes. Her hair was pulled into a messy ponytail, and she had dark bags under her eyes.

When Reina had first spotted Donna after walking through the door leading into the Inn, she just knew that her friend had guessed what happened from the knowing smile she'd tried to hide. She'd been in a similar state once or twice, after all.

Leon, on the other hand, had no idea what had happened and so he'd spent the past hour bugging her about it. Thankfully, for the sake of Reina's sanity and Leon's continued existence, they had just passed through the castle gates and spotted a familiar face.

"Hey, Ayla."

The young elf looked up from the book she'd been reading on the castle lawn and smiled. "Hey," she replied after closing her book and sitting it on her lap. "How're you feeling after your walk?"

"Like shit. My legs are killing me," was Reina's near-instant reply. Not only were her legs really sore, but so was a decent chunk of her other muscles.

"What happened to your legs? Did you fall or something?" Leon asked with genuine concern in his voice.

"Yeah, Reina. Did you fall or something?" Ayla said in a mock concerned tone.

Reina narrowed her eyes at the younger woman. She'd learned at breakfast this morning that both Ayla and Findral had overheard her and Torga's reunion. Actually, it seemed half the castle already knew about the two of them getting together. That didn't mean she was going to just tell them what happened behind those doors. Nope, that information was exclusive to her and Torga. "Yeah, you could say that," Reina mumbled.

"From the way you've been walking, you must have banged up your knees pretty badly. Would also explain why they're so red." Donna spoke up with an innocent smile on her face.

"I'll say. You wouldn't believe the screams and moans I heard last night. You'd have thought someone was trying to kill her," Ayla added with a similar smile on her face.

"Oh, bite me." Reina let out a frustrated sigh.

"Can't believe I'm saying this, but no thanks. I saw what happened to those poor ninjas, and I have no desire to end up on the receiving end of that." Donna hesitated for a moment, then a lecherous grin appeared on her face. "We'll, maybe a little bit."

"Hey, watch it," Reina warned.

"Oh, c'mon, Reina. Live a little." Donna threw her arm around Reina's shoulders and pulled her in close. "I know you've thought about it once or twice," she whispered into Reina's ear.

The hot breath on her sensitive ear caused Reina's face to heat up. She pushed Donna away before clearing her throat. "Actually, I'm glad I ran into you, Ayla. Have you seen Al—I mean, Torga anywhere? He was already gone when I woke up this morning."

"Dad was? Oh, right, the royal families of Asgard and Greece decided to have their peace talks today. The king asked Dad to join them, personally."

"Any idea why?"

"Nope, but knowing Dad, it's probably Odin's way of ensuring the Greeks won't try anything to stab them in the back."

"See, Reina. I told you it was nothing serious," Donna said reassuringly. "I'm sure everything will be alright. After all, Torga doesn't seem like the kind of guy to get himself in trouble without cause."

Reina and Ayla turned and gave Donna a wide-eyed stare.

"What?" Donna asked.

"Nothing. I just realized that you haven't had the chance to meet Dad yet, have you?"

"No, but I can usually sense these kinds of things," Donna explained.

Reina and Ayla gave each other a glance then started to chuckle.

"Oh, sweetheart. I have got to introduce you—the both of you, at dinner tonight. I'm thinking you'll be surprised," Reina said, not even caring that a bit of her former accent bled into her voice.

～ ～ ～

I grit my teeth and shoved down the all-consuming urge to punch Zeus in his perfectly sculpted face. The small meeting hall near the rear of Gungnir wasn't nearly big enough for eight people plus his overbearing ego.

Aside from myself and the blowhard in question, Odin, Frigga, and Thor were present for the Asgardian side. With Zeus came his wife, Hera, his daughter, Athena, and his son, Ares. A regiment of soldiers accompanied them across the border, but they were forced to wait outside Gungnir. Zeus protested this, stating that they needed their guards to prevent any assassination attempts, but Odin had given him enough face as it was.

The arrogant twat had showed up before sunrise with half his family in tow, demanding to know why the wedding hadn't been called off yet. How he'd known the wedding was still being planned, we didn't know. Though Odin didn't want to admit it, I assumed the obvious answer was correct.

Zeus had spies inside Taranis.

This led me down the rabbit hole of thinking about the numerous other hostiles that could have all manner of spies inside the city: watching, waiting, and plotting against us.

Taranis wasn't safe, for any of us.

"I'll not have my daughter's good name besmirched by some elf bimbo," Zeus growled, his fist hitting the table with enough force to crack the wood. "You'll hold up your end of the bargain, Odin. Or by the gods there will be war."

"I'll not force my heir into this political farce," Odin calmly replied, not even deigning to use the other king's name. "I told you from the beginning that the marriage would go forth, or be stopped, entirely at my son's discretion. To which—need I remind you—you agreed."

"That was before I knew of his—tastes," Zeus said disdainfully.

"Okay," I spoke up, unable to keep quiet any longer. "I was going to let the two of you argue this out, but I think I've heard enough."

"No one asked for your opinion. Unless you're an upstart king I somehow failed to take notice of, you have no right to involve yourself in a conversation between nobles. Begone." Zeus dismissed me with a wave of his hand.

I tightly gripped the arms of my chair, accidentally fracturing the wood beneath my palms. I stood up and placed my palms on the table. "I'm in a good mood and do not wish to ruin it by staining my hands with your blood, so I'll give you a simple warning instead. Lose the attitude, or I'll break you."

Zeus scoffed. He stood to his full height of seven feet and looked down on me with pure disdain. "Threaten me again, boy. I dare you."

"It wasn't a threat, your royal assness. I'm simply informing you that this course of action isn't wise."

"Is that so?" Zeus laughed. "Who is this, Odin? And why is he here?"

"He's Ayla's father. As for why he's here, that should be obvious even to you."

"So, you're the elf's father, are you? The one I was warned about."

"He doesn't look like much," Ares said, speaking up for the first time since the meeting began.

"I'm a grower, not a shower," I replied sarcastically. "Point is, I don't want to hear another untoward word about my daughter fall out of that gaping pit you call a mouth. You said you wanted a war, right Zeus? Keep talking and you'll get one."

"You, I like." Zeus smiled at me. "You've got courage; I respect that. But you're still involving yourself in matters far above your station. So, why don't you just—crawl back to whatever rock you live under and leave this to your betters?"

"Sure, let me know when she gets here, and I'll gladly leave it in her capable hands. Until then, I see none."

"Odin, this commoner is thinning what little patience I had left to put up with your outlandishness. Make a decision right now: Will there be a wedding, or will there be war?"

"Both, I think," Odin replied immediately. "You have placed demand after demand at my feet, and in some ways, I acquiesced to them. But that ends now. My son will wed whomever he so chooses."

"I see. Then there's no need for me to continue wasting time here." Zeus grabbed his wife by the arm and yanked her to her feet, then he motioned for Athena and Ares to precede him out the door. "You'll regret this, Odin. Mark my words, you'll regret this."

"That may be, but if there will be a war, then I'll deal with my regret over your maggot infested corpse."

Zeus gave us one final glance before leaving the meeting hall.

"Escort our guests back to their soldiers," Odin said to the table in front of him.

"*At once,*" a calm, almost emotionless voice replied from somewhere nearby. I assumed that to be Heimdall—Odin's right hand and Guardian of Asgard—or what was left of it.

"I have got to get him to show me how he does that," I said in awe.

"It's his birthright. There's nothing to teach," Thor replied.

"Shame. That's a damn useful skill," I sighed. I patted Thor on the shoulder, sent a nod to Odin and Frigga, then left the room with a request for them to inform me if the Grecians tried anything.

I stepped onto the deck and sucked in a mouthful of air. It wasn't necessary for me to breathe anymore, but the feeling still helped relax me. Not breathing just felt—wrong. I nodded to the few crew members I spotted on my way to the departure ramp and headed for the city.

Taranis was a beautifully strange place: Home to around fifteen million people, it was built with technologies from multiple different eras. On one street corner you could see shops selling swords, spears, small handguns, and rifles that fired the magical equivalent of a fifty-caliber round. My trip through the market this morning had me gawking like a tourist. I was sure I'd attracted my fair share of attention from the crowds, but I didn't care. Let them stare and giggle at me all they wanted; it was just the opinions of the unimportant.

Through one of the windows, I spotted a black, skintight leather suit. It was on a female mannequin about Reina's size, so I inevitably found myself imagining her wearing it—and then I somehow found myself inside the store.

"Can I help you?" a broad-shouldered older woman asked. She was wearing a stained white apron and had her hair tied into a tight bun behind her head.

"Sorry, I saw this armor through the window and couldn't help myself."

"Ah, good eye," she said in a friendly tone. "That's made out of wyvern leather. Tough enough to stop a blade or spear, though an axe could prove troublesome. More importantly, it's resistant to magic, so most small caliber magic rounds will bounce right off of it." She gave me a once over, then smiled strangely. "I must admit, I don't think I crafted one in your size. You'll need to give me a few days if you want one."

"No," I laughed. "It's for my wife. Actually, I'd need one for both my wife and daughter."

"I see. Well, you'll need to bring them in so I can make adjustments."

"When should we come by?"

"Whenever, child. I'm much less busy since my daughter took over the business."

I smirked at that. "I'll drag them by this afternoon."

~ ~ ~

"You know—when you said you'd drag them by, I never imagined you meant you'd literally drag them here," the old woman said while looking at the two women squirming to get out of my arms. "I'd assumed it was merely a figure of speech."

"It was. They're just embarrassed about being carried—"

"On that note—put me the fuck down, Albert! I swear to Christ, I'll kick your ass for this!"

"Who's Christ?" Ayla asked. Compared to Reina, I thought she was taking this whole thing in stride. Then again, she was used to riding around on my head, so being carried wasn't anything new to her. "Is that a human god?"

"I've never heard of them," the old woman replied. "Must be some newfangled god."

"What, no—Albert, put me down!" She sent a hard elbow into my temple—or I assumed it was meant to be; it's tough to tell when you can't feel it. I put them down anyway and gave Ayla a wink. She giggled at me, then forced a frown on her face and stepped out of my arm's reach.

Message received: Don't pick me up like that again. I didn't think she truly hated it; gods knew I'd carried her around enough back in my mercenary days to get her used to it. Then again, she was fifteen the last time I'd properly carried her around… Maybe she was too old for that now? I was having trouble remembering what was socially acceptable and what wasn't, specifically when it came to stuff like this. I suppose spending decades alone with only myself for company wasn't the best thing for my already lackluster grasp on human culture, and probably knocked what few screws I had left loose.

I'm still surprised I didn't end up as some hermit up in the mountains somewhere. But I think my ties to Ayla, Findral, and the others are what kept me from losing sight of myself.

I refocused on the conversations around me and caught the tail end of Reina and Ayla discussing price—which I'd completely forgotten about until now.

"A suit of this craftsmanship is worth every coin; I can promise you that," the old woman insisted.

"A suit of leather armor is not worth fifteen thousand gold. Especially not one made of wyvern leather. Drake leather, maybe—dragon leather, certainly—but not wyvern."

"Ah, but these suits were made out of the rare ice wyvern. They're rarely seen outside of the Jötnar home world, and I only came across it by chance when a group of adventurers returned from the ruins of Asgard. You miss out on this deal, you're not likely to get it again—"

"Wait, that's where you got the leather?" Ayla asked.

"Surprised?" The old woman smirked at her.

"Seeing as Dad's the one responsible for killing them, and thus all proceeds from the collection—and *sale*—of anything made from their corpses rightfully belong to him... Yeah, a little bit."

The old woman's face paled. "S-surely you jest. The adventurers are the ones responsible for killing the creatures. They even had the quest tag to prove it."

"I was there when he killed them." Ayla looked up at me then. "Tell her, old man."

"Did something like that happen?" I asked, genuinely confused by her statement.

"Of course! Don't you remember?"

"I think I see what's going on here. You don't wanna pay, so you're trying to pull the rhinox skin over my eyes. Well, it won't happen. Not to old Grissom."

"Wait—" I interjected. "Was that when I killed the ice dragon?" I asked Ayla, to which she nodded. I turned my attention back to the old woman—while dutifully ignoring the wide-eyed look of surprise on Reina's face—and nodded my head. "I do remember that. Sorry, my memory isn't what it used to be, I guess." I chuckled. "Old age will do that to you."

Grissom harrumphed and folded her muscular arms over her chest. "How convenient," she snarked. "Unless you can prove the wyvern and the d-dragon were killed by you, I'm not giving you one dull coin. You hear me?

Not one!" She placed her hands on my chest and shoved. All she succeeded in doing was pushing herself backwards, and tripping over her own foot, but I got the message loud and clear.

I shrugged in response to the glare she shot me, and escorted Ayla and Reina out of the store. "Don't worry, I'll find something else," I told them.

"Actually, old man, I don't really need anything else. The tortoise armor suits me fine; anything more would be overkill." Ayla waved my concerned look away. "I mean it. I don't need anything."

"Same here, Albert. I have my own weapons and armor," Reina added. "The suit I usually wear is made out of Boreal Lion leather, and my weapons are made out of Quicksilver. Besides, I have my own money. If I want something, I'll pay for it. No need for you to waste your money."

"You're sure?"

Reina quirked a brow and gave me a "really?" look. "Yes, I'm sure. You know I've always hated people buying me things."

"Oh—right. Of course." I chuckled. I guess I'd forgotten that. Reina was always fiercely independent and hated receiving gifts, or what she viewed as charity, from anyone. Christmas and birthdays usually turned into a knock-down, drag-out brawl between us because neither wanted the other to buy them anything. "Well, in order to keep this trip from being completely worthless, would the two of you care to join me for lunch?" I asked. To be completely honest, I was relieved to know that aspect of her personality was as how I remembered it. Given my memory problems lately, it was nice to know some things still made sense.

"Sure," Reina said with a kind smile on her face.

"I'd love to!" Ayla said happily. "It's been such a long time since we sat down and had a meal together!"

That gave me pause as I tried to remember the last time we'd sat down together and just ate for the sake of spending time together, and I realized that I couldn't. *Has it really been that long?* A horrified realization struck me, and I plastered a smile on my face. *I haven't taken her out for a quiet lunch—just the two of us—since I was inside the elf puppet.*

"Where should we go?" Ayla asked.

"Don't know—you've been here longer than I have. Any recommendations?"

"There's a great little dwarvish place around the corner. Reina, have you ever tried dwarvish food?"

"I have. I've actually been dying for some sweet rolls."

"I'm... kind of lost here, girls. Dwarvish food?"

"C'mon, old man. Don't you remember that little restaurant we tried back in Tialarthas? The one with the earth basilisk steak?"

"Come to think of it, I do remember something like that. Was that dwarvish?" I asked, the vaguest memory appearing in my mind.

"Wait, Tialarthas: As in, the place that up until a few years ago was overrun by the undead? You guys were there?" Reina asked, tilting her head adorably and looking up at me.

"There? We were the ones who solved their undead problem, weren't we, old man?" Ayla proudly announced, seeming to puff out her chest a little more.

"I do seem to recall that happening, yes," I laughed. It was nice to see Ayla acting her age again. Ever since

I'd awoken as a Serpentine dragon, Ayla had been desperate to display her maturity. So, it was a good sign that she was acting like the young woman she was.

"Well, this sounds like a story I need to hear." Reina winked up at me and gave me a crooked grin. She reached out and took my hand and we followed along behind Ayla as she recounted our adventures in Tialarthas.

CHAPTER TWO

I PUSHED REINA AGAINST THE WALL, TAKING BOTH OF her hands in my much larger one and pinning them above her head. I kissed her passionately, putting all of my bottled-up feelings into it as our mouths overlapped. This was both to show her how I felt, and to remind myself that she was real—and here—in front of me.

I released her hands, and she slowly lowered them to my shoulders, trailing her fingers through my hair, before stopping at the back of my neck and gripping the collar of my tunic. I placed my hands on the small of her back and pulled her against me. Her body was… much more delicate than I remembered. *No, I'm the one that changed. I'm no longer the man I once was.*

Time became meaningless as we stood there, in the room she'd been given by the king and queen of Asgard, making out like horny teenagers.

I paused in my efforts and allowed Reina to catch her breath.

"This—isn't—fair," she panted. "Why am I the only one gasping for air?" Reina directed the full force of her pouting face at me.

"One of the perks of my new body. Don't worry about it too much," I replied, smiling down at her. I used my thumb to wipe a bead of sweat off of her cheek, then I leaned down and kissed her again, much softer this time. Before I was trying to show the depth of my feelings, and what I'd been trying desperately to ignore since I'd lost her. That soul crushing loneliness only someone who's lost the most important thing in their lives could understand.

But now—I was just a man kissing his wife, and I loved her just as much now as I ever had before.

A series of rapid-fire knocks on our door pulled us out of our own little world and back into reality.

"I don't know who that is, and I don't care. But the world better be ending or so help me God, I'm gonna start wringing necks," I growled under my breath. Every time Reina and I tried to be alone, we were interrupted by something or someone needing Reina's immediate attention.

It was a bit of a pain in the ass being married to a hero, but oh so worth it in the end.

I stalked over to the door and pulled it open. I frowned at the teenage servant girl waiting with a cart of covered dishes. I motioned for her to step aside as I ducked under the door frame and looked up and down the hallway to see who was watching.

"Did you order food?" I asked Reina.

"No? Did you?"

"If I had, I wouldn't have asked," I snarked. I felt a smack across my rear end, and I raised an eyebrow at the servant girl, whose face had turned beet red. "We didn't order food; you should take this and go before you hear something that'll ruin your ears."

"Oh, I wouldn't mind," the girl who couldn't be any older than Ayla said in a sultry voice.

"I would." Reina said, stepping around my body to face the girl. With a smile on her face, Reina reached out and grabbed the door handle. She slammed the door in the girl's face then turned to me. "Being sarcastic, flirting with servant girls, what am I going to do with you?" she said with an exasperated sigh.

I snaked my arm around her waist, then picked her up and pulled her against my body. "The question, my dear, isn't what you're going to do with me, it's what I'm going to do to you." She squeaked in surprise as I tossed her across the room to land on the bed. Before she could move, I was on top of her again and I had plans to make her do much more than squeak.

~ ~ ~

I was tracing the lines of my wife's sleeping face with my eyes when an irritating voice intruded on my moment of peace.

"Oh, most powerful god of hunger, I beseech you! Appear before your most humble servant in his time of need!" the annoying voice yelled from the recesses of my mind.

I frowned at the interruption and shook my head. A few seconds later, the voice repeated itself again—and again—and a fourth time. By the six or seventh time, I'd given up trying to ignore it and had left the room so my grumblings wouldn't disturb Reina.

"Oh, most powerful god of hunger, I beseech you! Appear before your most humble servant in his time of need!" the voice yelled again. Only this time, I answered.

"Where are you?" I whispered.

The voice in my mind went quiet for several seconds. *"My lord?"* The voice replied in a much quieter tone.

"Where are you?"

I'm not sure how, but I could somehow *feel* the owner of the voice's panic as some kind of link connected us. I could see him now; an overweight old priest inside what appeared to be a dilapidated church. He was short, balding, and had incredibly pale skin.

I wondered where he was, and my "vision" responded by blurring momentarily. When it cleared, I was looking at a small church that sat on the boundary between an ocean and a mammoth mountain range. At one time, it must have been absolutely beautiful: The walls were made of white marble and some kind of dark purple stone that I couldn't identify, the floor was the color of fresh snow, and mesmerizing stained-glass windows lined the upper walls. But it was a mere shadow of its former self. Years of disrepair and abandonment had taken its toll on the once beautiful building.

The most surprising thing about my vision? I intuitively knew *where* the church was. It was like someone had programmed a set of coordinates into my brain.

"Y—You're not my lord."

"No, I'm most definitely not," I replied, returning my attention to the priest.

"S—stay away! Don't come here!"

"It's too late for that. Because I've found you." I teleported before I lost whatever hold I had on our link.

~ ~ ~

"You know, my wife would absolutely love it here," I said offhandedly. It truly was a shame that my first time visiting this holy place was being marred by the pathetic man currently groveling at my feet.

Now that I'd gotten a better look at him, I was absolutely certain that the man was a priest, or he was at one time. He may have worn the brown priest's garb, but he was a far cry from the priests I'd met in *either* life: His hairless head glistened in sweat, his three chins quivered in fear as he begged for his life, and the stench of piss surrounded him.

Even if he hadn't already annoyed the hell out of me, he wouldn't have made the best first impression.

"Forgive me, my lord, for I have sinned and called this demon into your most holy of places!" the man cried for the fifth time.

I stared down at the pitiful man. It hadn't taken me long to figure out that I'd somehow hijacked the prayers meant for another god of hunger. But I'd have to think on the how and why *after* I made the annoying man stop talking.

"Forgive me, my lord, for I have—"

"If you finish that sentence, I'm going to rip your tongue out and make you taste your own ass."

The priest's mouth snapped shut and he backpedaled away. His fat rolls heaved as his lungs desperately tried to pull in enough oxygen to keep him from passing out, but his fear would've made that a difficult task for someone *half* his size. So, he fainted.

That's just sad.

I stepped off the altar I'd appeared on and began looking around in earnest. The altar was on a raised dais near the rear wall. It held a statue that depicted a thin man in white robes standing tall above a mob of sickly looking humans. Just out of the humans' reach, he held a basket of fruits and vegetables in his left hand.

The statue wore a wicked grin as it watched the humans reach for the food.

And people call me cruel. I turned away from the altar. Just then, an idea formed in my mind. *Actually, this whole situation just might work in my favor.*

I walked over to the downed priest, intending to slap him awake—then I caught sight of my reflection in a broken mirror on the wall and realized why the priest assumed I was a demon.

A pair of glowing orange eyes met mine through the mirror and I grimaced.

Maybe I should fix that before I wake him up? It'd probably be easier for him to answer my questions if he wasn't so scared he fainted again... Less annoying that way too.

I created an image in my mind, then overlapped it with my reflection in the mirror.

The green lights my body was made of broke apart, twisted, then contorted into a much smaller form: that of a ten-year-old boy in clothes much too large for him. I didn't bother changing my eye color or trying to change the appearance of my clothes; the brown tunic and black pants I'd borrowed from Thor would serve me fine.

I ran tiny hands through my wavy brown hair to straighten it, then nodded to myself.

"Testing—1, 2." I shook my head at my voice and tried again. "Testing?" The high-pitched sound of a child's voice surprised me so much, I accidentally laughed out loud. *This is definitely going onto the "show Reina later" list.*

I walked over to the downed priest in my new, and hopefully less threatening, form and lightly slapped his face.

"Sir? Are you okay, sir?"

The priest's eyes opened, and his entire body jerked away.

"No! Stay away from me foul demon!" he screamed hysterically.

I pretended to be surprised and jumped away from the screaming priest. "Demon!? Where!?"

The priest seemed confused, then hurriedly looked around the room. "The demon! Where did the demon go!?"

"I don't know! I never saw it!"

The priest frantically scanned the ceiling and walls before he slowly climbed to his feet and hobbled towards the altar. "I must alert the most holy, at once!"

"Yeah, you do that."

The priest dropped to his knees and urgently began chanting the same prayer that had drawn my attention.

While the priest was chanting, I walked over to one of the pews and laid down with my feet propped on the armrest. *Not the brightest bulb in the room, is he?*

Not long after the priest began chanting, a glowing yellow portal appeared at the base of the altar and a startlingly tall and thin man stepped through. The man was eight or nine feet tall, with long black hair that hung down to his lower back, emotionless white eyes that lacked any sort of pupil, and sallow skin. He wore a snow-white robe that revealed his frail looking arms and pooled on the floor behind him.

Finally. I sighed. I stood up from the pew and made my way over to them.

"Why have you called me here, Robart?"

"My lord, I—"

"Was just leaving." I grabbed the priest by the neck of his robe and hurled him backward.

The priest slammed into the rotting double doors with a sickening *Crunch* and slid through the mud on the ground outside the church.

The god barely glanced towards the priest before his emotionless eyes zeroed in on me.

"Who are you?" he asked in a completely flat voice.

"Oh, you know, just a lost god looking for home."

"Do not joke with me, godling. Do you know who I am?"

I glanced over my shoulder at the unmoving priest, then back to the god.

"Obviously not the god of Weight Watchers."

A flicker of emotion entered the god's eyes before he could stop it. "I, am Jorthas, Elder God of Hunger and Pain!"

"Neat."

Jorthas took a deep, calming breath and glared over his hooked nose at me.

"Normally, I would cause you to feel the pain of a thousand deaths for annoying me." He took another breath, "But I am a merciful god. I will forgive you this once if you tell me who your patron is, godling."

"Well, gee-willakers, mister! That sure is awfully nice of ya!" I cheered. I shot the god a wide smile. "But wholly unnecessary," I sighed in my normal voice.

My small fist lashed out and slammed into the god's left kneecap. Jorthas' knee broke like a dried twig and he collapsed to the floor with a scream.

I quickly covered the god's mouth with my hand, pinned his body to the ground via an intense burst of gravity, and glared daggers into his eyes. "We're going to have a little chat, and this is how it's going to work: I ask a question, you answer me in ten seconds or less, or I break another bone. Any attempts to leave this place without my express permission will result in your immediate death. Blink if you understand."

Jorthas narrowed his eyes and I felt a slight pinprick of pain inside my head. So, I snapped his fibula with a well-placed stomp.

The god winced in pain, but he still refused to blink.

"Ah, almost forgot. You're a god of pain, so you're probably used to this, right?"

The god blinked.

"I thought so. Here's what I'm going to do. First, I'm going cut off your eyelids so you can't give in to me. Next, I'm going to break every bone in your body, while you resolutely stare at me in horror. Then, I'm going to cut off your nose, your lips, your ears, your fingers, and finally your toes. I somehow doubt that'll make you give in. So, then I'll start pulling out your veins—"

The god started to rapidly blink.

"I know, I know, you're a god of pain, so that paltry amount is *still* nothing to you, but I'm just getting to the good part. After pulling out your veins, I'll do my damnedest to shove Robart so far up your ass, you'll never get him out. Then, I'll—"

Jorthas screamed into my hand.

"You know what? You're right, talk *is* cheap. Let's just begin, shall we?"

Jorthas jerked his head to one side, freeing his mouth from my palm, and screamed, "Fine! We'll talk—we'll talk!"

"Great!" I cheerfully said. "Now, have you ever heard of a place called Earth?"

~ ∴ ~

Reina awoke to the smell of a bacon and egg-white omelet being waved above her nose.

"Morning, Beautiful. Hungry?"

"Course," she replied through a yawn.

She sat up in bed and gratefully took the proffered bowl from Torga's hand and nodded at the cup of juice he sat down next to her. She breathed in the smell and sighed in contentment.

"Thanks."

"Mmm-hmm." He sat on the foot of the bed and watched her eat for a while.

After a few minutes of comfortable silence, during which Reina finished off her omelet and juice, Torga asked, "How'd you sleep?"

"Fine. It got a little cold during the night, but I managed."

"Winter's coming," he replied around a yawn.

"Sleepy?" Reina asked.

"A bit, yeah. I didn't get much sleep last night," Torga admitted.

"Oh? Why, what happened?"

"Had to go make a noise complaint," Torga replied, a slight smirk on his face.

He's such a weird man, Reina sighed internally.

Chapter Three

THE NEXT DAY, I FOUND MYSELF STANDING BEFORE the king and queen of Asgard. I folded my arms across my chest and dug my fingers into my biceps. Odin was really starting to get on my last nerve, he was so conniving—actually, that might not be a strong enough word to describe the king, but I didn't have the vocabulary to express what I actually felt, and "He's a giant dickbag" wasn't elegant enough for the throne room, no matter how accurate it was.

"You're out of your mind if you think I'm leaving her again." I stared defiantly into Odin's eyes as I said this.

I wasn't afraid of the "King of nothing."

"You swore to us that if we took in Ayla, you would leave and never return. Now we overlooked your returning due to the circumstances surrounding the assassination attempt, but that is behind us now. The fact that you destroyed Asgard—our home for 1,000 generations—is still relevant. Will you keep your word and leave, or will we have to force you out?"

"You couldn't force out a dragon, let alone me. You have no power in this deal, Odin. No leverage, nothing to use against me."

"Really? Are you certain?" Odin waved his hand through the air, creating waves of magic that took the form of a still image. A picture of Ayla and Reina walking side by side through the marketplace hovered a dozen feet above the floor.

My fingers sunk deeper into my biceps. "Do not test me, Odin," I said quietly. "You will not like the consequences."

"Test you? Test. You? Do not test me, Serpent. While I appreciate what you've done for me and my family, that doesn't—will never—make up for your crimes. Not only I, but every living Asgardian wishes for your death. I'm simply warning you of what could happen, that's all."

"Warning received. May I go now, your 'Highness'?" He waved his hand in my direction, in a clear sign of dismissal. "That's very kind of you." I twitched my hand, forcing the gravity of the room to bend to my will. Odin was yanked out of his chair and pulled into my waiting hand. His head fit nicely in my palm, like a basketball or a melon just waiting to be popped. My aura began to lazily flow out of me, creating a visible ball of darkness around my body.

I briefly felt his magic flair in a desperate attempt to defend himself, but it was wiped away almost immediately under the onslaught of my aura. "To repay you for being kind enough to warn me of what could happen if I dared to stay near my own daughter, let me remind you of what you're dealing with." I squeezed his head, forcing a painfilled groan to escape his lips.

I absently noticed the guards advancing on me, but I paid them no mind. Let them come. More food for me. I shook my head. *What kind of thoughts am I having?*

"The—" I cleared my throat. "The only reason I've put up with your demands is that my daughter seems to have taken a liking to you. Remember that the next time you decide to threaten the safety of my wife and daughter." I released my hold on the gravity in the room and allowed it to return to normal.

I let go of Odin's head and watched him drop to his knees. His breath came in great heaves, and his entire body shook like a frightened rabbit.

I pulled my aura back and glowered at him. "The next time you need my assistance with the Greeks—remember this moment and go fuck yourself."

As I left the throne room, I bumped into Thor, Ayla's would-be fiancé, and nodded to him. He'd most likely heard what I'd had to say, but that was fine. It's not like I was trying to hide my disdain for his father, and while I held no ill will towards the queen, the fact that she let her husband act as he did, did not endear her to me.

Thor was... an intriguing amalgamation of his father and his mother. He was prideful, but he had the skills as a warrior to back it up. He was a good leader, and I was sure he would one day be a great king. However, unlike his father, Thor listened to Ayla. He took her words and suggestions seriously and he'd come to me for advice several times since my return.

Above all else, Thor loved Ayla, and that was all that really mattered to me. And as the father of the future queen, the more reasons the current king gave me to want a change in leadership, the more likely he was to simply disappear.

My power flared around me and I teleported away from the castle before I was tempted to speed things along more than they already were.

~ ~ ~

When my magic settled down again, I found myself standing in the living area of mine and Reina's shared room. I looked around for a few moments but didn't see anyone. The room appeared to be empty, though from the state of the clothes on the floor I assumed Reina was here, just in a place where I couldn't see her. "Reina?" I called out.

A few seconds later, she responded from the other room. The space we shared was really a small apartment: It had a living area, bedroom, and a private bathroom, which was a rarity. Because Reina had saved the life of their future daughter-in-law, she was given one of the better rooms inside the castle. I imagined Odin was probably regretting that choice now, but he could take those regrets and shove them where the sun doesn't shine.

I stepped into the bedroom and immediately spotted my dear wife. She was decked out in a skintight black leather bodysuit. A leather holster on her hips sported a pair of mag-pistols, while the holster slung over her shoulder to wrap around her back carried a much larger weapon: a mag rifle.

"Going hunting?" I asked.

"No, just thought I'd walk around my room wearing a full suit of uncomfortable battle gear," she deadpanned.

"Wise ass," I laughed. "Mind if I join you? I'm dying to get out of here."

"Sure. I was going to ask if you wanted to come anyway," she said as she finished lacing up her boots.

For probably the fifteenth time today, I found myself staring at the contours of her body, which were made all the more pronounced by the skintight leather bodysuit that showed off every breathtaking curve.

"See something you like?"

"Yeah, but it's covered up by this damn bodysuit."

She laughed at that. "Unfortunately, it's too much of a pain to take off and put back on. So, you're gonna have to wait until later to get me out of it." As she walked past me, she ran her hand across my chest, before trailing her fingers down my side and off of my hip. "Come along, big boy. We've got trolls to kill."

"Are we meeting Donna and Leon?"

"Yep, they're supposed to be waiting for us in the market district."

I caught up to her and wrapped my arm around her waist. I spun her around to face me, then cupped her head in between my hands. I kissed her long and slow as my power flared around me and we teleported out of the room.

As the kiss came to an end, and my magic returned to a sedated state, we appeared in the market district. At first, Reina seemed surprised and unsure of what to say about us suddenly appearing there. But she took the whole thing in stride.

"That's... convenient. If I'd known you could do that, I wouldn't have gotten dressed so quickly," she whispered into my ear before stepping away from me. She took me by the hand and led me through the throngs of people to the place where we were to meet up with her companions.

Chapter Four

"Now, remember to be on your best behavior," Reina reminded me.

"Yes, dear. I'll be good." I rolled my eyes. I didn't really understand why she was so concerned about me being on my best behavior. After all I was a likable person, right? It's not like I was planning to kill the sniveling little rat named Leon. So, what if he almost constantly flirted with Reina? I wasn't jealous. Nope, not me, not one bit.

The mobs of people walking through Taranis' market district floated around us, as if we were a giant stone in a river— or whatever the human equivalent was.

On our way to the tavern Reina's companions were boarding in, we passed by blacksmiths, armor smiths, alchemy stores, even a gunsmith, which Reina seemed particularly enthused about. I asked if she wanted to step inside and have a look around, but she turned me down flat.

"No, my mag-arms still have some use to them. They may not be the most powerful arms around, but they've served me well. I'm not interested in replacing them and needing to relearn the ins and outs of a new weapon with everything else going on."

I understood. It took practice to become familiar with a new weapon. It took even more practice to get to the point where your weapon was an extension of your body, and constantly switching weapons made that difficult. Forget what you've heard about being able to pick up a weapon and use it just because it's similar to one you're used to. Slight differences in weight and length could have a huge impact on the way a weapon handles.

Firearms were no exception to this rule, though for the most part they were more pick up and go than a "normal" weapon. They were designed, specifically, for inexperienced warriors to be able to use them to defend themselves. However, minor differences in the barrel length and weight can still affect the aim of the user. For example, if a gun was heavier or lighter than you were used to, it would affect your ability to draw it efficiently. And as someone who relied heavily on her ability to draw her weapon, Reina would only carry the weapon into combat if she trained with it for over two dozen hours.

That was how seriously she took her job, a trait that hadn't changed from when she was a doctor back on Earth.

When we arrived at the tavern, it was to the sound of drunken merrymaking, music, and the occasional brawl. I stepped onto the short deck on the front of the building, then made my way over to the western style swinging door hanging halfway up the door frame. I pulled it open and beckoned Reina in first. Never let it be said that my centuries as a serpent made me forget my manners.

As we entered, the tavern went silent as the grave as the inhabitants eyed us up and down. Oh, I'm sure we made quite the spectacle: Reina with her otherworldly beauty, and me with my freakishly pale skin and bright orange eyes. We looked like we'd walked straight out of a "serial killer and his victims" catalog.

If I was being perfectly honest with myself, I'd been expecting someone to mistake me for a vampire for a while now. The fact that it hadn't happened yet was either attributed to people's fear of offending me, or the citizens' ability to ignore the strange in favor of focusing on themselves.

"Oh, there they are," Reina said, pointing out a table near the front of the building, where Donna, Leon, Ayla, Findral, and Thor were all waiting for us.

I vaguely recognized Donna and Leon from the few times I'd seen them inside the castle.

Donna was, for lack of a better phrase, extraordinarily beautiful. With scarlet hair inlaid with white highlights, wide green eyes that made her look oh so innocent, a robe that made her look anything but, and a body built for sin. She was the party's sorceress, damage dealer, and resident nymphomaniac. Though, from what Reina told me earlier in the day, Donna's magic relied on her being... promiscuous.

Don't ask me how that worked because I didn't know or care to know. She hadn't tried to hit on me yet, but I didn't blame her. It took a special kind of person to find my form attractive, and I didn't blame—No, I couldn't blame—people for finding me monstrous. Besides, it's not like I wanted her to hit on me anyway. The fewer women who were interested in me in that sense, the easier my life was going to be.

Reina's other companion was a young man named Leon, and like most young men I had the displeasure of meeting, he thought with the head that was not attached to his shoulders. Even after being told about me and knowing what I could do, he continues to flirt with Reina at every available opportunity, and if it wasn't for Reina keeping me in check, I would have killed him already.

He was your standard Adonis type: tall, broad shouldered, flawlessly tanned skin, and shiny white teeth that made him look like he came right out of a toothpaste commercial.

He also wore this gaudy suit of plate armor that shined like a mirror in the daylight and he carried a longsword that was inlaid with gold.

He was the knight in shining armor that liked to fool girls with promises of adventure and love. He would sweep them off their feet… and deposit them right onto his bed, only to dump them the next morning.

In other words, he was the type of guy I hated most in this world and the last person I'd ever want to hang out with my family. Yet there he sat.

"Took you long enough."

"Thor!" I held my arms out wide and gave him a pleasant smile. "It's been only a day, but it feels like weeks. Glad to see you've finally stopped crying like a little girl."

"And you're still an intolerable asshole."

"If it isn't broke, don't fix it."

Thor opened his mouth to say something, but Ayla and Reina chose that moment to intervene. "Boys!" they yelled simultaneously.

"Thor, can you give us a few minutes?" Ayla asked him sweetly.

"But—"

"Please..."

Thor threw one last glare my way then walked over to the group of men standing guard at the front door.

"Must you always antagonize him?"

"Yes." I chuckled and pulled her into a hug. "I'm your dad. Not liking your boyfriend is kind of in the job description."

She laughed, rested her forehead against my chest, and closed her eyes for a moment.

"We'll give you two some privacy."

"No—" She pulled away and looked to Reina. "That's really not necessary."

Ayla looked up and smiled at me. "Well, I'm going to get going, now. Let you four get acquainted with one another."

"Thanks, Ayla."

"Of course!" she exclaimed. "By the way, don't forget that I'm trying on dresses next week. You better be there, Dad."

"Naturally."

"Good, I'm going to hold you to that."

"And I'm going to hold the both of you to your promise."

Ayla gave me a confused look, but after a moment of thought her eyes widened and her face turned slightly pink.

"I—er... I was hoping you'd forgotten about that."

I just quirked a brow in response and gave her an unamused look.

"We'll keep it," she sighed in resignation.

"I'll make sure they follow through with their promise, master Torga," Findral interrupted with a smirk in Ayla's direction.

"That's my girl."

"*Traitor!*" Ayla hissed.

Ayla stepped back and briefly glanced at Thor before setting her eyes on me. She sighed, then nodded at me.

She looked to Reina. "Keep an eye on him for me?"

"Of course. I'll make sure he stays safe."

Ayla snorted in response and walked away without another word.

"That's adorable," Findral sighed, then followed Ayla.

Reina looked after the two in confusion then glanced at me. "I missed something, didn't I?"

"She wasn't asking you to protect me. She was asking you to *babysit* me. The little brat."

"That says a lot about you, "Leon said with a clearly false smile on his face.

"You must be Leon."

"The one and only."

"Thank God."

I ignored Leon's reply and turned to look at Donna—

"Hi!" She waved at him.

"You're… barely dressed."

"Oh! It's my new dress. Do you like it?"

"Where's the rest of it?"

"It was made this way."

I glanced down at the deep cut of her robe that exposed *a lot* of cleavage, then back to her face and smiled. "You're going to be a pain in my ass, aren't you?"

"Huh?"

I ignored her and turned to see Reina giving me the stink eye. I leaned down and gave her a quick peck on the forehead without breaking eye contact with Donna and Leon, which elicited an involuntary smile from Reina and a frown of annoyance from them.

"This is going to be fun," I whispered into Reina's ear before kissing her neck, again without breaking eye

contact with her friends. Reina giggled at the kiss and they, as expected, briefly frowned at the contact.

"Oh, this is going to be very fun."

Chapter Five

THE FOUR OF US HEADED TOWARDS THE CITY gates. As we did so I pulled a pouch out of the bag I kept on my waist and fished out my ID. It was a little placard, no larger than your average business card back on Earth. While a normal ID would have the bearer's name, class, and job title, mine only held my name along with the words *Asgardian VIP* written in large black letters across the bottom of the card.

Thor explained that the ID would become useless when I left Asgard, but for now it would serve to get me in and out of the city as I pleased. It was something Thor had given me a few days after I returned from the Serpent King's challenge. He also explained that the guards were instructed to turn a blind eye to my activities so long as I showed them my ID.

I'm not sure what my future son-in-law believes I do in my spare time, but I wasn't going to look a gift horse in the mouth.

I showed my ID to the gate guards, then stepped outside the walls to await Reina. Her group had to go through a slightly longer process to get out than I did, but it was a difference of a minute and 1/2 at the most. Hardly anything to complain over.

And yet, that's exactly what Leon did. As soon as he stepped foot outside the city, he started complaining. He complained about the way the guards treated me, he complained about the fact that I was not carrying supplies, and if he could, I'm sure he would've found a way to complain about my blood pumping too hard or my lungs working too efficiently. As it was, he'd long since gotten on my nerves and was working on Donna's and Reina's nerves.

An impressive feat considering we'd only been outside the town for five minutes.

"Seriously, Leon. Shut up," Reina grumbled. "We get it, you're having a bad day. But if you keep complaining about him, I'm going to shoot you."

Leon folded his arms over his chest and started sulking. He maintained this pose for the entirety of our trip to the city's stables, and for half an hour thereafter.

As we drew closer to the location of the suspected trolls' nest, Leon seemed to come back to himself. He stopped complaining and grew serious as he surveyed our surroundings. About three miles from our destination, he threw up his hand and gave us the signal to stop. "Something's not right here," he told us. "The forest, it's… too quiet."

I shrugged my shoulders. "Truthfully, I'd be more surprised if you did hear anything."

"Insult me if you want, but do not make light of our situation," he whispered harshly.

"I'm not insulting you. Animals don't tend to stick around when I intrude upon their territory."

"Yeah," Leon snorted. "I'm sure it's all because of you. Seriously, Reina, this is the 'perfect husband' you gushed so much about?"

"I'm sure he has a good reason for saying so—right?" Reina asked me.

"Yeah, actually, there's something I wanted to talk to you about. You see, I—" A massive fireball appeared in the air behind Reina's head and my voice failed me.

Luckily, my power did not.

My aura rushed forward like a tidal wave, flowing harmlessly around Reina and company, and slamming into the fireball, extinguished it immediately.

In a surprising show of professionalism, Reina drew her mag-pistols and with her left hand, she ran through a series of rapid-fire hand signals. Leon drew his sword without a word and readied himself for battle and moved to the front of the group, while Donna started chanting to herself.

I watched all of this peripherally as I searched for the attacker. A few seconds passed and I still hadn't found any sign of them. I narrowed my eyes in annoyance at the enemy's ability to hide.

Though they could hide from my sight, they couldn't hide from Reina's. Such was the difference in our races. I watched as she quickly and efficiently locked onto a tree in the distance and clicked her tongue to get Leon's and Donna's attention.

Without missing a beat, the two shifted their positions to face the tree. Leon bent his leading knee until his head was way over the end of his foot. He held the longsword out to the side as he prepared whatever skill he was about to use.

The next thing I knew, his body blurred, and he was standing in front of the tree with his sword in a position closer to the ground.

He's fast! I internally exclaimed. I didn't expect him to be able to leave my sight, even for a moment, so I was more than a little surprised when he did. I idly wondered what kind of training he'd done to reach his current level, and if my wife and her companions were more powerful than I'd given them credit for.

A second later, the top half of the tree began to slide away from the base.

A white blur shot around the tree, flashed around Leon's back, then rushed towards us. I stepped out in front of Reina and raised my hand. I pointed my palm at the blur in the universal sign for "stop," but it ignored my warning.

Guess we're doing this the fun way. I pulled my fist back then sent a gravity-infused punch at the ground in front of it to halt its advance. A wave of super condensed gravity flowed out from my knuckles and met the blur head on—or it was supposed to. At the last possible second the blur stopped its forward motion and went straight up, easily passing over my attack and landing behind it.

Now that it'd stopped moving, I could make out some details about it. The first thing I noticed was the dress: whiter than fresh snow. It turned semitransparent as it fluttered with the breeze rustling the trees high overhead. In stark contrast to the dress, the woman's skin was darker than anything I'd ever seen, and bright red hair flowed freely from her head to cover her breasts.

However, all of that paled in comparison to the sheer power she emanated without effort.

If this woman wasn't a god, then I was a squirrel's backside.

I silently cursed my horrid luck.

"Mind telling me what this is about?" I asked the woman while ignoring the commotion going on around me.

The woman smiled brightly at me, which showed off teeth that would've looked more at home on a piranha. She slowly rose to her full height and spread her arms out wide, as if she were asking for a hug, then she swung both arms inwards and clapped her hands together.

I instinctively sent my aura forth to protect Reina and Donna: forming a hollow dome of darkness around them that rapidly devoured the ground beneath their feet, turning it into dust.

However, it served its immediate purpose, as the ground around the dome exploded not a second later. Something whooshed over my head a fraction of a second later. I couldn't see what *it* was, but *it* cleaved through the trees in a ten-foot line to either side of me.

"Not much of a talker. I get that." I released the dome before it could injure either of the ladies.

As the wind began to pick up, the woman's eyes narrowed into a thin line and her grin grew wider still. She clicked her teeth at me. The sound carried surprisingly well over the wind and rustling of trees.

I spotted a stupefied Leon staring at the woman's ass at the same time she did. *Shit!* I teleported over to him and managed to place my body between them just in time for the woman to clap her hands again.

My aura flared to life, forming a wall of darkness in front of me and absorbing whatever power she was using before it could get to us. Her grin grew even wider in response, almost to the point of splitting her entire head. She clicked her teeth again, then vanished with the breeze.

"What was that!?" Leon yelled.

I grabbed his arm and teleported us back to Reina's side. "Stay behind me," I told the three of them. "This isn't an opponent you can face." I reformed the hollow dome around us, this time making sure that it didn't touch the ground. This kept it from forming an airtight seal, but at least I didn't have to worry about their feet being eaten or the ground being destroyed.

"The hell we can't," Reina snarled. She pulled her mag-pistols free from their holsters and pointed them through the dome at the woman, who was calmly advancing on us. I wasn't sure how Reina could see her through the heavy darkness of my dome, but the two rounds she fired would have hit the woman in the chest if they hadn't been immediately consumed upon contact with my aura.

"Damn it!" she growled. "Torga, I know you're the one controlling this barrier. Open it so we can face her!"

"Not happening." I shot down her order. "I told you, this isn't someone you can face."

"I can fight, Albert."

"I know that—" Something heavy tried to tear into my aura but was devoured before it could do more than warp its shape. "But trust me on this one. The best thing you can do is wait here while I deal with them," I implored her.

She didn't lower her weapons, and she refused to look at me, but she didn't try to attack the woman either.

If she genuinely wanted to get out, all she had to do was walk into it. At that point, I would either have to remove it or allow her to be devoured by my aura—which wasn't going to happen. *Hopefully, she doesn't try to test that idea.*

I looked to Donna and Leon in turn and took their silence as agreement. Neither seemed eager to argue the point with me, but I had the feeling that if Reina pressed the issue, the two of them would ignore my request and follow her into battle.

I'll take what I can get. I nodded my head. With myself as the focal point, I willed my aura to rotate around the four of us. This would hopefully allow it to deflect anything that wasn't immediately destroyed.

"Don't touch the darkness. It'll protect you from her, but I don't have enough control over it to separate good things from bad. If you stick your hand through it, don't expect to get it back. I'll let you know when it's safe to pass through it again," I told them. They were so focused on the prima donna piranha that they didn't immediately react to my words, so I prompted them to answer with a quick "hey."

They nodded their heads but didn't look at me.

"Perfect. Wait here; this won't take long," I said. I focused all of my attention on the woman… I felt myself grinning from the anticipation of consuming another god.

I allowed the dome to dissipate, then exploded into motion. Leading the charge by blasting a wave of super condensed gravity at the woman, I allowed my aura to twist itself into a violent maelstrom that was forty feet wide and a hundred feet tall.

As I suspected, the aura washed over the woman— unable to do anything more than ruffle her hair. That was the final detail I needed to know who I was facing: The woman before me was indeed a goddess. And where there was one, more were sure to follow.

I need to hurry up and deal with this chick, then get everyone as far away from this place as possible. I led with a gravity-infused right haymaker. She ducked my punch and sent a surprisingly heavy blow into my ribs.

I spun with the momentum of my swing, shifting into my Naga-Hydra form in a swirl of green particles and letting loose with a barrage of energy breath attacks from my nine other heads that slammed her in the chest and sent her crashing through a tree.

This was one of the perks of normally being aethereal: My body could be anything I wanted it to be, and I could shift into other forms in a matter of seconds.

While I preferred my "human" form for everyday interactions, the Naga-Hydra form was the most versatile and most useful in combat.

Also, after living so long as a snake, I just didn't feel right fighting without a tail.

I launched myself into the air, fully prepared to blast her back into whatever mutant hellhole she crawled out of—but she'd vanished.

I heard a loud clapping sound a moment before something thudded into my body. I looked down and saw a dozen or so small cuts appear on my side. None was deep enough to draw blood, though they stung like papercuts.

It got through my aura?

"Reina, take the others and go!" I yelled.

Nine mouths opened simultaneously and fired beams of energy in the direction the attack had come from. A second later, something else hit me, coming from the opposite direction this time.

"Reina!? Did you hear me!?" I hollered, hoping she would answer. Rage began to fill me when she didn't respond. I knew I shouldn't do it, shouldn't take my eyes off the fight, but I had to make sure she was safe.

I turned—and gasped as three attacks hit me simultaneously from multiple directions, blasting me off my feet to land thirty feet away. I rolled with the momentum so I wouldn't be caught flat-footed, coming up with a roar and a wild gravity-infused punch. This time I didn't care about precision or control, I went for raw, unadulterated power.

A wave of gravity fifty feet across exploded out of my fist, rocketing into the distance faster than my eyes could track. Everything the wave touched was either flattened or reduced to splinters.

The forest was torn asunder.

I panted at the sudden depletion of energy within my body. Shifting back into my human form to conserve power, I stumbled over to the last place I'd seen Reina and the others. They were nowhere to be seen.

"Reina!" I screamed. "Reina, holler if you can hear me!"

The forest remained quiet.

"Reina…" I panted.

The scream that followed would have torn my throat to pieces if I were still mortal.

I picked my way through the destroyed section of forest until I found what I was looking for: the woman, pinned beneath a mound of rock and destroyed trees.

I growled low in my throat, wrapped my fist around her skinny neck, and yanked her free from her prison.

"Where is she!?" I roared in her face.

She weakly tried to pry my hand off of her neck, and I squeezed harder in return. I slammed her into the dirt, then mounted her. Placing a knee on either side of her chest, I wrapped my hands around her neck and pinned her in place.

"Answer the question if you want to keep your soul."

The woman's body relaxed beneath me, her arms splaying out to the side. She opened her mouth in a silent laugh, even as my grip tightened.

I felt the heat a moment before my world exploded into a haze of red and orange light. Fire swirled around me in a spiral for a second before suddenly turning into a tornado of flame. The red and orange quickly gave way to blue and black as the temperature inside the tornado skyrocketed.

I let out a rage-induced roar, followed by my aura ripping the flame vortex apart and creating a giant pit in the ground around me.

The clicking of teeth drew my attention. I looked up and saw a man standing in front of me. He was naked, though that didn't matter much since his skin was like a living bonfire. It was a miracle he didn't set fire to the very forest around us, but somehow not a single leaf or blade of grass that came into contact with him was burned.

Like the woman, his mouth was filled with rows of piranha-like teeth. Unlike the woman, his hair was a mass of ebony tresses that flowed down his chest and back.

Were it not for the bonfire, I would've assumed the two were also twins. The male was the spitting image of the woman, just larger and more muscular.

The male gnashed his teeth at me. I don't know what he was trying to say, but it was clear that he was pissed.

Good, then we were on the same page.

His body grew hotter as the orange and red turned to blue. Without warning, he pushed off the ground and dashed towards me. I had no time to react. He slammed into me and forced me to release my hold on the woman.

We crashed through half a dozen trees before he angled my body and drug me through the dirt. He stomped his foot hard onto the ground and spun, before slinging me through the air and throwing me away like I was some type of frisbee.

My body dug a massive trench in the ground as I hit and slid through the dirt.

I let out a pain-filled gasp as I climbed onto my knees.

The man was helping the woman to her feet. His enraged eyes were something I knew I'd never forget: with a vertical red pupil on a black iris.

A pillar of fire erupted behind them, and the man helped the woman walk. His eyes remained locked onto mine the entire time. As soon as they stepped inside the pillar, it collapsed in on itself and I was left alone, with only one thing reverberating through my mind: *I lost?*

I scrambled to my feet and leapt into the air. I rose above the treetops and called Reina's name as loud as I could.

I didn't get a response.

My chest began to heave as I struggled to keep myself calm. My body no longer needed oxygen to survive, but it seemed like it had forgotten that little tidbit.

My chest burned like someone had stuck a miniature sun inside my lungs. I fought down the sudden urge to flatten the area for fear of hurting Reina. Instead, I opted to fly as fast as I could through the forest in search of her.

She's gone, a little voice inside my head whispered. "No, she can't be! Reina!" I screamed. I accidently flew into a tree, reducing the ancient thing to dust as my uncontrolled aura consumed it.

"Reina!" I called again. "Please, answer me!" I searched the forest for a while before I crash landed back in the destroyed area where I'd fought the goddess and stumbled my way over to the last place I'd seen her. I hadn't found anything the last time I was here, but there had to be something!

I dropped to my knees and threw the fallen leaves aside. It felt like my entire body was shutting down as I clawed at the dirt. My vision tunneled as I haphazardly threw aside dirt and leaves. My failing sense of balance caused me to involuntarily sway from side to side, but I couldn't stop, not until I found her.

Boom!

I was thrown aside from a colossal shockwave that obliterated the forest.

I bounced off the ground once, twice, three times—***Crack*** I was embedded back first into the face of a sheer rock wall. The explosion, combined with the force of my crashing into the cliff facing, served to knock me out of whatever spell I'd been under.

I slowly pulled myself out of the rock. Once I was free, I crouched down and cupped my head between my hands. I inhaled, then exhaled, inhaled, then exhaled. *What the hell is wrong with me?* I wondered.

Was I actually under some type of spell? No, that couldn't be. I have an immunity to mind control. But, what else could it be? My regeneration should have healed any toxins or poisons, and that's if they somehow managed to pierce my scales and affect my body in the first place.

I pushed off the ground and rose above the treetops. Instantly, I realized the problem:

Gungnir, Odin's flagship and de facto command center, was now airborne.

For a moment I wondered what could have caused Odin to bring his spear to bear, but that question was answered almost immediately as well. From this distance, they looked to be bats or some type of small bird. But I had a good idea what they actually were: frost drakes.

And frost drakes meant that the Jötnar had finally found Odin's hideout.

Maybe...Maybe that's where Reina is. Maybe she heard the sounds of fighting and went to defend the city. It's possible. Regardless, I have to do something. I accelerated towards the city as fast as I could.

Hang on, Reina. I'm coming.

CHAPTER SIX

REINA SLID BETWEEN THE LEGS OF A LARGE, BLUE-skinned ogre and fired two rounds into its groin. The ogre wailed in pain and dropped to its knees in time for Donna's ice spike to pierce into its face and pin it to the wooden portcullis that served as the entrance to the city.

Not for the first time in her decade-long monster hunting career, she thanked the gods for enchantments.

Jötnar blood was essentially just liquid nitrogen playing pretend. A drop of the stuff on your skin could cause serious damage to creatures in the same Tier as the Jötnar, and outright kill a normal human.

Luckily, through the absolutely broken ability known as enchantment, the stupidly cold liquid slid off of her body without ever making full contact. It only took losing her outfit to an acid spitting lizard once before she insisted all of her clothes had this enchantment cast on them.

That was an embarrassing walk back to the Inn…

Donna sent a hailstorm flying into a troll looking Jötnar's chest, slowing it down enough for Leon to knock it on its ass with a heavy kick to its chest. A twitch of Leon's arm brought his sword to bear, and the troll's head was removed from its shoulders.

"Reina—" Leon caught a blow from a troll on the arm, which knocked him back a step. He quickly brought his sword up in an upwards swing that bifurcated the troll from groin to scalp. "I'll be the first to admit that I don't like Torga—but leaving him back there seemed kinda harsh. What if he needed our help?"

"Believe me, I hated it. But I have to believe that he can handle himself and focus on what I can do." Reina lifted the pistol in her right hand and blew a hole in an ogre's face, completely removing its left eye and a large chunk of skull. "As much as I wanted to remain by his side, I couldn't just leave these people to die for my own selfishness. He'll understand. Besides, I'm sure he would've done the same. He was never the kind of guy to let people suffer needlessly."

"The way you bolted for the gate, I thought you were mad at him for something and you just hadn't had the chance to tell us about it," Donna chimed in.

"What—No!" Reina ducked to avoid the wild swing of an eyeless troll with large ebony horns and fired a round into each of its knees, then one in between its horns. "Why would I be mad?"

"Well, I'm sure I don't know. Perhaps that little show with the black aura seeping out of his skin and the manic look in his eye had something to do with it?" Donna continued. "You wouldn't be the first person to realize their spouse wasn't who they thought they were. Happens more often than you'd think."

"And I'm sure catching them in bed with you had absolutely *nothing* to do with that assessment, did it?" Reina sarcastically replied. She ducked a wild swing from a blue-skinned human-looking Jötnar, then stepped into its chest. She hooked its arm with her bicep, then simultaneously stuck her leg between its legs, twisted her hips, and ducked. It was lifted off the ground and slammed headfirst into the unforgiving cobblestone of the main road.

"Less often than you'd think," Donna laughed.

"I'm sure—" Reina punctuated her statement by firing a round into the Jötnar's face for good measure. The fall had probably killed it, but she wasn't about to risk it getting the drop on her later because she'd wanted to save a bullet.

Mag-pistol magazines were loaded with the condensed form of the wielder's magic anyway, so she wasn't wasting a precious resource. Give her ten minutes and she could refill all twelve of the magazines she carried on her. The same rule applied to her rifle magazine, each of the ten rounds took about five minutes to replace due to their density. She could refill all five rifle mags in a night, though she'd be out of commission until late in the afternoon in order to replenish the lost mana.

Reina placed the barrel of her pistol under the last Jötnar's jaw and pulled the trigger, dousing herself with its blood. The blood felt like she was dunking her head in ice water, but thanks to the enchantment it couldn't hurt her.

"You know—" Donna panted. "You never answered my question."

"Eh, I was a bit too busy saving your ass."

She turned her ass in Reina's direction and wiggled it a bit. "How can I ever repay you for saving my ass?" she replied with a coy smile on her face.

Reina rolled her eyes and holstered her pistols. "You could start by giving back the ten gold I loaned you last week."

Donna's only response was to pout at her. They caught their breath then began jogging towards the sound of battle.

"You know, I've been thinking—" Leon muttered.

"That's dangerous," Donna quipped.

"Bite me."

"In your wettest of dreams—"

"Children, can we get back to the matter at hand?" Reina interrupted them. "What is it Leon—What is it, boy?"

"Oh, shut the fuck up," he said half-heartedly. "I was thinking: What if the quest to scout the troll's nest was a trap to get us—or more specifically, Torga, out of the city?"

That brought Reina up short. Not because of the impossibility of someone knowing that they'd be the ones to take the quest, and then Torga would agree to come along… But because in spite of those points, it was somewhat believable.

Thinking on it even further, maybe it wasn't so impossible after all.

If they knew Torga would follow Reina without question, then the most difficult part was making sure they'd agree to take the quest. But even that could be explained by a simple bribe. Especially when you consider the fact that the quest came via request, so all it came down to was getting them to accept it… And knowing Donna and Leon, all it would've taken was a pretty attendant in a short skirt being the one to ask, to get them to agree. Then all the attackers would need to do was distract Torga long enough for the siege to get underway… Which a fight with a freaky piranha woman would almost certainly do.

"Shit, he's right. This was all a setup from the very beginning. Somebody played us for fools," Donna spat, coming to the same conclusion Leon had.

They fought their way through the city, stopping to help anyone they could along the way, until they eventually arrived at the market district, which was usually the most populated section of the city at this time of day.

What they found almost made Reina lose her lunch. Ghouls, hundreds of ghouls, fought to get inside the building housing the adventurers guild while the bodies of those unlucky enough to be caught in their way lay half eaten on the ground.

Before they could shake off their surprise at the sheer number of ghouls present, a petite creature with the lower body of a goat and the upper body of a rather well-endowed woman landed in a crouch beside Reina. She wore a sheer nightgown that barely hid her private bits from view and a dark hood that covered the entirety of her head and neck. She wielded a vicious looking morning star in her left hand and a steel shield in her right.

Wasting no time, Reina immediately drew her pistols and began firing.

The creature dodged the first three rounds as if they were in slow motion, then she raised her shield and deflected the rest.

Realizing she wasn't going to get anywhere with the pistols, Reina shoved them back in their holsters, leaped over a preliminary swing from the creature's morning star, and pulled her rifle from over her left shoulder while simultaneously kicking off of the goat woman's shield to gain some distance.

Reina performed a quick tuck and roll as she hit the ground, coming up onto her knee and training her barrel on the creature's left leg.

Boom!

The ground shook with the force of a massive explosion, causing Reina's aim to veer off at the last second and hit the ground a dozen paces behind the goat woman. She mentally cursed whoever caused her to miss, then slid the rack back and chambered another round—all in less than a second.

Goat woman was even faster.

Reina didn't bother trying to bring her rifle back on target— she knew she'd be gutted before she could. Instead, she dodged to the side, narrowly avoiding a blow that would've popped her head like a tomato and brought the butt of the rifle around like she was swinging a baseball bat.

Reina caught the underside of goat woman's jaw and sent her head skywards. Then she hurriedly switched grips and pointed the barrel at her chest. Reina pulled the trigger and blew a hole the size of a coconut in between her breasts, then she stepped forward and went for a field goal.

Reina hit her hard enough between the legs to lift her body off the ground and make it collapse in on itself.

Goat woman landed in a heap with her head between her legs and Reina let out a sigh of relief. "Thanks for the help you two—" She got hit in the face hard enough to pop the cartilage in her nose and send her crashing into the dirt. Reina rolled with the impact to minimize the time she was defenseless and quickly brought her rifle to bear on the exact duplicate of the woman she'd just killed.

Reina looked over her shoulder and caught sight of Donna and Leon fighting other copies of the same woman, and while Donna seemed to be holding her own, Leon was defending in lieu of attacking.

"Leon, fight back you idiot!" Reina yelled before firing her rifle at a goat woman's right leg, which was dodged with little effort.

"But I've never hit a woman before!" he hollered back. His goat woman used her morning star to rip the longsword out of his hand, then swung wildly at his face. Leon yelped as he dodged out of the way.

"Yeah, I noticed!" Reina kicked a goat woman's legs out from under her with a drop spinning sweep, then pushed off the ground to right herself and smashed her boot into the goat woman's midsection, sending her flying into a brick wall a few feet away. "Try harder!" Reina ended this one's life with a twitch of her trigger finger, then moved to help Leon.

"Reina, behind you!" Donna yelled. She fired a massive ice spike over Reina's shoulder, who leaped out of the way for good measure.

Reina landed on her back and pointed the barrel of her rifle at the large, hooded man standing sedately in front of her.

The most frightening thing was the fact that if not for Donna's warning, Reina never would've known he was there.

He stood over seven feet tall and was clearly thickly muscled as his heavy, hooded cloak was pulled taut over massive pectorals and impossibly wide shoulders. The axe he carried was the size of a grown human: Its shaft was made from some type of light wood and strange runes glowed in a faint blue light. The blade was easily the size of a child's torso and was forged from some form of wickedly sharp black metal.

"I'm gonna need you to follow me, lass," a silky-smooth voice said from beneath the hood.

"That's not gonna happen," Reina growled as she climbed to her feet and pointed the rifle at the man.

"I wouldn't be so sure about that," another voice, this one more childlike and clearly feminine, said from behind her. A heavy blow to the back of Reina's head sent her into the ground and into blissful unconsciousness.

~ ˜ ~

I scanned the busy streets for any sign of Reina and the others from my position, high above the tallest tower. Any ice drake stupid enough to get in my way was devoured by my aura without hesitation. I didn't have time to be dealing with their bullshit.

"Torga!?"

My head rotated to locate the source of the voice... *There: by the castle.* I dropped out of the sky like a meteor and only began to slow once I was fifty feet from the ground. I landed in a crouch and listened to the sounds of fighting within the city.

"Torga!?!" The voice screamed, louder this time, a clear indicator that they were close. The voice sounded feminine and remarkably familiar. *Lena?*

I raced towards the direction the voice had come from. Less than a minute later, I was standing outside the large steel doors that led inside the castle.

Lying just outside the doors with her face to the sky, was Lena. All around her lay the dead and dying bodies of Jötnar soldiers, while just inside the door lay the bodies of the castle's servants.

"Lena!?" I yelled. I ran to her side and lifted her head enough to sit it on my lap. My face was splattered with blood as she coughed.

"Torga?" she whispered. Her voice was hoarse, and her face was heavily bruised and blistered… And those weren't even the first things I noticed. She had a bloodstain on the stomach of her gray robe that was slowly growing larger before my very eyes.

"Can you heal yourself?" I asked softly.

She minutely shook her head. "I haven't got the magic."

"What if I—"

"No," she cut me off. "I know what you're thinking, and it won't work. As I am now, your magic is too powerful for me. My body won't be able to take it."

"Lena, I—I'm sorry. I should've been here."

"It's not your fault." She placed her palm against my cheek. It was soaked in blood, her blood, or the blood of the Jötnar, I didn't know. "I'm sure you would've been here if you could, Torga. That's just the kind of man you are."

I bit back my immediate response and just nodded my head.

"Torga, oh, thank the gods—Mom?" a girlish voice said from behind me. "Mom!? She's over here!" the voice exclaimed.

I heard the sound of multiple people running over and looked up: Hali, Solon, Talia, and Fenris arrived and I was violently shoved by Fenris. He took my place without a word or acknowledgment of my existence and clutched onto Lena's body as if he were adrift at sea and she was his only lifeline.

Which, in a way, she was.

Hali began pumping as much mana as she could into her mother's body, but after ten seconds none of the wounds seemed to be closing.

"Torga, where's Reina?" Fenris asked.

"I—I don't know."

"What do you mean you don't know?" he yelled. "She's a healer, right? Go get her so she can fix this!" he demanded.

"I don't know where she is!" I yelled back. "I came back to the city looking for Reina and found Lena like… this."

"Then, what are you standing around for? Go find her!" he screamed at me, then in a much softer voice he said, "It's alright, baby. We'll find Reina and we'll get you fixed up. Don't worry, okay? Just—Just stay with me. Torga, go get her, right now!"

"Findral, take to the skies. If you find Reina, bring her back here. No matter what."

"Right away." She turned away from me before leaping into the sky. With a single beat of her batlike wings, she was gone.

"I'm gonna go too," I told them. "Fenris, I swear, I'll bring Reina here as soon as I find her."

"You'd better," he said softly. He pulled on Lena's body until she was almost sitting in his lap and tightly held onto her.

I couldn't bear to watch them anymore, so I left in search of Reina.

Memories of the days I spent with Lena came unbidden into my mind: every laugh, every argument…

Every time she helped pull me out of the darkness within my own mind. Lena was one of the first friends I made when I came to Yggdrasil, and I'd be damned before I let her go out like this.

~ ~ ~

The first thing Reina noticed upon regaining consciousness was the nearly unbearable heat surrounding her. Every breath felt like she was trying to push hot coals out of her throat; any exposed skin was cracking from the severe dehydration she was experiencing.

Oh, and her arms and legs were bound.

How long was I out? Under normal circumstances, it should have taken hours, if not days for Reina to get to this level of dehydration. However, judging by the overpowering warmth in the air, and the fact that the inside of her armor felt like a swamp, she could have been unconscious anywhere between fifteen minutes to an hour.

Reina forced her blurry eyes to focus as she took in her surroundings: an uncountable number of gray-skinned people walking along an ebony-colored stone path lined with snow covered trees greeted her... Except they were on the ceiling. The snow was the purest white she'd ever seen, the trees were easily several hundred feet tall, and the people walked in a single-file line down the center of the path.

Reina couldn't stop the gasp of awe that escaped her lips.

"Look who's finally awake." An uncontrollable shiver raced down Reina's spine. Power: Wild, untamed, and ancient beyond anything she'd ever experienced permeated the voice.

Reina was afraid.

A woman who appeared to be about Reina's age crouched down to look her in the eyes. Her own eyes were made of solid gold. At first, Reina thought they were prosthetics, and then they rotated to look at something behind her and she knew they were real—or at the very least, they gave the woman some form of sight.

Aside from her freakish eyes, and the feeling that she could wipe Reina from existence by accident, she looked like your average, everyday human woman. Maybe a little on the thin side, but her wavy black hair spilled over her shoulders and she wore a black business suit— Reina's eyes widened as she realized that the woman was wearing an honest to god black tuxedo, complete with a silver tie and golden cufflinks.

"Who are you?... Why do this?"

"It's nothing personal. We needed to bait someone out of hiding and you were the easiest way to do it." She grabbed Reina's bound wrists and pulled her into a sitting position.

What could only be described as a hellscape greeted Reina as she looked out over the edge of either a plateau or some kind of small mountain: Black clouds went on for an eternity in every direction, massive fireballs fell from said clouds almost continuously, monstrous creatures of every shape and size soared through the sky on colossal bat wings and crawled along the walls. The wails of those unlucky enough to be grabbed by the creatures echoed in her ears.

"I'm definitely not in Taranis anymore. Am I…In Hell?" Reina whispered.

"Good guess, but Hell is actually a few thousand miles and a layer down from here. We're currently at the intersection of Tartarus and Hel: the one with one L and a few billion tons of snow."

"Does that mean I'm dead?"

"Hardly," the woman scoffed. "This is one of the few places in the realm where a mortal can survive... if only just. If this plateau we're on was two feet higher or lower, you would either freeze to death in seconds or you would boil from the inside out. "

Reina's mouth suddenly went bone dry, and she was almost positive it wasn't because of the heat. "Look, there must've been some mistake. I've done a lot of bad things, sure, but I've done just as much—if not more—good things." Then Reina remembered what the woman said about her being bait. "Who are you trying to bait? I don't think I know anyone that would warrant such a plan from someone of your… power," Reina said, having to force the last bit out around a tongue that was refusing to cooperate.

"I thought that'd be obvious, but okay," the woman said sensibly. "We're attempting to convince your dear friend Torga to surrender himself to us."

"Torga—Why?" Reina asked a little too loudly. But she couldn't help herself: Why was someone this powerful worried about him surrendering?

"Why?" she echoed. "Because we'd rather not face the devourer in combat. Sure, we'd probably win, but not without injuries—or possibly even casualties. Getting him to surrender ensures we all survive the night."

"What'd you call him?" Reina asked. The woman wasn't making any sense. First, she referred to him by name, but then she called him something like "the devourer." What was that supposed to mean?

Was Torga in some kind of trouble? Was he a criminal of some kind?

No, surely not. The Albert Reina knew was an honorable man. He'd never get involved with something like this.

The woman was quiet for a long moment, then she reached behind her back and pulled out a thin piece of stone that could've been mistake for a piece of notebook paper.

"What's this?" Reina asked her.

"Read it."

Reina looked at the rock.

"It's gibberish."

"Give it a minute," the woman told her.

Reluctantly, Reina did as she was asked.

At first, the lines on the stone were unintelligible scribbles. But all it took was a single blink, and the words suddenly made sense. Without realizing it, Reina began reading what was carved onto it.

[Name: Torga]

[Race: Demon Serpent]

[Alias: The Devourer, Orochi, World Eater]

Her eyes widened bit by bit with each line she read until she reached the bottom.

[Wanted dead or alive. Reward: 1.5 trillion Celestial Spirit Coins.]

Torga, what have you done?

Chapter Seven

I HOVERED HIGH ABOVE THE ROOFTOPS WHILE frantically scanning the streets for any sign of Reina and her friends. Every moment felt like an eternity with the knowledge that Lena's life hung on my ability to find them.

What if I can't? What if she dies before I can find her? I shook the thought from my mind. I couldn't allow myself to start thinking like that. I was sure she was around here somewhere. I just needed to follow the sounds of gunshots—which the city was conspicuously absent of. *C'mon, Reina. Give me a sign or something.*

"Torga—" Findral said as she flew up to me. A grim expression cast a shadow over her otherwise beautiful face and made her look like she wanted to commit murder. "I found them."

That works, I internally sighed. "Judging by the look on your face, I'm guessing Reina isn't currently trying to save Lena's life, is she?"

A shake of her head was enough to almost break me.

"What happened to Reina?" I asked, and her expression noticeably softened.

~ ~ ~

I wrapped my fist around Leon's throat, lifted him off the ground, and pushed him against the wall in front of me. The brick building obtained new spiderweb cracks from the point of impact, but I honestly didn't give a shit about it or the rapid purpling of Leon's face.

"You were supposed to protect her," I hissed into his ear. He didn't seem to notice.

"Stop it, you're killing him!" Donna yelled as she fought to escape Findral's grip.

I grit my teeth at the thought of letting him go but realized I must. My anger at him could wait until later. Right now I needed him alive to help me find Reina. Through a ton of effort, I managed to loosen my grip enough for him to breath, eventually getting to the point where I could allow him to stand on his own two feet.

"My apologies," I said through clenched teeth. "It's been a rough day. And as far as I can tell, it's not going to get any easier now that *someone* allowed my wife to be dragged through a portal to who knows where."

Leon coughed as he sucked in a few breaths. "We— we were dealing with our own problems at the time," he wheezed. "Which you would have known if you'd actually been there instead of fighting with the scary teeth lady in the forest. This is on you, not us—"

I put my fist through the wall beside his head.

"You think I didn't want to be?" I ground out. It was a struggle to keep my aura contained with him throwing my failures in my face. "I've been looking for you three ever since you vanished into thin air. Now, I know I told you to go, but—"

"Bullshit," Leon spat. "You told us to wait and watch so you could show off. It was Reina who decided we'd be better off leaving to help the people of the city."

I stared at him for a long moment before I looked to Donna for confirmation. She nodded her head in agreement with Leon.

When exactly did they leave? I wondered. I stared into his eyes and thought about calling him a liar. Surely Reina would've left a sign of some kind to tell me where she was going, right?

Unless it was destroyed when the forest was flattened? Was that it? Did I simply miss it in my frantic state?

"Torga?" I heard Findral call.

"What?" I tore my eyes away from Leon and looked at her. She was still holding Donna by the arm, though both she and Donna appeared to be staring at something just out of my field of vision. I stepped out of the alley and followed their line of sight to the roof of a nearby building.

"So, the devourer shows himself." The large hooded man Leon had spoken of was crouched on the edge of the roof, looking down at us. "Do you have any idea how long I've been looking for you?" His voice radiated a power the likes of which I'd never felt before. It was enough to send shivers down my spine.

I clenched my fists until my knuckles cracked.

"Where's. my. wife?"

"I can see I've struck a nerve," the big man laughed. "Understandable. I'd probably feel the same way if I'd been unable to protect what I cared about," he said more seriously.

His tone pissed me off, not because he was making fun of me. But because he sounded genuinely sympathetic.

"If you understand how I'm feeling, then give her back." I stepped in front of Findral and Donna, using my body to block them from his sight. "Findral, take them and go find Ayla."

"I'm not leaving you," she immediately denied my request.

"I'm not asking you; I'm telling you. I've already lost my wife. Don't make me lose one of my daughters."

There was a moment of silence as she processed what I had said, then she let out a long sigh. "Fine, but you better come back alive. And don't let it take weeks for you to return, this time. Lena's life depends on it." Without giving me a chance to respond, Findral, Donna, and Leon vanished in almost simultaneous pillars of fire: one of Findral's newer tricks.

As far as I could tell, it worked much in the same way as the normal teleportation spell, though it appeared to be much more limited since Findral was only able to teleport a couple hundred feet at a time.

"Smart of you to let them go," I told the man.

"Aye?" he chuckled. "I lose nothing by letting them go. After all, I'm only here because you are. If you hadn't caused such a ruckus, I would've been on a beach somewhere in the silver city, sipping virgin made honey wine and enjoying the company of some beautiful angels." He stepped off the roof and crashed onto the cobblestone road with a heavy thud. The thick stone beneath his feet fractured beneath his weight, letting me know that his appearance wasn't as simple as it first appeared.

"Instead, I'm here in some backwoods piece of shit town that's on the verge of war because some two-bit minor god decided to interfere with mortal affairs. Didn't anyone ever tell you that that was a no-no?" He lifted his meaty hand and grabbed the cloak that hid his face. With an easy tug, the fabric tore free from its bindings and I got my first look at the man responsible for taking Reina.

Surprisingly, he looked a lot like Leon in the face. Very "pretty," if that's what you wanted to call someone who looked like he could've been an Olympic body builder: He was a foot taller than I was, extremely broad shouldered, legs like tree trunks, and arms bigger around than most men's heads. And all of that was crammed into a suit of armor so thick, it'd take an anti-tank round to pierce it. He took a single step forward, and he was suddenly bearing down on me. "Allow me to introduce myself. My name is Ruknar, god of strength and the honorable dead, at your service." He showed me a surprisingly elegant bow for one his size.

"Torga, pissed off husband."

"Don't be modest, now, you're so much more than that. You, my hungry little friend, are Orochi: The god of serpents, and the chaotic king of destruction," he said in a tone that sounded almost giddy.

"What are you talking about?" I asked, genuinely startled by what he'd called me. "My name is Torga—Tor-Ga, not Orochi."

"If you say so. Truth be told, doesn't matter to me what you call yourself. All that matters is that I was asked to bring you in, and I kinda have a 100% success rate to uphold. I'm sure you'd understand my desire to hold on to that record, yes? So, why don't you just surrender? Come in quietly and you have my word that the feisty elf bitch will be returned quickly and unharmed—" His words were cut off as my right fist slammed into his left cheek. His head was thrown to the side and he stumbled back a step. I pulled my left arm back and stepped forward to execute the follow up.

"Torga!"

I paused mid-step, with my arm still in position to launch a punch, as Reina's voice pierced through the rage I'd been feeling ever since she disappeared. Without warning, Ruknar's arm blurred, then a massive fist was bearing down on me. I quickly raised both arms and took the blow on my forearms.

If I'd blinked, I would've missed the moment Taranis faded like a mirage and I ricocheted off a mountain, landing heavily in some kind of rock canyon. The rough stone gave way to my nigh-impenetrable scales and splintered like a glass window.

∞∞∞∞∞∞∞

Warning!
Access to the Yggdrasil system has been lost!

∞∞∞∞∞∞∞

I slid to a stop after destroying a few hundred feet of the canyon floor. *What happened? Where—where am I?* I climbed to my feet after a long minute of staring at the pitch-black sky overhead. Vertigo hit me as soon as I straightened up, and I collapsed onto one knee.

"Not bad." A loud crash announced his arrival, the stone beneath his feet shattering from his very presence. "I thought for sure that would've killed you."

"Dis—" I had to stop speaking in order to spit out the amber fluid that was filling my mouth. "Disappointed?"

"Hardly. I've never been happier to be wrong," he said jovially.

My vision swam for a moment and I had to force it to focus on him. I couldn't allow myself to be surprised like that again. To that end, I began the process of shifting into my Naga-Hydra form: It was the most appropriate for battle and my other heads could be used as meat shields if necessary. "AH…" Pain unlike anything I'd ever felt coursed through my body the moment I attempted to shape-shift. This wasn't a physical pain; my body had long since grown too durable for me to process pain.

I felt it in the very fabric of my being, almost as if I were feeling it in my soul, instead of my body.

"Oh, that's my bad. Guess I forgot to mention that you can't use your powers here," he said in a tone that was full of amusement.

"What're you talking about?" I muttered through gritted teeth.

Was I always so heavy? I struggled to my full height, and almost buckled under the weight of my own body. I swayed heavily from side to side, but I eventually managed to take the two steps that separated us before Ruknar stuck his arm out and placed it on my shoulder, halting my steps and helping me remain standing.

My left arm blurred into motion and smashed into his face with all the force I could muster, and yet, the god of strength barely flinched. A backhand struck the right side of my face and knocked me flat on my ass.

"No no no no no no. This isn't the way it's supposed to go," Ruknar growled. "You aren't supposed to be this weak." He grabbed the front of my tunic and lifted me to my feet. "Are you really the devourer?" I could see the anger in his eyes growing with every second that passed. He wrapped one fist around my throat and lifted me off the ground, in an almost perfect copy of the way I'd been holding Leon earlier, and held me aloft without any visible effort. Which was damn near impossible given my weight—or, at least I'd thought it was.

He drew back a fist and sent it flying into my stomach. My body was propelled backwards with so much force, I didn't get the chance to see the canyon around me move. I was just suddenly falling onto my face after bouncing off the canyon wall a hundred feet away.

I struggled to lift myself back into a kneeling position, but soon found it was a wasted effort. He grabbed the back of my neck and picked me up like I was a sack of potatoes.

Despite struggling to free myself, I was unable to move my head as he forced me to look him in the eyes. He made a disgusting noise at the back of his throat, then I felt something wet stick to my face.

The bastard spat on me…

As if that wasn't enough, he lightly tossed my paralyzed body aside to land face first on the hard stone.

"You can come out now. I'm done here," Ruknar growled to seemingly no one.

"Your personality is as shit as always," a woman sighed from somewhere nearby. "If you wanted a challenge, then why'd you use the mirror? You knew the effect it'd have on him."

"Because he's the Devourer, damn it! What kind of world destroyer hesitates at the sound of a woman's voice?"

"I don't know." I felt someone stroke the back of my head. "I thought it was kind of cute, the way he's so single mindedly focused on her… If only you worried about me half as much," the woman said quietly, while still stroking the back of my head.

"Don't start that mess again. We literally talked about this the other day: Why should I worry about the safety of someone stronger than me?"

"You're right, you shouldn't… If your goal is to sleep on the couch for the next millennia."

I felt someone grab a fistful of my hair and lift me off the ground. Since I was still unable to move, I was forced to watch as a beautiful woman in a black tuxedo held me aloft with a pleasant smile on her face. "Hello, Devourer." She said in a too sweet tone. "Welcome to Tartarus."

"Tartarus?" I asked. "I'm—in the underworld?"

"So, you know where you are. That's good, saves us some time. We have someone waiting for us and I'd hate to leave her unattended for too long. Never know what kind of beasties would consider a young elf to be a delicacy worth dying over." While still holding me by the throat, she slightly bent her knees then jumped. Within moments, we were airborne and flying out of the valley.

I had Naunet to thank for it, but yes, I knew where, and more importantly what, Tartarus was.

According to Naunet: Tartarus is one of the near infinite layers of the underworld. However, that name was a bit of a misnomer since it wasn't technically under anything. The underworld was actually inside Yggdrasil's trunk and was divided into layers that spanned the length of the world tree.

Tartarus was also known as the prison of the gods. While it wasn't one of the more "brutal" layers of the underworld, it was infamous for its ability to reduce even the mightiest beings in existence into weak children— due in no small part to the way Tartarus absorbed a person's power and used it to create all manner of monstrous creatures to defend it.

Before I knew it, the woman touched down and released me. I landed on my side and dug my fingers into the granite ground to stop my forward momentum. I skid to a stop a few feet beyond her and dug my toes into the ground to prevent me from going any farther.

"That's a nice look in your eyes," the man laughed, a moment before his big meaty fist slammed into my face with enough force to knock me off my knees and send me rolling across the ground.

Through the haze of a possible concussion, I thought I heard someone scream my name just before I passed out.

~ ~ ~

"And with that, it's time for me to go," the goddess told the mammoth sized man.

Reina ignored their byplay and sprinted over to Torga's side. Her magic was ignoring her call in this godforsaken place, so she was stuck doing this the old-fashioned way. A cursory glance revealed two major problems that needed to be addressed: *He's showing signs of severe trauma to the skull. Concussion is certain, cerebral edema is likely.* She tentatively prodded his neck and immediately found another problem. *His C-7 and C-6 vertebrae are misaligned. Hard to tell if they're fractured or merely dislocated... Or both.* She quickly removed her satchel and grabbed the small first aid kit she'd cobbled together from various alchemy shops.

She pulled out a small dagger, pausing briefly to recall the first time she'd held it. This dagger had been with her from the very beginning and had saved her life on numerous occasions.

Reina only prayed it would do the same for Torga.

Something grabbed her arm just before she could make an incision and jerked the dagger out of her hand. "What're you planning to do with this?" the man-shaped building asked.

Reina moved away and glared at him, making sure to show him just how much scorn she felt towards him. "You bastards did this. If I leave him alone now, he'll die long before you can turn him in for the reward."

The god simply shrugged his shoulders and showed her a crooked grin. "Then he dies. The reward is the same whether he lives or dies."

"Why not just kill him then? Why take the chance?"

The god leaned down and looked Reina in the eyes, that irritating grin never left his face as he said, "Let him try. I put him in that state once. I'll do it again."

Reina had nothing to say to that. He was right. And confirming that redoubled her hatred towards the narcissistic god.

"Nice eyes," he chuckled. "I'm sure you'd like nothing more than to take this dagger and cut my head off, right?"

Reina remained silent.

"'Tis a shame you'll never get the opportunity." He slid the dagger into a loop on his belt and winked at her. "You'll get this back if, and only if, you prove that you can be a good girl." With that last infuriating remark, he walked over to a rock a dozen or so feet away and sat down to watch them.

Reina stroked Torga's head and breathed out an anxious sigh. Deciding that she couldn't just sit by and watch as he hemorrhaged to death, she focused on doing whatever she could to keep him comfortable. Ayla had once told her that Torga was an anomaly, that he frequently did things that defied reason and logic.

She scooted even closer to him and prayed to whatever god was listening that he'd live to do it again.

Interlude: The Vestiges of a Broken Man

"Fenris!" Uriel called as he raced over to the despondent man. He grabbed Fenris' collar and spun him to face him. "Get ahold of yourself!" Uriel screamed. Fenris couldn't remember when, but at some point, he and Lena had been dragged inside the castle's throne room and dumped with a gathering of civilians. Over Uriel's shoulder Fenris could see a large group of Asgardian troops fighting alongside his children, Ayla, Thor, Leon, and Donna, to hold off a small army of Jötnar soldiers and keep them from taking the throne room.

"I—I can't leave Lena's side. She needs me," Fenris lamented. He wanted to fight beside his children and the other warriors, but a part of him screamed not to leave. If he did, he was sure something bad would happen.

"Fenris…" Uriel grimaced, his face twisting into something unrecognizable. "That's enough. We need your help or we're going to be overrun."

"No! I can't leave her. I can't." A sharp pain spread across Fenris' face as the sound of clapping rang in his ears. Uriel shook out his hand and stared down at him.

"She's dead. Lena is gone and if you don't get off your ass and help us hold the room, we will be too."

"No. She's not dead. She's just sleeping until Reina gets back and heals her."

"Fenris—"

"No!" Fenris shouted, clutching Lena's body tightly to his fur covered chest. "You'll see, as soon as Reina comes back, Lena will open her eyes, and everything will be fine."

"Fenris, I loved her too, but you have to face reality. I mean—look at yourself." Uriel beckoned Fenris to look down at his body. "You're shifting back. Without Lena's magic to balance your own, your body is losing its ability to hold that form. In another fifteen minutes your claws will start to cut into her flesh—" Fenris quickly moved his fingertips away from her skin. "And you'll start to lose your sense of being. I don't need to remind you what happens after that, right?"

"No. I remember clearly." Most people called it mana corruption, but it had another name: druidic withdrawal. Sixty percent of druids had animal partners, thirty-five percent had monster partners, and a lucky few managed to partner with a sentient creature. Regardless of class, there was one condition all druids feared, and that was druidic withdrawals. The longer a druid and their partner stay bonded, the more intertwined their mana becomes. This gives myriad benefits to the bonded pair and is what allows beings like Fenris to shift form. However, should their partner perish, the backlash of the interwoven mana unraveling has been known to outright kill druids and send their partners into a frenzy.

And Fenris knew, without a shadow of a doubt, that he was no exception. Lena's death was like a poison... in more ways than one. It was just as toxic to Fenris' mind as it was to his body.

Hali moved to Fenris' side and placed her hand on his arm. She was trying to maintain a look of confidence, but the loss of Lena had hit her just as hard, if not harder than it had Fenris. Even so, she agreed with Uriel. "He's right, Dad. Let's focus on getting her out of the city and then we can give her a proper burial. Okay?"

Fenris sucked in a shaky breath. He nodded his head. "Okay." He turned to Solon and handed over Lena's body.

"What're you doing?"

"I'm giving you the opportunity to give your mother a proper burial." Fenris reached up to his shoulder and pulled his shirt over his head. His partially transformed body free for all to see as coarse black fur had sprouted all over it and his musculature had begun to tear itself asunder as it struggled to take on a new shape. With Lena's magic, this process was painless and near instantaneous. Without it—the cracking of moving bones and the pain and fear filled whines that escaped from Fenris' throat were enough to give onlookers shivers.

When he was done, Fenris struggled to his full height and looked down on his children. "When the time comes, take the others and flee," he growled. He stepped over them and approached the ongoing battle for the door. As he walked, Fenris thought he could hear Hali calling his name. He strained to hear her over the sound of his own heart pounding in his ears. Her words finally came through, and tears fell down his lupine face. He knew he wouldn't be able to do what she asked, but he wasn't about to let his children know that.

"Of course. Take care of each other until we meet again." Fenris looked over his shoulder and imprinted the sight of his children and wife in his mind.

He knew he would need it to focus the rage: The enemy in front of him would soon know why Wargs were a race to be feared, and the cowards that left them to die would be reminded of what it meant to face a husband's wrath.

He threw his head back and let out an ear-splitting howl. He poured everything he was feeling into that howl, all the anguish and the rage stored within his heart that was just waiting to break free.

The howl was so soul wrenching that even the Jötnar paused in their massacre to stare.

His eyes grew hazy, and before Fenris could lose what little control remained, he rushed the attackers and began ripping them to shreds.

With the desperate strength given to him, as a man who wanted to protect what little he had left, the Jötnar at the door stood no chance before Fenris' wrath.

He slaughtered them like they had so many innocents, and then he fled from the throne room without looking back. Fenris had decided that he wasn't taking any prisoners. Any Jötnar unlucky enough to be caught by him was devoured before they could put up any semblance of a fight, and then he would move on to the next one.

The Jötnar had unleashed a beast amongst their number and this beast would go on to become something talked about in legend through hushed whispers, even invoking its name brought fear and dread to those who heard it.

But that is a tale for another time.

CHAPTER EIGHT

WHEN I CAME TO, THE FIRST THING I NOTICED was the shaking. My head was being cradled against someone's chest, yet they were shaking. Were they afraid of something? I opened my eyes and turned my head so I could see their face—

"You're awake." A sickly looking Reina met my eyes, and it all came flooding back to me.

The first thought I had was that I needed to get away from her as quickly as possible before my aura devoured her. The second thought I had was if it hadn't done it while I was asleep, it wasn't going to. Which raised the question, why?

I carefully pushed away from her and sat up. "Where are we?" I looked around and compared my surroundings to the last vestiges of my memory: We were in a cave— well, calling it a cave was being generous. It was more like an indent in the side of a giant glacier. Reina debriefed me on everything that had happened since she'd been grabbed.

I looked out the opening. From what I could see outside, we'd been dropped off in some kind of frozen tundra and left to die: Hundred-foot-tall pine trees, and massive pillars of crystal-clear ice stretched towards the pitch-black sky. The only light came from massive fireballs that streaked across the sky every few minutes and illuminated the pillars in a dazzling display of multicolored light.

"It's beautiful, isn't it—" A coughing fit interrupted her.

I got up and inspected her: Her skin had taken on a slight bluish tint, her supple lips were cracked and blistered from the cold. I reached inside me for my magic. It didn't come. "Come on," I hissed. "Work." I tried again… and again. Nothing came out no matter how hard I tried. "God damnit!"

"It's okay. My magic isn't working either. If it was, I wouldn't be in this state." She laughed weakly. "Besides…" She pointed off to the side of our little cave. She'd managed to fashion together a small fire pit from the branches of the nearby pine trees but hadn't been able to get a fire going. "It's like fire doesn't exist in this place. No matter how hard I tried, I couldn't even get a spark."

"Can I try?"

She lifted a semi-frozen eyebrow at me, then laughed. "Knock yourself out. You get a fire going and I'll do that thing with my tongue you like so much."

In spite of the situation, I found myself chuckling at that. I made my way over to the fire pit and checked to be sure that all of the pine needles she'd collected were spaced out enough to allow oxygen to flow beneath them, then I started working at it.

After almost twenty minutes of wasted effort, during which Reina began to shiver to the point I could hear her teeth clicking together from over ten feet away, I was forced to accept the fact that we had to find another source of warmth, and fast.

"Are you sure you're not cold?" Reina asked. It was an easy question to answer: No, I wasn't cold. Ever since my ascension, my body felt neither warmth nor cold. It was incapable of feeling such things. I paused as I realized something. If all of our abilities were gone, then why *wasn't* I cold?

But how to explain that to her? I couldn't just come out and say it without telling her *why* I wasn't cold, and Reina wasn't an idiot. If I gave her some half-hearted excuse, she'd know instantly and would be rightly pissed that I was keeping something from her. "No, I'm not cold," I finally said, deciding to just rip the band aid off and get it over with. "My body doesn't get cold."

"Really? How come?"

"I'm... not quite as human as I look."

"Well, obviously. I've never seen a human do half the things that I've seen you do. So… what are you?"

"That's hard to explain." The unsaid bit was "without transforming," but I'd been trying to do that for a few moments now and even that proved out of reach for the time being.

"Torga, with everything that I've seen since I was reborn on Yggdrasil, I don't think you can surprise me anymore."

I was silent for a moment. "I'm a Quasar Serpent. Oh, and the gluttonous dark god of hunger and gravity," I told her honestly.

Reina's eyes widened and her mouth fell open. She stared at me for a long minute without making a sound. Then she laughed. "Sorry, I tried to keep a straight face, but I just couldn't do it. That's a good joke though, had me going for a second."

"But I'm serious."

"Sure, you are," she sighed. "Fine, if you don't want to tell me, that's alright. I'm sure I'll needle it out of you eventually."

"I'm sure you will," I muttered. "So, we can't stay here."

"No, we can't. Unlike some people—" she shot me a weak grin—" I'm freezing my ass off over here. If I were a human, or even a normal elf, then I would be suffering from severe hypothermia or already dead. I'm lucky to have only lost feeling in my extremities."

"Can you walk?"

"I think so." She attempted to stand but couldn't get her feet under her. I caught her before she could land on the ice and pulled her into my arms.

"You thought wrong."

"Shut up."

I smiled at her. I set her feet and helped her stand while I took off my pants.

"Whoa, now I'm down for some playtime after the day we've had, but at least let me get feeling back in my legs first."

I bonked her on the head. I pulled off my shirt to go with my pants, leaving me in only a pair of wool under breeches, then slung my pants around her hips and fashioned a crude harness for her out of my clothes. I lifted her onto my back then tied everything off, so she was sitting with her legs around my waist and her arms around my neck. I did a few test bounces to see how secure she was, and only started moving once I was satisfied.

"Hang on."

"Is there anything else to do?"

"Run your mouth, apparently." She snorted at me, then snuggled closer to my back.

"You're warm," she whispered.

Of course, I was. I had two stars inside my body. "Good; focus on my warmth and try to ignore everything else. I'll get us out of here in no time."

"Mm, I'm counting on you."

I left the cave at a dead sprint to build up speed. Once I had a clear path through the trees, I jumped with all my might. I had to quickly catch myself on the lowest branch of one of the trees.

Guess my strength is gone too, I groaned internally, then leaped down and resumed sprinting. *Never thought I'd say this, but damn do I miss being a giant snake.*

~ ~ ~

I slowed to a light jog to get my bearings. I'd been jogging for hours, yet nothing had changed. The sky was as dark as it ever was, and the trees and glaciers continued to loom over us like silent watchers. To that point, aside from the trees themselves, life didn't seem to exist in this place. I hadn't seen a single animal since I woke up, which meant finding a village was a pipe dream. Of course, at this point I'd settle for a mad hermit living in a wooden shack. Anyone that could tell me the way out of here would be a godsend.

"What's that?" Reina asked, tapping me on the shoulder to get my attention and pointing at a spot on the horizon.

I could see a dozen or so humanoids trudging through the snow. They appeared to be naked, which made sense since they were most likely souls of the dead. However, as my eyes trailed over the woman walking near the end of the line, I realized that I recognized her. "Isn't that the shopkeeper? The one selling the wyvern armor?" I asked.

"I think so. It's hard to tell from this distance," she replied. Her voice was stronger now that the warmth from my body had time to spread to her.

"They seem to be going in the same direction we are," I pointed out. "Do you think we should follow them or pick another direction?"

"Might as well follow them," she said. "The alternative is wandering around until we starve to death." She had a point. While that wasn't an option for me, it was a very real threat for her. Especially in this situation, when food was even more of a necessity due to her body expending so much energy to keep her warm.

I jogged over to the procession of souls and fell into step behind them. They paid us no mind as they continued to shamble forward. I glanced over my shoulder at the ground behind us in the hopes that they would've left a trail I could follow. Unfortunately, I wasn't so lucky. Though the snow was disturbed as they walked, the moment their feet left the ground it was as if nothing happened.

"What do you think killed her?" Reina quietly asked.

"Does it matter?" I didn't see the point of her question. "She's dead either way. Whether from a building falling on her head, or at the hands of a Jötnar. It doesn't change where she ended up."

"I suppose. I just don't like the idea of her suffering. Sure, she was kind of annoying, but she didn't deserve to be killed by the Jötnar."

"Don't think about it," I said, shrugging my shoulders.

"How can you say that? We knew that woman—talked with her just yesterday—and now she's dead."

"Yeah, that happens sometimes," I told her. "People die every day. This time, it just so happened to be someone we knew. And if we're unlucky, the shopkeeper won't be the only familiar face we run into."

"I didn't realize you were such a pessimist…" her words trailed off as if she didn't want to finish her thought. But enough was said for me to get the point. She was disappointed in me.

I sighed.

This was something I hadn't accounted for. In all the years I'd spent dreaming of our reunion, I never once considered the most obvious problem: the age difference between us. Reina was still so young. While she accepted that bad things happened to people that didn't deserve it, she still allowed it to get to her, still allowed herself to feel pity for them, to empathize with them. Even after a decade of wandering around Yggdrasil, she was still the same woman who threw herself into traffic to save a small boy.

Suppose that's why she was chosen to be a hero and I wasn't.

I watched the forest for a while longer before I allowed myself to relax and settle into a comfortable pace. Reina didn't say a word for well over an hour. I'd started to believe she'd fallen asleep.

Another coughing fit hit Reina a few minutes later.

"You okay?" I asked.

"Yeah… Yeah, I'm fine. Don't worry about it." She snuggled closer to my back. "Mind if I take a nap?"

"Sure," I chuckled. "Go for it. There's no reason for both of us to be bored out of our minds."

"Thanks." Reina kissed my cheek, then rested her head on my back. A few minutes passed before I heard soft snores coming from my sleeping wife's mouth, and I smiled. *Yet another thing that hasn't changed.*

CHAPTER NINE

"I**T'S GETTING WORSE**," I TOLD REINA AS I HELD her hair out of her face. I felt myself grimacing as I watched her expel what little food she had left in her stomach into the snow. I glanced up and watched as the shambling souls moved further away from us.

Once she was finished, Reina wiped her mouth with the sleeve of her bodysuit before nodding her head.

"Not even going to deny it?" I asked.

"What would be the point? Lying to you in this situation isn't helpful to either of us."

No kidding. Reina's condition had continued to deteriorate over the last few hours, and I had a sinking suspicion that it wasn't just the cold affecting her anymore. Though the freezing temperatures clearly weren't helping, being a living person trapped in the underworld couldn't be healthy.

"We need a new plan," I said. "One that gets you out of here as soon as possible."

"Thanks for stating the obvious, babe. In other news, it's cold as hell. Now that we've both made pointless statements, do you have a plan?"

I frowned but remained silent.

"Yeah, didn't think so," she snarked. She held her glare for several seconds, then sighed and dropped her head. "I'm sorry. I shouldn't take my frustrations out on you."

"Don't worry about it. It's my fault you're in this situation to begin with, so getting yelled at is the least of what I deserve."

Reina grabbed my hand and showed me a weak smile. "It's not your fault. Whatever you may have done in the past, I'm sure you did for the right reasons."

If only you knew… Lately, I found myself thinking of the choices I'd made. The friends I'd left behind, the enemies I'd killed— the innocents I'd killed. What reason did I have? Survival? Did I truly need to kill them in order to survive or did I kill them just because I could: because it made me feel powerful—invincible.

I found myself unable to look at her, but I knew I needed to tell her before she found out some other way. "Reina, there's something I have to tell you. And I'm really not sure how to say this, but—"

"Torga, shut up," she whispered.

"No, I need to say this. It's important."

"This is too."

I looked up to meet her eyes, but noticed she was staring at something over my head. I twisted around to see what had captured her attention and felt myself stiffen as I prepared to move.

So much for being alone out here, I thought as I climbed to my feet and placed myself between her and the creature in front of me. Standing on a pair of twig-like legs with arms to match, it wasn't much taller than my human form—somewhere around seven feet or so. But that didn't mean it wasn't dangerous. The creature had a coat of thick brown fur that hung off of its wiry frame in strands that exceeded a foot in length. Its face was equine in shape, resembling that of a horse or perhaps an extremely large deer. Given the three spiral antlers on its head that resembled drills, I was leaning towards calling it Deer-face.

It was cute in a way, but the way its beady black eyes regarded me set my teeth on edge. After a few seconds of checking me out, the eyes slid off of me and landed on Reina.

"Do you think it's tracking the souls?" Reina asked.

It opened its mouth to reveal teeth blackened from rot and screamed like a banshee. It moved its arms to its sides, revealing a double-headed battle axe resting in its left hand, which it then hefted onto its shoulder.

"No, I think it was tracking you." It took a step forward, but I was quicker. I jumped forward and swung my left arm into motion, smashing into the creature's face with enough force to make it stumble.

The damn thing snorted at me.

I cursed. "Reina, you need to get out of here!"

"Fat chance." I heard Reina's voice a second before I felt her use me as a springboard. She leaped into the air and planted both of her feet in the creature's face, forcing it to stumble back even further. That was when the creature got mad. It let out a sound like the wail of the damned, then lifted the axe into the air and swung it at Reina's head.

Reina ducked the axe and stepped into the creature's personal space, preventing it from being able to use the axe effectively. She let loose two rapid fire punches into what would have been the liver of a human, dodged a second swing of the axe, then exploded into motion with a flurry of punches and kicks at its legs and pelvis region.

Unable to just sit back and watch, I stepped around to its side and wrapped my arms around its waist. I hauled back on it, pulling it away from her in time to help her avoid getting an axe to the head, and was rewarded with a fur covered fist to the face for my trouble.

I felt pain from the blow and was almost driven to my knees as a result. It lifted its axe and drove the handle into my back. I grunted but held on.

"Torga, get down!"

At the sound of Reina's voice, I twisted my body until my hip was in line with the creature's and pulled down on its neck with my right arm. At the same time, Reina tackled the creature, wrapping her arms around its chest and forcing it backwards through the momentum of her jump.

The combined might of both of our weights threw the creature off balance. It landed on its back in the snow and I wasted no time in taking advantage of it. I scrambled to cover its body with my own then planted my right knee under its left armpit and my left knee under its right armpit.

My fists came crashing down on its face like a landslide. I swung and swung and swung. I kept swinging even after my fists were covered in bright amber blood. Unfortunately, it wasn't the creature's. The skin on my knuckles tore as my broken bones pierced through the much weaker than usual flesh. I grimaced but kept swinging, my bones becoming makeshift daggers that couldn't manage to pierce the thick fur.

The creature roared in my face. The next thing I knew, I was flying through the air. I crashed through the trunk of a pine tree, bouncing a few times in the snow before sliding to a stop twenty feet away. I rolled to my feet and sprinted at the still rising creature.

I noticed Reina was doing her best to keep the thing down, but her body must've been weaker than we thought because she was having trouble putting enough strength into her blows to really do any damage. The creature came up swinging its axe, narrowly missing Reina as she dove to the side to avoid it. She scrambled away from Deer-face, ducking behind a tree for some measure of cover, while I approached it from behind. I grabbed the arm wielding the axe and thrust my elbow into it. Now, that wasn't enough to make it let go of the axe, but it did piss it off enough for it to change its target.

While I was still holding onto its arm, it lifted me into the air and swung me into the tree Reina was hiding behind. I felt a couple of my ribs break, but for the most part I ignored that. My body was already working to repair the damage anyway. With absolute regeneration as one of my traits, it would take a lot more than a broken bone—or thirty—to keep me down for any length of time. And since our traits were the only things we got to keep in this place, my regeneration was the only weapon I had until I figured out how to revert to my true form.

Deer-face pulled me away from the tree, only to slam me into it again, and again. Reina quickly came to my rescue, jumping onto Deer-face's other arm and using her weight to twist it around and save me from yet another meeting with the tree. While still being held aloft, I wrapped my legs around the creature's arm and pulled until its elbow straightened out, then I kept pulling until—

Crack

The arm holding me dropped, which also caused the axe to fall free from Deer-face's grip. Quick as a flash, Reina slid beneath me as I fell and scooped up the axe before I could land on it. She came up swinging, hacking into the creature's flank with everything she had while I kicked its legs out from under it, causing it to land on its stomach. Poor old Deer-face wailed in pain as the axe blade bit into its back, sinking to the middle of the axe head on one particularly vicious swing. Sickeningly sweet-smelling black blood spewed from the open wound, shocking both Reina and me into inaction—for a moment, anyway. As soon as she regained her composure, Reina went wild on Deer-face, hacking away at its legs, back, arms, and neck. She left deep wounds everywhere she hit, but the stubborn bastard kept moving. "Hey." I held out my hand as I climbed to my feet and Reina tossed me the axe without a word. I pretended not to notice the exhausted look in her eyes as I snatched the axe out of the air and raised it above my head. I drove it deep into the back of Deer-face's skull. Its body spasmed for a moment, then it grunted in annoyance and tried to roll onto its back, almost throwing me to the ground in the process. *Damn. What the hell is this thing made of?* I wrenched its head to the side, via the axe still implanted within its skull, then flipped it back onto its stomach. I planted my foot on its back to hold it steady while I imagined myself cutting firewood.

"Let's see how long you can keep going, eh?" I told the creature. I brought the axe down with a mighty swing, ignoring its pitiful wails of pain.

~ ∻ ~

I don't know how long I stood there swinging that axe, but by the time I was done, old Deer-face wasn't moving anymore. Which wasn't surprising, considering I'd hacked off its head.

I tossed the axe to the side and moved to check on Reina. She was sitting in the snow with her back resting against one of the pine trees. She hadn't said a word since she'd given me the axe, apparently resigning herself to letting me deal with the creature.

"I'm fine," she told me. "Just cold."

"Then you're not fine, are you?"

"Can you stop doing that?" she yelled. She jumped to her feet and advanced on me. "Ever since we got here you've been treating me like I'm an invalid. So, I'm cold, who gives a damn!? Did you forget that I've been an adventurer for ten years? That I hunted monsters for a living? You think I've never been cold before? Even before that, I was a field medic. Did you forget that I served in the same places you did?"

"Not quite."

"Close enough. I'm not a delicate little flower that'll let you put her in a vase while you do everything yourself."

"It's more of a sack, really."

"I'm not joking with you, Torga. I'm sick of it. You may be more powerful than me outside of this place, but in here, we're in the same boat. I fight just as well, if not better, than you do. And another thing—"

"You're right," I sighed.

"What?" she sputtered, clearly caught off guard.

"I said you were right. I'm so used to fighting alone, that I forgot you can fight too." I explained. "I was alone for a long time, Reina. And during that time, the only thing that kept me going was my desire to find you and keep you safe… and I failed at that. I let you get taken right out from under my nose. And after you'd been taken, I failed to save you. I let my pride swell my head and affect my ability to fight." Now that I had started talking, I found it difficult to stop. This was something that had been building for a long time and I needed to say it. "Aside from Ayla and Findral, you are the only person that I trust unequivocally—and that's why I have to tell you the truth, to make you understand it."

"What are you talking about? You never say stuff like this. We would spend days arguing because you pulled the same stunt back when we were humans. So, I guess I'm just wondering where this is coming from."

I started backing away from her. "That's just it. I'm not that guy anymore." I picked up the axe and walked over Deer-faces' corpse.

"What are you doing?" she asked.

I ignored her. I stuck my hand into the bloodied stump of Deer-faces' neck and pulled a hunk of meat away from the rest. I pulled the axe up next to me and used it like a saw to cut the meat free. It came away with a wet popping sound and I stuck it into my mouth.

"Oh, God…" I heard Reina gag. "How can you eat that?"

"I'm a monster," I said simply.

"Sure, and I'm the tooth fairy."

I ignored her in favor of shoveling more meat into my mouth. Surprisingly, Deer-face didn't taste awful. There was a subtle flavor of rot mixed into the meat. I didn't mind that though. After several mouthfuls, I had an idea. I grabbed the fur at the base of its neck and pulled on it. I began using the axe as a skinning knife and tried to remove as much of the fur as possible without damaging the coat. It was slow going—incredibly slow going—but I was hoping to get the entire pelt off in one piece so she could wear it like an oversized cloak.

"Oh, for Pete's sake. Here, use this," she said, holding a dagger out to me hilt first.

"If you had this…" I trailed off, accepting the knife, and stabbing it into Deer-face's back. "Why didn't you use it during the fight?"

"I didn't think of it," she admitted after a moment. "It's been more of a lucky charm for so long that I forget about it… sometimes."

"Okay," I said, accepting her words. It's not like I hadn't forgotten blatantly obvious things before.

"That's it? 'Okay,' and we're done?"

"Yep," I said as if it were the most obvious thing in the world.

"You really have changed."

"Was I truly that bad?" I asked as I got back to work skinning the creature.

"It's not that you were bad. You just had a way of obsessing over details like that. I've always known that it came from a good place. It was just an annoying part of your personality. If left unchecked, you could be the most domineering person I knew, and I'm including my father in that list."

I snorted at that. "That's a bit harsh."

"Maybe so, but it's accurate. You could be far worse than Dad ever was."

"Name one time that I was worse than that son of a bitch."

"Well, there was the time you made your Lieutenant cry for accidentally knocking me over. Dad was a bastard, but he didn't lay into people quite like you did."

I scoffed. "Which Lieutenant was this again?"

"I'm talking about Lieutenant Davis. You know, the six-foot-eight guy who challenged you to a fight on his first day."

I stopped what I was doing and looked up into her eyes. I'd forgotten about Lieutenant Davis. He disappeared a few months after his promotion to Lieutenant and, well, out of sight, out of mind.

"Whatever happened to him?"

"He came to me one day and apologized for what he'd done, then requested transfer to another unit on the grounds that you made him feel uncomfortable."

"And it was granted?"

"Course it was. You're a difficult man to work under and the brass knew that."

I just wish they'd had the decency to tell me that. I shook away the thought and finished up what I was doing. I couldn't change what happened in the past, even if I wanted to.

I handed the knife back to Reina and asked her to take a step back. I grabbed the pelt and pulled it free from the bloody meat beneath it. It wasn't much to look at: Deer-face was far too skinny to make a proper coat, but with a little bit more work I could probably make a blanket. At the very least, that would be better than the makeshift harness we had now.

"Think you can skin the arms and legs?" I asked her. Her response was to quirk an eyebrow at me and scoff. "Right, well, while you do that, I'm going to clean this and get it ready for you to wear." I carved a few pounds of meat from Deer-face's back, then moved off to clean the pelt.

"Ugh—right." She waved me off and got to work.

~ ~ ~

When we were done, I stood back and looked at our handiwork. The fur pelt took a while to clean, but now that it was done, it looked like a big fur blanket. It was large enough on its own to cover her entire body and protect it from the elements. But thanks to skinning the arms and legs, Reina also had arm and leg warmers to keep her limbs from succumbing to frostbite. It didn't look great, but it was functional.

"Looks good on you."

She rolled her eyes at me, but I caught the smile that flitted across her lips. "It's like something I would find in my dad's old office. He would've loved this," she said, raising the edge of the blanket and giving it a little shake for emphasis.

"Putting aside your father's 'appreciation' for animals. How does it feel?"

"I'm absolutely disgusted by it. Aside from that, it's perfectly fine."

I nodded to show I was listening. I picked up the axe from where I dropped it and began to move when I had an idea. I walked back over to the corpse and used my axe to finish snapping off the antlers on top of its head, then I handed them to Reina.

"Daggers?" she asked.

"Think you could use them that way?"

"Sweetheart, I could use a spoon as a dagger if I was motivated enough."

"Good girl." I gave her a quick pat on the head and then we moved out.

Ding!

I stopped moving the moment I heard that sound. In front of me was a pop up covered in static, almost as if the signal was choppy.

∞∞∞∞∞∞∞

You have eaten the following race for the first time. Helheim Guardian: Tier 6

Note: The guardians of Helheim are responsible for removing any intruders who do not belong inside the afterlife. As a reward for slaying one, a portion of your powers has been unlocked.

∞∞∞∞∞∞∞

"Fuck yeah!" I hollered.

"What—What is it?" Reina asked.

"A portion of my powers is being unlocked because I ate a piece of old Deer-face over there."

"What—Really!?"

Another pop up appeared in front of me.

∞∞∞∞∞∞∞

Name: Torga

Race: Quasar Serpent/Gluttonous Dark God of Hunger and Gravity (Minor)

Classification: Tier 10(+1)

Level: 100(?)

Experience: N/A

Titles: Destroyer of Asgard, The Dark Serpent, The Unwavering One, Royal Serpent, Free, The Devourer of Worlds, God of Hunger, God of Gravity

Stats:

Kenneth Arant

Physical

Strength: ∞/85

Endurance: ∞/85

Dexterity: 1,051/51

Speed: 1,583/83

Mental

Intelligence: 74

Wisdom: 51

Charisma: 31

Resistances

Elements: 90%

Divinity: 90%

Mental: 60%

Immunities

Mind Control

Illusions

Disease

Skills: Major Stealth, Heat Detection, Absolute Gluttony, Absolute Growth, Greater Petrifying Gaze, Superior Acid Venom, Detect Concealment, Energy Breath, Fly, Magic Enhancement, Elemental Manipulation, Omnipotent Control over Hunger and Gravity, Shapeshift, Aethereal Form, Size Control

Traits: Dark Gluttonous Aura ∞, Growth +1,000, Forever Growing, Indomitable, Absolute Regeneration,

Ageless, Oxygen Independent, Self-Sustaining, God of Hunger, God of Gravity

∞∞∞∞∞∞∞∞

"Reina?" I muttered after reading the pop up and seeing all but one of my skills scratched out. "I don't think we're quite as screwed as I thought we were."
"Yeah?"
"Oh, yeah."

Chapter Ten

EVER TRIED TO RUN THROUGH WAIST HIGH SNOW AT a dead sprint? It's not easy. Especially when you're being chased by three of Helheim's guardians. Though they make for great motivational tools.

With Reina slung over my left shoulder and the axe in my right hand, I sprinted through the snow in a desperate attempt to get away from the guardians. One on one, or rather two on one in our case, we could handle a single guardian easily. We could handle two guardians if we pushed ourselves, and I resigned myself to being mortally wounded. Attempting to take on three guardians was suicide, no if, ands, or buts about it.

I looked over my right shoulder and immediately wished I hadn't. The three guardians seemed to glide over the snow as they chased us like pissed off wraiths. Much like the Jötnar, the guardians only shared a passing resemblance to one another. All of them were outrageously skinny and had that weird horse/deer head, but the similarities ended there.

The closest, and thereby the fastest guardian had four arms and four legs and wielded a hammer in each of its four hands. It had two horns on its head, each barely more than a few inches long. It was the first guardian to join our little parade and had been chasing us for something like twenty minutes.

The second guardian to start chasing us had two legs and six arms. It didn't seem to wield any weapons, but with six arms it most likely never needed one. On top of its head, in between its two beady black eyes, was one two-foot-long antler that reminded me of a rhino's horn.

The third guardian was a full-blown quadruped and lacked any arms to speak of, making it look almost exactly like a normal deer, if you somehow ignored the six beady black eyes and its two mouths. It made up for its lack of arms with a pair of antlers that stuck out to either side of its head about 3 feet. Each antler had dagger-like protrusions that pointed forward end up, giving this guardian the ability to gore whatever it ran at.

"They're gaining on us!" Reina yelled.

"I figured. It's kind of hard to run like this!" I yelled back.

"What's that supposed to mean?"

"Means we need to come up with another way to do this, or we're going to get caught," I said, looking around for anywhere to hide.

"You know, I'm surprised we ran from the first one. If we stayed and killed it, we probably wouldn't be in this situation right now," she said.

"Considering how long it took us to kill the last one, I'd rather not tangle with another one right now. And judging by how quickly the other two joined in, they weren't that far away. We would've had all three of them on our asses before we knew what to do with the first one."

Reina was quiet for a few minutes, then she suddenly piped up with, "Think they can climb?"

"Haven't seen a reason why they wouldn't be able to!"

"Think they can climb *that*?" she asked, pointing a finger to our left at a massive pillar of ice that jutted from the ground.

"Reina, I don't think *I* can climb that."

"Do you have a better idea?"

Of course, I didn't. If I did, I wouldn't have changed directions and started sprinting right for it— "Incoming! Duck left!" Reina screamed. I quickly followed along with her warning and swiveled to the left, ducking my body down as I did.

"Gah!" A hammer zipped past my head not a moment later, smacking into my shoulder and knocking me to the ground. Luckily, I managed to hang on to the axe, but Reina fell into snow that came up to her chest, sinking to the ground immediately.

The three guardians let out what could only be described as a victory bellow. I looked back and saw they were quickly gaining on us, especially the hammer guardian, who had its three remaining hammers raised above its head in preparation for bringing them down on mine.

I rolled to my left just as it brought two of its hammers down on where my back would have been, avoiding the blow and getting closer to Reina at the same time. I swung my axe back, striking one of the guardian's front knees with the side of the axe head since I couldn't risk getting the blade stuck in its tough muscle. The knee bent at an awkward angle and the quadruped guardian fell to the side, hollering all the while as it attempted to stop itself. Reina put the finishing touches on the strike by planting both feet into its chest, toppling it backwards and away from us.

I scrambled forward and started running, only slowing long enough to allow Reina to jump onto my back. I picked up the pace as I put everything I had into running for the mountain of ice. Pulling slightly ahead of them, I could hear the guardians' wails of anger growing in intensity as I neared the pillar.

They're pissed. Despite the situation, I almost wanted to laugh. Had I finally lost my mind after all this time? I didn't really want to think about the answer to that question, so I pushed it down and ignored it. I could worry about my sanity, or lack thereof, later. Right now, I had other things to worry about.

Not allowing myself or Reina to die anytime soon was at the top of that list.

When we drew closer to the pillar, Reina pointed out something strange with our tagalongs. Namely, that they had begun slowing down and giving up the chase. As we came within a few hundred feet of our destination, only the hammer guardian was still following us. However, even it broke off as soon as we came within a hundred feet of the pillar, disappearing into the forest of pines as quickly as it had appeared. I slowed my run for only a few moments, then I sprinted at the ice wall without a care or thought of slowing back down.

"What is it? Did you see something?" Reina asked.

"No, that's the problem. Creatures like those don't just stop chasing us for no reason."

"So, what's your plan?"

"To get my ass up that pillar as quickly as I can, and hope that I'm near the top before whatever scared those guardians off comes back. Hang on!" I jumped as high as I could and swung the axe with all my might, driving it into the ice and using it as a pick as I began scaling. It was a bit difficult at the beginning, but I soon got the hang of prying it loose and jumping in order to gain height. Within a few minutes, I was already several tens of feet up the side of the ice wall. After a few minutes of doing this and climbing until I could see over the tree line, I'd grown confident enough in my process to try jumping over a dozen feet at once.

It didn't work out quite as well as I had hoped. "Ho—ly," Reina grunted as the axe cracked the ice and slid free. We fell almost twenty feet before I regained my wits and shoved the axe back into the ice, almost causing me to lose my hold on it. I used my feet to slow my fall and eventually stopped sliding.

"Done a lot of climbing, have we?" She let out a trembling laugh.

"Not since I got arms and legs," I laughed. I twisted my body around until I could see over the tree line behind me. Every few seconds, the innumerable ice pillars of Helheim would light up with an orange glow as a fireball from Tartarus traveled across the sky like a shooting star. I let out a sigh as I watched the red and orange reflect off the ice crystals on the ground and off the pillars.

"You know what, I'm not even gonna ask," Reina groaned. She rested her chin on my shoulder and tightened her hold around my waist and neck as she hugged me. "You know, for such a dull and dreary place that's out to kill us, it has its moments."

"Yeah... Reminds me of an island I went to once."

"Really?"

"Yes. It was as deadly as it was beautiful and if I hadn't gotten lucky, I probably would have died there.

For a while, I thought it would've been a great place to take you."

"What for?"

"I was going to ask you to marry me again."

"… Was?" she asked with a note of hurt in her voice.

"How about we get you out of the cold before we have that talk." I pulled back on the axe and used the momentum to launch myself upwards. Reina didn't say another word for a long time after that.

~ ~ ~

I pushed the axe into the ice and leaned back so I could see where I was going. This particular pillar went on for what felt like miles, and even after climbing for hours, at least, I didn't seem to be any closer to the top than I was when I started. The only evidence that I'd been climbing at all was the fact that the trees beneath me were little more than specks. I repositioned Reina, who was resting against my chest instead of hanging off of my back, in order to make it more comfortable for me to hold her. She'd fallen asleep not too long ago, which slowed down my climbing speed since I could no longer just leap up, but she needed the rest.

I knew we would eventually need to climb back down, so I didn't want to climb too high. But I also wanted to be high enough off the ground that I didn't need to worry about the guardians or whatever other creatures prowled those pines. At our current height, I felt like we wouldn't need to worry about being sniffed out by any creature that happened to come across us. Whatever had run those guardians off still worried me, but I had to think of Reina.

"Hang on; you'll have a place to sleep soon," I whispered to her. She mumbled a bit in her sleep but didn't wake up. I let out a tired sigh as I fought to keep myself awake, then I continued to climb. I wasn't just climbing blindly, though. I had a destination in mind. There was a spot, about four or five hundred feet above me, that looked like an indent or some type of cave system. Hopefully abandoned like the one I woke up in, but if it wasn't, I would try to remedy that as soon as possible.

I climbed for a while longer, eventually reaching the indent and pulling myself over the lip. I laid Reina down on the edge, then placed my body in between her and the opening: it was much deeper than I had originally thought, more of a cave rather than a mere indent. It was several dozen feet deep, about twenty feet tall, and fifteen feet wide. It was easily large enough to hide us from the elements, but that's what worried me.

Something like this didn't usually happen naturally, in my experience.

I took a few breaths to ready myself and allow my arms to rest. I moved Reina away from the edge and set her against the wall, making sure the guardian pelt was wrapped tightly around her to stave off the worst of the cold. After ensuring she was comfortable, I moved deeper into the cave to investigate the cause of its size. Were it not for the flashes of orange light coming from outside that lit up the entire pillar like a beacon, the cave would have been pitch black. As it was, I could see fine. Though, that also meant whatever had made this cave could see me just as easily.

I pressed on towards the rear of the cave. As I drew closer to where I believed the owner would be waiting for me, I held the axe in front of me to make it easier to defend myself in case of an ambush. After a few minutes of walking, I began to see signs of life: a long guardian pelt laid out next to the wall, a few weapons scattered about on the floor, several guardian corpses strung up from the ceiling. But the most telling evidence was the man waiting for me at the rear of the cave.

He was tall and emaciated with sallow skin and a long nose. Two bone-like protrusions stuck out from the sides of his head and curved forwards, resulting in wicked looking horns. And what truly caught my eye about the man were his glowing red eyes, which stared at me as if I was his greatest enemy.

"Hello, Torga. I thought I recognized your voice." I recognized *his* voice immediately. But I was wrong in my initial estimate. I wasn't his greatest enemy—I was his biggest mistake.

"Niabus," I growled. "What the fuck are you doing here?"

"Waiting for you, obviously." He smirked.

CHAPTER ELEVEN

"I'LL KILL YOU," I HISSED.

"Before that, would you mind hearing me out first?"

"How did you find me?"

"Lucky guess," he sneered.

I sprung off the ground and launched myself at him. I grabbed his shoulders and used my momentum to slam the two of us into the rear wall. Once I had him against the wall, I clutched his throat with my left hand and pulled my right fist back for a haymaker that would cave his face in.

He threw my arm off and slipped to the side, forcing my face to hit the wall behind him. Two sharp pains lanced through my sides as he sent a pair of quick punches to my ribs, then he headbutted me, which forced me to take a step away from him.

I knew I couldn't give him a minute to recuperate or I'd lose. Stepping into his personal space, I fired off an elbow at his throat, striking his carotid and throwing his head to the side to bounce off the ice wall. Though he was taller than me by a few inches, in these confined quarters, I had little issue keeping him off balance enough to rain down blows upon him.

Every attempt of his to regain balance resulted in me slamming him into the wall again—and again. After about 40 seconds of getting smacked around, he finally managed to lock down my wrists and gave me a solid shove. I slid across the floor, bouncing off the far wall and almost losing my balance in the process. However, the moment a solid right hook landed on my left cheek, any balance I had left was thrown out the window. I was knocked off my feet and sent skidding across the slick floor.

Niabus was quick to follow me, catching up to me the moment I stopped sliding and placing his foot on my throat.

"Are you ready to listen yet?" he asked, pressing harder on my throat for emphasis.

I grabbed his ankle so he couldn't withdraw his foot and punched the side of his knee. It made a harsh cracking sound, then bent in the wrong direction. He gasped as his knee gave out and he collapsed on top of me. I grabbed him by the horns on either side of his head, and tossed him off of me, before quickly pinning him to the ground with my elbow against his throat. I lifted my left leg and kneed him in the side as hard as I could.

He cursed in pain, then threw an elbow that hit me in the temple. I saw stars as I fell to the side, landing on the cool floor beside him. Niabus sat up with his hands on his throat, gasping for air.

"You're—you're a vicious bastard—you know that?" he said in between coughs.

"That's hilarious coming from you," I said sarcastically. I rolled onto my side with the intention of punching him again, but he was suddenly gone. I looked around the cave and found him crouched against the rear wall. He had his hand wrapped protectively around his throat, and he was eyeing me up and down.

"I'm not sure what I did to piss you off, but we can work things out, right?"

"Oh, you aren't sure, huh? Come on, Niabus, you don't really expect me to believe that you don't remember selling me out, do you?"

"Ah," he said, acting as if he'd forgotten the whole thing. "I didn't realize you'd made it that far." He sighed. "I was… a different person when I set that in motion. My sister had yet to prove how vicious and manipulative she'd become. You have to believe that I deeply regret what I've done, and I hope we can work through this for the greater good."

"No." I replied, climbing to my feet. "There is no 'greater good' that can make me forgive what you did. You sold me out to Orochi, literally planned my death just to get what you wanted. I can't forgive that."

"That's kind of hypocritical coming from you. I might not have seen everything that's happened, but I know for a fact you would have done the same and so much more if Reina's life had been on the line. So, let's stop with the hypocrisy and get down to business, or shall we stand here and argue until her life *is* on the line?"

I bared my teeth at him. "Explain."

"Are you going to listen? I'm not going to waste my breath unless you swear to me, on your life, that you will hear me out without interruption."

What I wanted to do was to rip his damn head off, but what I actually did was nod. "You have one minute."

"That's more than I need. We are in Helheim, Torga. Helheim, in case you weren't aware, is a place meant for only two types of people: gods and the dead. This place seeks to turn Reina into one or the other, and since she isn't a god…" He trailed off.

"So, it is killing her." I wanted to deny it, call him a liar, and attack him for everything he's done, but I knew deep down that he was telling the truth. The signs were all there—the general weakness, the coughing, the lethargy. This place was killing her, and it was my fault. I collapsed into the wall and slid until I was sitting on the floor. I ducked my head, unable to look at Niabus for fear that he would see my weakness.

"Torga, listen to me. You can save her— well, with my help you can. All you have to do is listen to me."

I glanced up at him and felt my rage swell at what I saw. Niabus was enjoying this. The wide smile on his face was evidence enough of that. But that didn't mean he was lying. As it was, I'd been presented with a choice—do Niabus' bidding or figure out a way to save Reina myself. Since I'd already tried one of those two methods and ended up almost killing her… I feared my only recourse was to try the other option, and once again subject myself to the machinations of this bastard.

I stood and approached him. "I'll do as you say, but at the first sign of betrayal or if she dies—I'll kill you. I'll slaughter you as many times as it takes to break your mind and your spirit. And then I'll devour your soul. I can promise you that." I held up my hand for him to shake and waited.

"We're in agreement then," he said with a smile. He took my hand in his own, and the deal was sealed.

～ ～ ～

"I'm confused. Who are you and why do you know Torga?" Reina asked. Her voice was noticeably duller than before, with little inflection. The same decline was evident in her eyes. They were tired, as if she hadn't had any sleep in days. The dark circles under them added to the impression that she was on death's door.

"He's the god that summoned me," I explained. "We've—I decided to ask for his assistance and he agreed to help us."

"Just like that?" she asked skeptically. "I didn't realize you had a god on speed dial."

"It's complicated. And as much as I'd like to stay here and tell you all about it, we are on a bit of a time crunch. Niabus has informed me that you are dying. This place is slowly killing you and if we don't get you out of here soon, you'll be stuck here for eternity."

"I'm dying? Don't you mean *we're* dying, or is this another 'perk' of your mysterious race?"

"You haven't told her." Niabus Said, his voice full of amusement. "I thought you were smarter than that."

"No, I have told her. She just didn't believe me." I sighed. "Why don't we talk about this once we've started moving?"

"I'm not leaving until you explain everything," Reina stated hotly, her eyes unwavering in their determination. And I knew then that she already knew— at least, she knew a part of it. I'm not sure how, and I'm not sure for how long, but she knew I wasn't what I was supposed to be.

"What I told you before is the truth. My race is something called a Quasar Serpent, and I'm a minor dark god. I told you this before, but you didn't believe me."

"Because it's unbelievable. People can't just become gods."

"Actually, they can, and quite easily at that. All it takes is intelligence, charisma, and a ruthless drive to be more powerful than everyone around you. As long as you meet those three qualifications, then it's not difficult to become a god. That's why there's so many living out their lives across Yggdrasil."

"Well, there's a lot fewer now than there were when you were still alive."

"What's that supposed to mean?"

"You faded them?" Niabus asked. I thought he would be upset that I'd killed some of his fellow gods, but if anything, he sounded... proud?

"A couple here and there," I admitted. For the next half hour or so, Niabus and I took turns explaining the innerworkings of Yggdrasil to Reina and the way gods came into being. She was quiet throughout our explanation, only interrupting to ask a question three times—two of which were about my time in the King's Challenge. When we'd finally finished our explanation, Reina looked shaken up. She wasn't panicking, but you could tell from looking at her that she wasn't happy with the information.

"Let me see if I've got this straight," she finally said. "The man I fell in love with as a young girl, has become God—"

"Lowercase G," I interrupted. "I'm a minor god, and not a particularly powerful one if my recent win/loss streak is to be believed."

"Okay, so you've become *a* god of hunger and gravity... what does that mean for us?"

"I'm not following," I said stupidly.

"You're immortal, Albert. I'm not."

"But you can become a god too. I'll help you. Then we could spend eternity together."

"I have no intention of becoming a god. But it's not even that. If it was, I'd learn to deal with it. I'd bet good money an elf marrying a god wouldn't make Yggdrasil's top ten 'weirdest pairings' list. It's the fact that you're a murderer with a body count higher than—God, any war I've ever heard of."

"Alright, I can understand your point. And I agree I've made some mistakes, okay? I was in a bad place for a long time, driven to the point of insanity multiple times because of my hunger, and the situations I found myself in. But I did what I did because I wanted to find you again. Every battle I fought, every person I've killed—they were all so I could be with you again." I reached out to take her hand, and it was slapped away at the last moment. Reina glared at me in a way she'd never done before, and my stomach fell.

"Don't you dare blame that on me," she snarled.

I pulled my hand back without breaking eye contact. "You're right. It's not your fault. It was never your fault." I stood up and made my way over to the entrance to the cave. "Niabus, would you mind carrying Reina while we descend? I don't believe she wishes for me to touch her at the moment."

"Would be my pleasure," Niabus smirked. He reached out for Reina to take his hand, and she accepted it. As he lifted her into his arms, she never broke eye contact with me, and I couldn't tell if that was a good thing or a bad thing.

I turned away from her and stepped off the edge. My body quickly reached terminal velocity, and I hit the ground a few minutes later. My weight caused the ground beneath me to crater, and the snow beneath my feet to explode outwards, filling the air with a cloud of white powder. A few seconds later, Niabus and Reina reached the ground and the phenomenon repeated itself.

Niabus walked out of the cloud of snow, carrying Reina as if she weighed nothing. For her part, Reina was hanging onto Niabus' neck like she was trying to break it.

"We need to move quickly. There's no telling when Sarthaal will return," Niabus muttered.

"What's a Sarthaal?" I asked.

"Not a what; a who. Sarthaal is something of a protector in these lands. Hates trespassers though, so it's best if we get out of here before we're discovered."

I felt myself involuntarily twitch at the information. I braced myself for what I was sure to come—

"What are you doing?" Niabus asked.

"Waiting on Sarthaal to show up and attack us."

"Why would he show up now?"

"Isn't that the way this works? You tell us about a dangerous enemy, and they show up unannounced?" I asked.

"Torga, this isn't a television show. It's not gonna appear just because you say its name," Niabus replied sardonically.

I looked to Reina for assistance, but she seemed hell bent on ignoring me. She was standing at Niabus' side with her guardian cloak wrapped tightly around her. *She won't even look at me.* "If you say so," I sighed. I moved to follow them but caught myself looking at Reina as we walked.

I understood her anger. I'm sure if the roles were reversed, I would be having trouble accepting it as well.

But what I wouldn't do is get angry about something she'd willingly shared with me, and then blame it on her for me not believing it. I shook my head. *Either she'll get over it and we'll go back to the way things were, or she won't. That doesn't change my mission. After all, I've been resigned to a life protecting her from the shadows for over a century. I'll protect her from the gods and see her back to her teammates whether she wants me to or not. Then, and only then, will I take a concede and leave her side.*

I eyed Reina's back and wondered if this wasn't what was supposed to happen. Now that she knew what I was, and I wasn't referring to my title as a god, I didn't have to hide it anymore; didn't have to hold back.

INTERLUDE: ANCIENT HISTORY

A FEW HOURS AFTER REINA'S AND TORGA'S disappearance, Donna and Leon were still fighting to clear out as many Jötnar as they could. They weren't getting paid for this, but they owed it to the Asgardians to help them. After all, were it not for their mistake, maybe this wouldn't have happened.

Maybe Torga and Reina would've been here to stop the invasion before it even began.

Donna shook her head to get that thought out of her mind. She didn't have time to think. Such luxuries were reserved for when she wasn't fighting for her life.

Donna swayed back, avoiding the nasty looking hammer wielded by the Jötnar: a five-foot tall, blue-skinned, goblin looking creature wearing a mismatch of metal armor. Over a dozen of these creatures had chased them into a small alleyway, though only seven of them still remained.

She spun her staff in a circle, using the rotations of her wrist to build up momentum so when she brought the end of the staff down on the Jötnar's helmet it would do enough damage to at least stun it for a moment.

The helmet echoed like a gong, and the Jötnar inside it wailed in agony as its eardrums burst from the vibration. Donna followed up by using her staff to make two quick strikes to either side of its helmet. The Jötnar went cross-eyed as its brain bounced around inside its skull.

The Jötnar pitched forward, flailing its arms in an attempt to keep from falling over, but Donna caught it in the throat with the butt of her staff. She grimaced as she heard the Jötnar's neck break. She came back with a sideswipe that knocked the Jötnar off center, depositing it onto the ground and out of her way.

Donna glanced around for her next opponent and found one rushing at her. She brought her staff up, spun, and parried a sword that would've cleaved her head in two. She maintained her spin and brought the staff around to sweep the legs out from underneath the Jötnar. As soon as she stopped spinning, she started whispering a spell under her breath.

She planted her staff between its legs, then vaulted over it and drove a kick into the chest of another. The second Jötnar stumbled backwards, his thin body unable to withstand the force of the kick.

Donna wasn't done yet, though.

She finished the spell and twisted her staff so that the butt smacked into the Jötnar's pelvis and kept going. A highly concentrated beam of heat scorched the ground and sliced the Jötnar from pelvis to scalp. The smell of burnt flesh filled the air as both sides of the Jötnar were cauterized immediately.

"Leon, duck!" Without waiting to see if her partner had moved, Donna dropped to a knee and spun her staff over her head. The heat being whipped through the air slashed apart anything that got into its way. This included the buildings that surrounded them, a couple of streetlamps, and three Jötnar necks. The intense heat left a trail of molten stone and fire in its wake. She was thankful that this section of the city was mainly a residential district. Most of the people living in this area would've been evacuated already, so she could use her magic with impunity.

She released her spell and dropped her staff almost in the same instant. Her magic had been exhausted by the spell and it would take a while for her to recuperate the lost mana.

Luckily for her, Leon was there to pick up any slack.

He clashed blades with two Jötnar at the same time. Neither party could push the other back, but Leon had a few tricks up his sleeve. For starters, he took his left foot and used the guiding lanes that were a Jötnar's legs and brought his boot straight into one of their frozen berries.

With the one Jötnar taken care of for the moment, Leon was able to focus on the other. He quickly overpowered the other goblin creature and pinned it against the wall. He brought his elbow across its face, breaking its nose and knocking out a few of its needlelike teeth. Then, for good measure, he grabbed its sword with his gauntlet-covered hand. He placed his own sword across the Jötnar's throat, then punched it.

The blade was pushed through the tender but cold flesh as easily as if it had been a sheet of paper.

Leon drug the sword across the wall, not having to worry about dulling the blade due to the powerful enchantment protecting it, and then slashed across the other Jötnar's torso. The blade cleaved from its right shoulder to its left hip, bifurcating the two halves and causing freezing cold blood to spray into the air as its still-beating heart pumped what was left of its blood out of its body.

Leon quickly covered his face with his gauntlet, hissing as a few droplets landed on the unprotected skin of his face.

Leon cursed at the pain. "I'm telling you, Donna. If my face gets scarred because of this crap, I'm going to find a way to bring these bastards back to life just so I can kill them again."

"Woe is the world that has to live with your scarred face," Donna replied sarcastically. She took another glance around the alley; it would've been annoying if they'd left one of the Jötnar alive just so it could ambush them later.

"All right, I think that's all of them. We should get a move on before we run into anymore Jötnar." Donna left the alley and started walking towards the center of the city. It took her a few moments, but she soon realized that something wasn't right.

She returned to the alley and found Leon standing in the same spot where she'd left him. He had one gauntleted hand running through his hair, presumably in a vain attempt to keep it at least somewhat presentable.

"That's a wasted effort, don't you think? There are no barmaids for you to seduce here," she joked.

Leon didn't react.

Donna put her hand on his shoulder and shook him.

He didn't budge. In fact, pushing on his shoulder felt like she was trying to push over a large stone.

Has he been cursed? she wondered.

She lifted her hand and opened her mouth to chant a spell—then her eyes landed on one of the flames caused by her spell.

It wasn't moving either.

She only knew of one phenomenon that could do such a thing and if she had been a few years younger, she would've dropped to her knees and prayed that she was wrong. Slowly, so as to not be considered a threat, she released her staff and allowed it to clatter to the ground. She lifted her hands above her head and slowly turned to face the mouth of the alleyway.

A tall man was standing there, a kind smile on his face. His shoulder length curly black hair hung loosely over his face, hiding his right eye from her sight. The man was broad shouldered, with a well-defined chest, which she could see because he was only wearing a white robe that hung down to his knees and a pair of rough looking sandals.

He wielded no weapons, and wore no armor, but he terrified Donna more than anything she'd seen in her travels with Reina.

"Hello, Donna. I'm happy to see you again." The man stepped into the alley. His presence grew stronger the closer he moved, and Donna found herself walking backwards to stay away from him.

"Spare me your lies. You and I both know you're not happy to see me." Donna continued to walk backwards until she inadvertently bumped into Leon.

"Oh no, I'm happy you're here. Things just haven't been the same without you around."

"I bet." Donna glanced over her shoulder at Leon, and for just a moment, she thought about leaving him and running.

But she knew she couldn't. She couldn't abandon him and escape alone.

She'd be lucky to escape at all.

"So, what drew you out of the silver city?"

The man's smile grew predatory. Though he may have looked harmless, Donna knew that was just what he wanted people to see; it's what every one of his kind wanted people to see.

The people whose ageless beauty rivaled that of the elves, whose ingenuity rivaled that of the dwarves, whose appearance on Yggdrasil caused a war that lasted for centuries.

"The judges have asked that I bring you back in one piece. For old times' sake, and to ensure the safety of your friend there… please do not struggle." A pair of wings burst from his back, completely blocking off any chance she had of getting around him. The wings were light itself, though most mortals would've seen them as merely white.

The man reached Donna and placed a hand on her shoulder.

"Good choice," he told her. Then he reached around her and placed a hand on Leon's shoulder.

Donna grabbed his wrist and squeezed, bringing his attention back to her. "You said you wouldn't hurt him."

"And I won't. But you are not the only one the judges wish to see."

"What—" The alley was filled with a ray of light for only a fraction of a second, but in that time, the three of them had vanished.

CHAPTER TWELVE

I KNEW I WAS LYING ON MY BACK ON A COOL SURFACE that was as smooth as glass. The sky above me was pitch black, with a million-billion twinkling lights of every color imaginable swirling around a pale colored tree adorned with silver leaves and limbs that spread out in every direction. The sound of waves crashing into a cliff at the edge of my hearing caused my body to involuntarily relax and I slowly drifted back into unconsciousness.

"Hey..."

I felt something poke me in my side.

"Torga, are you still alive?"

My eyes snapped open and I grabbed whatever was poking me and ripped it away from the spindly limbed shadow standing above me. I swatted at the shadow with the thing in my hand, a wasted effort since it passed through the shadow without hitting anything.

I attempted to climb to my feet, but the entire world seemed to be spinning constantly. I ended up stumbling backwards into something sturdy, and possibly made of wood. I had to close my eyes and lean against the thing to ride out the sudden onset of nausea I was feeling. I slid down with my back pressed firmly against it and leaned my head back.

After several minutes passed without the feeling going away, I opened my eyes and for a moment I forgot all about the nausea as I became mesmerized by the thing's—the tree's—beauty. It was probably only twenty or thirty feet tall, but every other branch seemed to stretch out far beyond what I could see with my eyes. The leaves on the closest branches glowed with an ethereal luster and cast a silver light on everything within a three-hundred-foot radius around the tree, which had the unfortunate effect of revealing two things. The first was that the tree, and therefore I, was sitting on a large hill overlooking an endless abyss that seemed to stretch on for eternity.

The second thing the light revealed was that the only thing protecting the hill from the void was a low dividing wall composed of glowing white bricks. The wall was only a dozen feet tall, but it stretched out as far as I could see in either direction. Without the wall, I had the strangest feeling that the tree wouldn't be able to survive in this place.

"Incredible, isn't it?" I glared at the shadow for disturbing my ability to watch such a thing of beauty. A pair of fleshless hands extended from the shadow. They were followed by an elegant top hat, and I found myself wanting to groan in disbelief.

"Hello, Amaar."

"Hello, Torga." Amaar looked down at the thing I was holding and moved his hands in a "give it here" fashion. "Would you mind giving back my cane?" I grunted and tossed the cane to the dapper skeleton, who caught it and bowed low with a flourish.

"You know, you're shorter than I remember," Amaar muttered after returning to his full height. He shrugged off my glare and made his way over to my side. "We need to talk," Amaar finally said after sitting down next to me. He took off his hat and placed it in his lap, then leaned his cane against his shoulder.

I'd never known the death god to be so reserved. I doubted he would have given me such a courtesy before. He'd always seemed like the type of god that did whatever he wanted, and consequences be damned. But now—he sounded like a tired old man.

That probably seems weird considering he was a skeleton, but it was the image that popped into my head.

"What about?" I asked, half out of curiosity and half out of fear. Anything that could put Amaar into this state couldn't be a good thing. Amaar motioned to the border between the light cast by the tree, and the darkness beyond the dividing wall.

"Welcome, Torga, to the birthplace of creation." As if it were waiting for that moment, a waterfall of multicolored light fell from the sky; it was as wide as anything I'd ever seen, and its beams illuminated everything for miles around.

Amaar stood and motioned for me to follow him. I was too awestruck to form any questions, so I did as he asked.

He led me to the dividing wall and beckoned me over to take a look. I had to fight to keep my jaw from dropping at what I saw: Every light I'd seen since waking up earlier wasn't *just* swirling around the tree... They were falling into an inky black ocean that continuously crashed into the bottom of the low dividing wall. As I watched the lights spiral into the water, I noticed a pattern emerge. The lights closest to us always appeared to be moving deeper into the darkness of the ocean, while the lights furthest away seemed to be moving upwards, into the sky.

"What are they?"

"The lights moving upwards are newly created realities. Soon, they will give birth to their very own Yggdrasil and life will be born anew."

"And the lights moving into the water?"

Amaar didn't say anything for a while, choosing to watch the lights as they moved throughout their cycle. "They are realities reaching the end of their existence. Whether because life has died out or some other fate befell them, they are brought here to be destroyed."

Those are entirely different realities? "Then... That tree is—"

"Yggdrasil, yes. Smaller than you imagined?" he asked, a trace of his old humor seeping into his voice.

I looked over my shoulder at the beautiful silver tree and nodded. "Much."

"Appearances can be deceiving," Amaar snorted. "That tree carries the weight of all creation upon its branches and has never once wavered in its duty to support it."

"… Why am I here?" I muttered. "I assume there's a reason you pulled me away from my wife's—from Reina's side?"

Amaar gave me a pitying stare and sighed. He placed his hat upon his head and pulled the brim down over his eyes. "I brought you here to give you two warnings: one from me, and one from someone with a vested interest in your life. First, my warning: Do not blindly place your trust in Niabus. He wants only one thing in this life, and there's a decent chance you'll eventually stand in the way of his ambition."

I already knew I couldn't trust Niabus as far as I could throw him, so I thanked him for the advice and didn't think much more about it.

"As for the other…" He sighed. "It doesn't end well for you. Give up and move on with your life."

"What's that supposed to mean? What doesn't end well for me? Who told you to give me this warning?"

"I dare not speak for this person… but, if I were to hazard a guess, they are referring to your current path in life. As for who they are, I cannot say."

"Can't or won't?" I questioned bitterly.

"I can't, but even if I could, I wouldn't."

"You can't? You're *the* god of death. You could obliterate any god I've ever met without even trying, and yet *you* can't do something? Why?" I asked, my voice getting louder with every word. I couldn't help it. I'd had enough life altering events in the past few days to last an eternity. And now he shows up with this crap?

"Because they asked me not to," Amaar said, his voice quiet and full of… sadness? Pain? "Never mind that, it's not important. What is important is that you wake up before a group of nasty troublemakers find out you're here."

"Troublemakers?"

"Yes. Of course, since your arrest was most likely arranged by them, it'd be almost impossible for them not to know."

"My arrest, what does that have to do with anything—" My brain turned on and I remembered the words of my captor, Ruknar. *"Don't be modest, now, you're so much more than that. You, my hungry little friend, are Orochi: The god of serpents, and the chaotic king of destruction."*

"Oh—*Oh*." I hissed. "So, I was arrested because of Orochi?"

"Most likely." Amaar nodded his head. "The journey ahead won't be an easy one, Torga. It's going to be incredibly dangerous for you and the people around you. Everyone you've killed, every enemy you've made over the course of your travels—they're *all* in the underworld. I'd be willing to bet that some of them are already aware of your presence in Helheim and Orochi has plans to tell the rest."

"Why help me? Why tell me all of this?" I asked suddenly. "I know you were told by *someone* to give me a message, but you didn't have to tell me everything else, so, why?"

Amaar shrugged. "Let's call it repayment for showing a jaded old god something he'd never thought he'd see again and leave it at that."

"If you say so," I sighed.

Amaar lifted his cane with one hand and pressed the butt of it against my chest. "Remember my warnings, Torga. They just might save you. Oh, and don't forget to breathe," Amaar said in an amused tone.

"What—"

I felt the cane tap against my chest, and then I was yanked backwards; my body came close to crashing into Yggdrasil, but I was deflected off of a transparent dome of magical energy and ricocheted off into the darkness.

I flew, faster and faster—faster than I'd ever gone before. The darkness around me seemed to warp time as I passed through it for what felt like an eternity. As I flowed, I began to see shapes and colors I'd never seen before. All of that came to an end as I felt my momentum stop… I was out of the darkness now; instead, floating above me was a large white moon. Its surface was marred by craters from an eternity of debris forcing its way through the moon's atmosphere and slamming into the surface. I don't know how I knew, but I somehow thought that if I turned around, I would see the Earth.

I didn't get the chance. I fell, gravity suddenly pulling me away from the moon at speeds I never would have believed possible. I felt myself get caught in the gravity well of a large brown planet, but my speed was such that I wasn't pulled in. Instead, I was slung around the planet and shot off into the distance.

I clenched my eyes shut as I felt myself losing whatever tenuous grasp of sanity I had left.

"Breathe, Torga." Amaar's voice ripped through my panic. I involuntarily did as he said. My momentum was broken; I felt myself floating in place for several seconds before I dared open my eyes.

The world had been painted gold, astral bodies floating past as if they were being pulled along by a slow moving river. Planets, moons, asteroids, all had been painted gold. Or maybe it only appeared that way because of the massive flame that burned around me.

I was enraptured by what I saw. If I were to die right now, everything leading up to this point would have been worth it just to see this. *"This is what it means to truly become a god. Very few of my so called 'brethren' ever get to see this,"* Amaar told me. *"You've barely scratched the surface of the power lying dormant within you. Your path is fraught with danger, but if you make it to the end... This will be your reward."*

The world of gold shifted instantly, and I found myself in a world of mirrors—no, not mirrors— multicolored crystals so pure they gave off a mirror-like shine. I floated past an oblong emerald and stared at my reflection, and my reflection stared back. Hundreds of thousands of different Me's stared back. I only got to see my reflection for a few seconds, but even in that breath of time I noticed there were differences between myself and my reflections. Namely, some of them weren't identical to me. There were Serpents, Nagas, Dragons, Humans, Elves, I even saw one cat-like creature staring at me with amber colored eyes.

"Look away," Amaar's voice warned. *"That is a gate to the multiverse. Best not look into it for too long, lest you become trapped within."* Reluctantly, I tore my gaze away and shut my eyes.

However, they did not stay that way for long. My eyes snapped open as I felt my body being ripped apart. I looked down at my right hand and saw that it had split into eight replicas of itself. The same was true for the rest of my body, though the furthest replicas would be broken down and reduced to ash, only to be replaced by a new one at the front of the line. My body was in excruciating pain, but even that was gone in a flash and I found myself floating alongside a giant eyeball of the purest red. Its pupil, though slitted, was liquid gold.

I was grateful that it didn't seem to pay me any attention.

I thought maybe Amaar would tell me about it, but he was strangely silent. Seconds passed as I left the eyeball behind and sank to the bottom of an ocean comprising every color imaginable; every drop of water was a different color, every layer a different shade.

Then I stopped moving, and I found myself in what I can only describe as a cave full of atoms. Energy bounced between the various masses, only to be bounced off to some unknown location. An instant after I stopped moving, I felt as if my body was being sucked through a straw and I was pulled down into a puddle of green goo. The green transformed into orange, the orange transformed into blue, and the blue transformed into white.

I opened my eyes and stared at the ceiling of a rather small ice cave. I twisted my head to the side and saw Reina and Niabus sleeping on opposite ends of the cave. I stood up; climbing onto shaky legs as I fought to maintain my balance. After almost falling twice, I held onto the wall and used it to move towards the exit.

I need to kill something. I stumbled my way out of the cave, making sure to grab the axe as I went, and set out on my first hunt of the day.

The sights and sounds of whatever Amaar had done to me were still fresh in my mind, as I spotted a guardian and rushed it.

CHAPTER THIRTEEN

I STUMBLED BACK INTO THE CAVE WITHOUT LOOKING at anyone. I had gaping wounds all across my body healing as I walked, and my vision was so blurry I thought I might vomit, but I'd done it. I pulled along the corpse of a guardian with my right hand. Its head was missing, courtesy of the axe I wielded in my left hand, and there was a gaping hole in the side of its chest where I'd sunk my fangs in and injected as much venom as I could.

Oh, how I missed my venom. It was one of the truly useful things about being a snake, and one of the few things I'd never regretted unlocking.

Ding

A pop up appeared in front of my eyes and my already half-dazed smile grew even wider.

∞∞∞∞∞∞∞

For consuming another guardian, another of your skills has been unlocked and is available for use.

Name: Torga

Race: Quasar Serpent/Gluttonous Dark God of Hunger and Gravity (Minor)

Classification: Tier 10(+1)

Level: 100(?)

Experience: N/A

Titles: Destroyer of Asgard, The Dark Serpent, The Unwavering One, Royal Serpent, Free, The Devourer of Worlds, God of Hunger, God of Gravity

Stats:

Physical

Strength: ∞/85

Endurance: ∞/85

Dexterity: 1,051/51

Speed: 1,583/83

Mental

Intelligence: 74

Wisdom: 51

Charisma: 31

Resistances

Elements: 90%

Divinity: 90%

Mental: 60%

Immunities

Mind Control

Illusions

Disease

Skills: Major Stealth, Heat Detection, Absolute Gluttony, Absolute Growth, Greater Petrifying Gaze, Superior Acid Venom, Detect Concealment, Energy

Breath, Fly, Magic Enhancement, Elemental Manipulation, Omnipotent Control over Hunger and Gravity, Shapeshift, Aethereal Form, Size Control

Traits: Dark Gluttonous Aura ∞, Growth +1,000, Forever Growing, Indomitable, Absolute Regeneration, Ageless, Oxygen Independent, Self-Sustaining, God of Hunger, God of Gravity

∞∞∞∞∞∞∞∞

I lifted the corpse in my hand, brought it to my mouth, and ripped out its heart with my teeth. The heart tasted awful; it was rotten and was bursting with the foul-tasting blood. I didn't care.

I dropped both the corpse and the axe by Reina's side, then walked out. I couldn't stay here, I had too much energy, too much anger. If I stayed, we would only get into another fight. Better for me to leave and take out my aggression on something that deserved it. I stepped into the biting winds and lifted my head to the sky. I sucked in a deep breath, then let it out slowly. *Time to hunt.*

I took off at a slow jog, being careful not to burn more energy than my body could regenerate at any given time. It wouldn't be a smart idea to get stranded out here and not be able to find my way back. To that end, I also took the time to mark trees every hundred or so feet so I wouldn't lose track of where I was and where I was coming from.

I ran for a long time before I found another guardian. This one was as tall as the trees and about fifteen feet wide, with eight spider-like legs coming out of its underbelly. Despite its size, it was moving quickly through the forest. I knew that at my current size and strength, there was no way I could kill it—at least, not immediately. So, I had to focus on crippling it first, and what better way to cripple a spider than to rip off its legs?

I just had to remember to avoid the fangs. Or in this case, the eight-foot-long claws that came out of each foot.

I leaped into the air, grabbed the lowest branch of one of the trees, pulled myself up, then leapt to another branch, this one slightly higher up. I repeated this until I was closer to the guardian's height, then I just focused on catching up to it, as it had traveled quite a distance in the time it took me to climb to the top of the trees.

Let me tell you, jumping from branch to branch isn't nearly as easy as elves made it look.

I jumped after it as fast as I could, each leap carrying me over a dozen feet at a time. I was quickly catching up to it, until one of the branches I landed on snapped in half and I fell over twenty feet, slamming my stomach into one of the thicker branches below. I was lucky that branch hadn't snapped as well, but if my plan was to work, I needed to be as high as possible. So up I went. I climbed to the top of the trees and continued my running jumping combo.

It took another five minutes, but I finally caught up to the spider guardian and ran alongside it for a minute or two. I wanted to make sure that I had the timing right, because I definitely didn't want to have to do this again.

I shifted my body as soon as I landed on another branch, and then leaped toward the spider guardian. I landed on top of its back and was forced to dig my nails into its fur in order to avoid sliding off the other side. Pulling its fur was all it took to alert the guardian of my presence. If I didn't want to get thrown off, I'd have to work fast. I jumped towards one of the legs and wrapped my arms and legs around it. I sunk my fangs into it, injecting as much venom as I could manage, then swung around and jumped back towards the body. I repeated this two more times before the guardian got wise and moved one of its legs right as I jumped towards it. I missed, of course, and slammed into a tree on the other side of the guardian, almost falling to the ground below.

But my work was done. My venom was like acid in its veins and ate through the tender flesh beneath its skin, causing the three limbs to detach and fall to the ground. Taking out three of its eight legs had thrown it off balance and made walking difficult for the large creature.

Of course, I could have simply taken out the bottom of the legs, and it would have been far easier to do. But I didn't want to risk it breaking off one of its own limbs just to avoid falling over. Now that it was off balance, I could go for the lower parts of legs and bring it down easier than if I'd left the first three alone.

I dropped to the ground, using the snow as a cushion to absorb most of my weight, and then I took a few moments to take a few bites of one of the detached legs before I ran after the spider guardian. It knew I was after it now and was determined not to let me get at its back a second time. It turned to face me, allowing me to see its head for the first time, and I realized how spiderlike it actually was. It had eight arachnid-like eyes; four on each side of its head, and a pair of large mandibles that stuck out from its jaw. I couldn't tell for sure if it had fangs or not, but I was going to err on the side of caution and assume it did.

I dashed underneath it, diving to avoid a wide slash from one of its legs, then rolled to my feet and came up swinging. I struck the inside of one of its legs with my right palm and realized my mistake immediately.

I was way too weak to even attempt to break off a leg through sheer force. Instead, I would have to do it the same way I broke off the first three. I wrapped my arm around one of the legs and was towed into the air for my trouble, but it didn't matter. My fangs sunk in just as easily in the air as they would have on the ground.

What I wasn't prepared for was for the guardian's leg to detach at a joint above me and drop to the ground. I hit the ground hard enough to daze me for a moment, which just so happened to be the exact amount of time the spider guardian needed to stomp me into the snow. In spite of its massive size, the spider guardian's legs were very dexterous, or so it appeared after four of them stomped on my back in rapid succession.

I rolled to the side after the 4th leg came down on my back, and pushed off the ground, throwing myself towards one of the trees. I ducked behind the tree for a second, then started climbing.

I needed to get higher—it held the advantage on the ground with its longer reach—but if I could get to its back then it would lose that advantage. Something heavy struck the opposite side of the tree and broke it off at the base. I had to leap from the tree quickly or risk falling to the ground again and being at the mercy of the spider guardian's legs. I grabbed hold of a limb and swung myself up, then resumed climbing. Trees on either side of me were smashed to splinters one after the other. In less than ten seconds, over twenty trees had been destroyed, with my tree following soon after. This time I didn't have the luxury of being able to jump to another tree, so I was forced to ride it all the way to the ground.

I leapt off at the last moment to land in the snow, rather than be crushed by the tree.

I knew I couldn't afford to sit around, so I started running almost immediately. Good thing too, as the spider guardian's foot stomped on the tree half a second later. There was no doubt in my mind that if I'd been under that tree when that foot came down, I would have been reduced to paste, and absolute regeneration or not, that would have sucked something awful.

I dove behind a tree to avoid the guardian's gaze, then used the tree line to put some distance between us. If it couldn't see me, it couldn't catch me.

Crash!

The cacophony and ear shattering sounds forced me to look over my shoulder and what did I see: The guardian, caring not for the safety of its body, as it shoved over any tree in its way in order to run after me.

Ever seen a spider scurry across the ground so fast you lose track of it? Well, this was a lot like that… Only about a million times worse since this particular spider was over a hundred feet tall.

Ding

Yeah, yeah, skip to the bit where I get my skill back, please!

∞∞∞∞∞∞∞∞

Name: Torga

Race: Quasar Serpent/Gluttonous Dark God of Hunger and Gravity (Minor)

Classification: Tier 10(+1)

Level: 100(?)

Experience: N/A

Titles: Destroyer of Asgard, The Dark Serpent, The Unwavering One, Royal Serpent, Free, The Devourer of Worlds, God of Hunger, God of Gravity

Stats:

Physical

Strength: ∞/85

Endurance: ∞/85

Dexterity: 1,051/51

Speed: 1,583/83

Mental

Intelligence: 74

Wisdom: 51

Charisma: 31

Resistances

Elements: 90%

Divinity: 90%

Mental: 60%

Immunities

Mind Control

Illusions

Disease

Skills: Major Stealth, Heat Detection, Absolute Gluttony, Absolute Growth, Greater Petrifying Gaze, Superior Acid Venom, Detect Concealment, Energy Breath, Fly, Magic Enhancement, Elemental

Manipulation, Omnipotent Control over Hunger and Gravity, Shapeshift, Aethereal Form, Size Control

Traits: Dark Gluttonous Aura ∞, Growth +1,000, Forever Growing, Indomitable, Absolute Regeneration, Ageless, Oxygen Independent, Self-Sustaining, God of Hunger, God of Gravity

∞∞∞∞∞∞∞∞∞∞

Are you fucking kidding me!? I internally screamed as a skill that did absolutely nothing to help me out of my current situation was the one I'd unlocked. *Screw it!* I accelerated to my top speed with one thing on my mind.

Getting the hell away from that spider.

CHAPTER FOURTEEN

"So... want to talk about it?"

I looked over my shoulder at Niabus and frowned at him. I turned my face away and looked out the entrance of the cave. It was my turn to keep watch to make sure guardians didn't ambush us, and it didn't help that we were in the middle of a blizzard, so I didn't appreciate being distracted by useless talk—which Niabus seemed to be full of lately.

I'll admit, Niabus was being surprisingly helpful when it came to taking care of Reina: He didn't argue, didn't make threats; he just nodded his head and did as I asked. Which made me all the more suspicious. It didn't match up with what I knew about him. Niabus was always detached. Even when he was trying to be helpful, I didn't see him emote or show concern... Yet, all of a sudden, he was acting like a concerned friend?

I didn't buy it.

"No, I'd rather not."

"You lost," he muttered. I knew it wasn't a question, he was stating a fact.

"That's becoming rather common lately. What's your point?"

"It's getting to you. I can see it and she can see it."

"My hearing must be going, because I still haven't heard your point."

"Fine, here's my point. If we don't hurry up and get her out of here she's going to die and her soul is going to be trapped in Helheim forever, and you going out and challenging every guardian you find to a fight to the death isn't going to get her out of here any faster."

"I've heard your point and taken it into consideration," I told him. I picked up the axe that I had sitting beside my foot, and then stepped out into the storm. I felt a hand land on my shoulder a second before I was spun around.

I glared first at the hand on my shoulder, then the owner of said hand. "Take your hand off of me."

"Are you going to pull your head out of your ass or are you going to run back out there and get yourself killed? Which is it because if you're going out there to commit suicide, I'll just kill her right here and now and be done with it."

"No, I'm not going to commit suicide. I gain power by killing them, more power means her chance of survival goes up. If you finally have a plan to get her out of here, I'd love to hear it, but so far all I've received are platitudes and excuses."

"Excuses? That's rich coming from you," he laughed condescendingly.

"I know, and right now it's like I'm looking in a mirror." I knocked his hand away with the handle of the axe and grabbed his throat with my free hand. "Now, do you have a plan to get her out of here or not?"

"Yes, I do."

I shoved him back towards the cave. "Then start talking." I walked over to where Reina was sleeping and woke her up. Though she was a bit groggy at first, she came fully awake when I told her that Niabus had a plan to get us out of Helheim.

"To my knowledge, there are only two ways out of Helheim without outside help. The first is to find death's elevator: It's basically the way the death gods travel to and from the underworld. It runs through every level of the underworld, but its location is randomized every day. The other... is with help from the lord of Helheim."

"Who's the lord?" Reina asked before I could.

"Her name is Gamos, and she's something akin to royalty in these parts. I only know a few ways to get in touch with her, all of which require a fair bit of walking."

"Perfect. You start walking, Reina and I will wait here."

"That's not the way it works. If I leave here, there's no telling when I'll make it back. Or if I'll ever even find my way back. It's better if we all go."

"That's crap and you know it. I travel out every single day and always find my way back. The only reason you wouldn't find your way back is if you chose not to return."

"Can we make it before I die?"

"Don't listen to his bull crap, Reina. You're not going to die. If I have to, I'll keep killing guardians until I regain my ability to fly and I'll get you out of here that way. Let him run off on his own; we don't need him."

"But it's getting harder and harder to find guardians, you said so yourself. How can you be sure that you'll be able to fly again before I'm dead?"

I grit my teeth but couldn't refute her point. The order in which my skills were unlocked was completely random, as far as I could tell. I had no guarantees that I would be able to fly before her body gave out, but I didn't like the idea of Niabus leading us to someplace only he knew about.

"Fine, but you're going to tell us where we're going before we leave. I'm not letting her out of this cave just so she can blindly follow you out in the middle of a snowstorm."

"Of course. I wouldn't dream of leading you down the wrong path."

So, he says. Personally, I was almost positive that that's exactly what he was doing. I just had no proof. And my credibility with Reina had fallen off as of late, so she wasn't likely to go along with what I was saying without evidence that he was trying to lead us on a wild goose chase.

"The place we're going to is known as Soulsden, and it's where Gamos lives," Niabus finished. He had a toothy grin on his face and his thin eyes showed his amusement. I knew I couldn't trust him one bit, and he knew that, which is why he targeted Reina and worked to get her approval. He knew that I'd go along with whatever she said. I felt my blood boil. I knew what he was saying was garbage, and I was being forced to swallow it or risk losing her.

I returned his smile with one of my own.

His smile faltered, his eyes widened minutely, then he looked away. "We'll leave once we have everything packed up." He turned his back on us and walked off, moving deeper into the cave, presumably to pack up his own stuff. He didn't carry around much, but he did have a few things in a fur sack stashed in the back of the cave.

"You're too harsh on him," Reina said quietly.

"You only say that because you weren't there. If you'd known what he did, then you would be on my side."

"You think he hasn't told me what he did? We've been living together in a cave for over a week. Do you think we haven't talked?"

"If you know what he did, and you're still willing to say that I'm too harsh on him, then maybe you've changed more than I thought you had."

"What's that supposed to mean?"

"You're a smart girl, figure it out." I left her behind and entered the forest. If I was lucky, I could find a guardian wandering around the outskirts of our little territory. Even if I didn't find anything, it would get me away from her before I said or did anything I would regret, so it was worth the effort.

I entered the forest at a jog. I'd mapped out a territory that spanned about 5 square miles. If I ran straight, without any breaks or distractions, I could cover the entire thing in about fifteen minutes. Hopefully, that would be all the time I needed to calm down. Otherwise I'd kill Niabus before he had the chance to lead us to Soulsden and if he was dead, then Reina and I were back to gambling our lives away on random chance.

I stopped running as a sound in the distance caught my attention. It was very subtle, and were it not for my past hunts I would have missed it. It was the sound of a guardian grunting in pain, and it was close... perhaps a little too close.

We'd never had one stray this near camp before.

I was simultaneously elated and terrified.

What if it'd found the camp while I was away? Would Niabus bother to protect Reina, or would he leave her to fend for herself?

Wasn't that what I was doing right now?

Damnit. I sighed. *What the hell am I doing?* I tightened my grip on the axe handle, then started following the sound of breathing. I would kill this guardian and then I would return to her side. No more of this solo hunting business. I wasn't an edgy teenager pissed off at their girlfriend. I was her husband. And I'd been leaving her safety in the hands of someone else.

Well, no more.

I rounded a tree and came nose to chest with a ten-foot-tall brick wall with fur. The guardian was built like a gorilla; with a huge barrel chest, equally large arms, and short legs that barely touched the ground. It seemed to walk on its fists rather than on its legs.

It let out a bellowing roar, then swung one of its massive arms and backhanded me. Luckily, I was able to get the axe up in time to take most of the blow on the handle. The axe managed to not be split in two by the train that just hit me, and I was knocked away to carve a trench through the snow.

I rolled onto my feet and faced the guardian, axe in hand. All it would take to kill it was for me to sink my fangs into its neck. Conversely, with those thick arms it wouldn't be too difficult for it to rip me in half.

All the more reason for me to get in close.

I dashed towards it. It lifted its arms into the air with both fists tightly clenched, ready to bring them down on my head at any moment.

So, I threw the axe at it. It wasn't pretty. The axe didn't even stick in, but when I throw an axe at you and I hit you square between the legs... You're gonna notice.

And it did notice.

Its beady black eyes tracked the axe as it fell into the snow. Then it gave me a confused look, as if to say, "Was that supposed to do something?"

Yes, it was supposed to distract you long enough for me to get within arm's reach of you. And it did.

I put everything I had into a shoulder charge and tackled it. My shoulder hit it dead center and forced it to take a step back. It was about like running into a massive rock, but thanks to my regeneration healing any internal injuries, I didn't have to spare time thinking about what to do next.

I scooped up the axe, waved around a wild swing, jumped to avoid its hand as it tried to grab my feet, then used the momentum from my drop down to drive the axe into the top of its head.

However, it batted me away at the last second, forcing the axe to stop a hair's breadth before it cleaved its skull completely in two.

I lost my grip on the handle as I was sent flying backwards. The axe remained stuck in its head, and the creature seemed to show very little interest in pulling it back out.

Good. Made this next bit a little easier.

I rolled to my feet and sprinted back into battle.

I sidestepped a hammer fist that would've turned me into a pile of goo, then stepped around behind it and leapt onto its back. Using its long fur to maintain my grip, I scaled the creature until I was directly behind its head. Then I wrapped my arms around its throat, put my feet into the small of its back, and put all of my strength into pulling its head backwards.

The guardian was surprised for a moment, but then it started clawing at my arms with its nails. If the guardian had been trained to fight, this move wouldn't have worked at all because it would've been able to stop me.

Once I'd pulled its head back far enough, I let go with my left hand and placed it on the handle of the axe. Then I let go with both hands, grabbed the axe, and kicked off the guardian's back, wrenching the axe through the top of its head and out the back.

Its head split into two pieces, each side lying on a shoulder as if the guardian were a massive flower in bloom.

That description is a bit morbid, but it's what popped into my head when I first saw it.

I knew I couldn't rest yet. These guardians were insanely durable, just splitting its head might not be enough to kill it. I needed to make sure that both sides more completely detached before I could rest.

⁓ ~ ⁓

I brought a chunk of the guardian's brain up to my mouth and sank my teeth into it. It was a bit weird eating a brain. I had originally tried to eat it like it was an apple, but that just seemed wrong somehow.

I know I know; I'm eating its brain. What does it care?

Well—

Ding

ꝏꝏꝏꝏꝏꝏ

For consuming another guardian, another of your skills has been unlocked and is available for use.

Name: Torga

Race: Quasar Serpent/Gluttonous Dark God of Hunger and Gravity (Minor)

Classification: Tier 10(+1)

Level: 100(?)

Experience: N/A

Titles: Destroyer of Asgard, The Dark Serpent, The Unwavering One, Royal Serpent, Free, The Devourer of Worlds, God of Hunger, God of Gravity

Stats:

Physical

Strength: ∞/85

Endurance: ∞/85

Dexterity: 1,051/51

Speed: 1,583/83

Mental

Intelligence: 74

Wisdom: 51

Charisma: 31

Resistances

Elements: 90%

Divinity: 90%

Mental: 60%

Immunities

Mind Control

Illusions

Disease

Skills: Major Stealth, Heat Detection, Absolute Gluttony, Absolute Growth, Greater Petrifying Gaze, Superior Acid Venom, Detect Concealment, Energy Breath, Fly, Magic Enhancement, Elemental Manipulation, Omnipotent Control over Hunger and Gravity, Shapeshift, Aethereal Form, Size Control

Traits: Dark Gluttonous Aura ∞, Growth +1,000, Forever Growing, Indomitable, Absolute Regeneration, Ageless, Oxygen Independent, Self-Sustaining, God of Hunger, God of Gravity

∞∞∞∞∞∞∞

I smiled so wide I thought my cheeks would split. Finally, I wasn't bound to my weak human form anymore.

I immediately activated the shapeshifting skill and reveled in the feeling of my body tearing itself apart. My legs fused together to form a long tail that extended well over a hundred feet. My rib cage broke as new bones were created inside my chest. Those bones then burst out beneath my arms and revealed themselves to be another pair of arms. I felt an intense pain in my head as two bonelike protrusions burst through my forehead and slightly curved backwards. My face elongated as a third bonelike protrusion pierced through the top of my nose to form a horn. I felt my teeth sharpen to a razor's edge and multiply until my entire mouth and throat were covered in razor sharp teeth.

However, all of that paled in comparison to the feeling that settled inside my body, as the black hole that replaced my stomach was recreated in all its glory.

My Naga form hadn't changed much since my ascension. I now had extremely thick scales on top of my hands and up my arms that reminded me of a set of gauntlets. These new scales were darker in color than the rest of my scales, being closer to black than green. Orange veins ran throughout my body, courtesy of the two stars that replaced my eyes. Each star filled me with magic beyond what most people could comprehend.

After being trapped in that weak body for so long... God was it good to be back. But I couldn't risk Niabus knowing which of my powers I had regained. I needed as many tricks up my sleeve as I could get in case he decided to turn on us.

So, with the future in mind, I forced myself back into the weak human body before trudging back to the cave.

Chapter Fifteen

UCK LEFT, JAB RIGHT, STEP BACK TO AVOID WILD swing, jump forward and sink my teeth into its throat. I poured my venom into what should be the guardian's carotid artery; each milliliter of the highly acidic venom scorched its veins and devoured its flesh. I closed my mouth and ripped out its throat. Its blood soaked me to the bone, propelling me even further into an anger fueled frenzy.

For days we'd been traveling through the forest, and for days I'd had to watch Reina's body waste away as the icy air sucked the life out of her.

I let the guardian's corpse fall to the ground and spun in search of my next victim. Two other corpses greeted me, each lying in a mangled mass of unrecognizable fur and meat. Movement off to my right drew my attention and I spun, ready to take the head off of anything in my way. I stopped my fist the instant before it made contact.

"What?" I asked sourly.

"Are you quite done?" Niabus asked. "You've been suicidally attacking these guardians since you woke up."

"Yeah, well, maybe if they weren't so close to camp, I would be able to leave them alone," I sniffed. My statement was entirely true. These three guardians were less than a hundred and fifty feet from where Reina was sleeping. Had I not been around to intercept them… I glared at Niabus, knowing full well he would have left her to fend for herself.

Niabus looked around at my handiwork, then smiled and said, "Your powers are coming back."

"Somewhat," I allowed.

"That's good. They'll come in handy soon."

"Oh?"

"If I'm right in my guess, then we're about twenty miles from Soulsden, and one step closer to getting the two of you out of here."

"Do you really expect me to believe that you're not coming with us?" I snorted derisively.

"Whether you believe it or not isn't any of my concern. I'm not leaving with you or rather, I can't leave. Not yet."

"Okay, I'll humor you. Why can't you leave?"

"I'm looking for someone." He shrugged. "Just remember that it's none of your business and I'd prefer to keep it that way." Niabus smiled at me.

"Whatever you say," I laughed. Niabus left with a halfhearted wave and a quiet goodbye. I turned back to the corpses and observed them for a moment, we needed meat. Specifically, Reina needed protein and a lot of it if she expected to survive out here. Her body was already beginning to eat the layer of fat above her muscles, giving her an emaciated appearance. It was so bad, her eyes had begun to sink into her skull, and she claimed to have lost all feeling in her fingertips.

If we didn't get some protein in her soon, she could have severe nerve damage that would last the rest of her life. And as someone who suffered from nerve damage in my previous life, that was not something I wished for her to experience.

Mine was due to shrapnel penetrating my head, but I'm fairly certain the principle was the same.

After skinning, butchering, and eating the hearts of the three guardians, I wrapped the meat in one of the pelts and carried it back to camp. I found Reina sitting next to a pine tree, cocooned in a bevy of pine needles, tree bark, and fur pelts.

I greeted her with a nod, which she didn't return, but I couldn't be bothered to complain anymore. She was mad at me. I understood that. I couldn't let my feelings get in the way of her survival anymore. With that in mind, I carried the meat over to her and dropped the pelt bag at her feet.

She eyed the meat tiredly; unable to muster up the energy to even complain about the blood soaking into her boots.

"You're going to eat some of this even if I have to force it down your throat," I told her. I reached into the bag and pulled out a palm sized mass of meat. Reina scoffed at the sight of it and turned her head to the side.

This was a game we'd already gotten used to. She refused to eat because the raw meat made her want to vomit, but she needed the protein to survive. It became a game of "How can I make her eat this without causing her to hate me more than she already does?"

The answer?

Don't worry about it.

If she hates me, she hates me. Only thing I can do is do my best to keep her alive until we get out of here and then leave.

"OK." I put the meat to my mouth and bit off a decent sized chunk. I chewed the tough meat until it was tender mush, then I grabbed her face and turned it to face me. I mashed our lips together and spat the food into her mouth. Before she could spit it out, I put my palm over her mouth and forcefully tilted her head back. "Swallow," I said in a harsh whisper; each syllable was pronounced slowly, so there could be no mistake. She swallowed the meat, and I removed my hand.

The moment my hand left her mouth, a string of incredibly diverse curses left her mouth. I had to admit, I was impressed. She swore in ways even I had never heard before, and that was saying something.

"You're an asshole," she growled.

I took the opportunity to shove more meat in her mouth. "I've been called worse. Now, chew that up. And don't bother spitting it out, I'm going to scoop it up and shove it back in your mouth If you do."

"Why did I ever find you charming?"

I smiled bitterly. "That's a good question." I shoved more meat in her mouth and forced her to chew. "When you figure that out, let me know." She stopped protesting a few minutes later and settled for grumbling under her breath in between bites of the guardian meat I shoved into her mouth.

Once I'd gone through several palm sized pieces of meat, I stood up and moved away from her. Reina said nothing about this, though I did catch her eyeing me once or twice. It was… rough seeing her so wary of me, but this had to be done or else she would starve. It's hard to describe the pain of starvation to someone who'd never experienced it. Despite Reina's background, this was her first time being truly hungry and I could tell she didn't know how to react to it. That's why she was fighting me about eating the meat; she still had her "preferences" and she chose to eat for pleasure as well as necessity. I'd discarded such ways of thinking even before my transition from human to serpent.

I settled against a tree a dozen or so feet away without saying a word. After another twenty or perhaps thirty minutes, Reina closed her eyes and drifted off to sleep. I followed soon after, closing my eyes and hoping for dreams of a less complicated time.

Ding

∞∞∞∞∞∞∞∞

For consuming another guardian, another of your skills has been unlocked and is available for use.

Name: Torga

Race: Quasar Serpent/Gluttonous Dark God of Hunger and Gravity (Minor)

Classification: Tier 10(+1)

Level: 100(?)

Experience: N/A

Titles: Destroyer of Asgard, The Dark Serpent, The Unwavering One, Royal Serpent, Free, The Devourer of Worlds, God of Hunger, God of Gravity

Stats:

Physical

Strength: ∞/85

Endurance: ∞/85

Dexterity: 1,051/51

Speed: 1,583/83

Mental

Intelligence: 74

Wisdom: 51

Charisma: 31

Resistances

Elements: 90%

Divinity: 90%

Mental: 60%

Immunities

Mind Control

Illusions

Disease

Skills: Major Stealth, Heat Detection, Absolute Gluttony, Absolute Growth, Greater Petrifying Gaze, Superior Acid Venom, Detect Concealment, Energy Breath, Fly, Magic Enhancement, Elemental Manipulation, Omnipotent Control over Hunger and Gravity, Shapeshift, Aethereal Form, Size Control

Traits: Dark Gluttonous Aura ∞, Growth +1,000, Forever Growing, Indomitable, Absolute Regeneration, Ageless, Oxygen Independent, Self-Sustaining, God of Hunger, God of Gravity

∞∞∞∞∞∞∞∞∞∞

Good. Another step closer to freedom.

At the rate I was unlocking my skills, if I only had another week—No, another five days—I knew I could unlock the rest of them. Since unlocking absolute gluttony, I had regained my previous strength and durability, which made hunting down guardians a breeze.

And this string of good luck all began when I unlocked shapeshifting and returned to my true form. It was a bit sad to think that I, who spent over 80 years of my life as human, now thought of my serpent form as my "true" form, but that's just how it was.

This human body was not the real me, not anymore. How I longed to return to my Naga, but until I was sure that Niabus wouldn't stab me in the back at the first opportunity, I couldn't afford to let him know how many guardians I'd killed. Especially since I devoured all but two of the ones I'd killed over the last few days to keep up the facade that I was weaker than I really was.

If Reina found out I was keeping such information from her, it would only validate her feelings that I couldn't be trusted.

Granted, I was keeping a secret from her, but it was for our own good. She wouldn't understand that; Niabus had somehow managed to brainwash her into believing that he was a "good" person.

I'd never heard such an unfunny joke before.

I shut my eyes and fully committed to falling asleep.

If Niabus was right, and we really were so close to Soulsden, then we might be out of here as early as tomorrow.

What would I do then?

It was obvious to anyone with a pair of eyes that Reina didn't want me around anymore. She would be perfectly content if I vanished and never returned.

Well, I wasn't gonna fight her on it.

There were people in this world who knew what I was, and loved me for it anyway. And I'd rather spend my life with them, than chase after someone who didn't want me around.

I let out a shaky breath and put my arm over my eyes to block out the light.

Yeah, that was why…

INTERLUDE: OROCHI'S MISDIRECTION

A YOUNG MAN OF ELVISH DESCENT LEANED against a massive door. There was nothing extravagant about the door itself; it was just a door. However, the door was located in a place without light. There were no walls, windows, ceilings, or floors in this place either. It was a pure void the likes of which could only be found in one place.

The Palace of fate.

The youth looked around, as if to make sure no one was coming, then he took a circular object out of the right breast pocket of his suit and pushed it against the door as quietly as possible.

Seemingly useless symbols appeared in rapid succession across the front of the object. However, the elf knew better. The object was akin to a magical lock pick, the symbols were various frequencies any enchantment on the door could match.

If the elf attempted to open the door right now, an alarm would go off somewhere in the Palace, and Seraphim, the Angels of fate, would swarm the elf within moments and attempt to cart him off to who knows where.

But this was Orochi, and he had no intention of going down without a fight.

Sure, he would not be happy about having to fight. But he would still wipe out any who stood in his way.

Orochi adjusted the glasses sitting on the bridge of his nose with the palm of his left hand. He didn't need them to see, of course. But the enchantment on them allowed him to see the traps that he was sure were nearby.

Not that anyone would pay him a second glance even if he did set off an alarm. After all, he was just a guy leaning against the door to one of the most well protected courtrooms in the universe. And he was supposed to be here. Well, the intern he killed was supposed to be here. But since he was kind enough to loan Orochi his face, no one would pay attention to someone like him.

There were certain perks to being a dark god, and that was one of 'em. People were all too happy to loan you almost anything. In fact, Orochi thought they were just dying to give him what he wanted.

Who was he to decline their gifts?

Click

Orochi smiled as the enchanted lock on the door came undone.

He quickly stuffed the circular device into his breast pocket and stepped inside. The inside was almost identical to the outside, save for a rectangular tower that stood in the middle of what Orochi assumed to be the room.

He reached up and pressed a button on the side of his glasses, which activated the enchantment. The lenses flashed red and he could see runes floating across the room. The runes were also scattered across the floor in various combinations that Orochi couldn't decipher.

Luckily for him, he didn't need to. He only needed to avoid stepping on them.

With that in mind, he made his way across the room to the tower. He took extra care not to touch the floating runes either.

He reached out and placed the palm of his hand against the tower. A bright light flashed as lime green lights lit up inside the room.

Orochi smiled.

A screen appeared in front of Orochi's face and with a simple motion, he summoned a keyboard in front of him. Symbols appeared on the screen that Orochi could only read because his glasses were still active.

He typed in a few dozen commands using the keyboard. Upon pressing the final key, a small slot appeared in the tower.

Orochi reached into his pants pocket and withdrew a small, pink, rectangular object. He shoved it into the slot on the tower and then stood back.

The device went to work. Almost immediately, the number of symbols on the screen multiplied by a factor of ten and flashed by in sequences that Orochi couldn't hope to keep up with.

Orochi stood by and watched as the symbols flashed on the screen for over ten minutes, and then it was done. The device ejected itself from the tower and disintegrated instantly, leaving no evidence of its presence.

A flashing red button greeted Orochi on the screen, but it wasn't an alarm, it was a file: Specifically, it was Orochi's file.

Orochi began typing more commands into the keyboard. As he did, changes in the file became evident as line by line, Orochi merged two files together: His and Torga's

Once he was done, he stepped back, and this is what he saw.

∞∞∞∞∞∞∞∞

Name: Orochi

Race: Demon Serpent

Classification: Dark God

Aliases: The Devourer, Torga, World Eater, Albert Robertson

Possible fate lines: Herald of Ragnarök, Father, The Lone Survivor, Hero's Husband.

∞∞∞∞∞∞∞∞

'Tis truly a pity. How can someone with so much potential be relegated to the duties of a mere breeder? Orochi internally sighed. He found a few of Torga's other fate lines interesting; for example, he'd never heard of the lone survivor. Fate lines usually show your greatest achievement at the moment of your death, so it was odd for the word "survivor" to be present at all.

Orochi glanced at the "hero's husband" and "father" fate lines and shook his head. Such pathetic fate lines for one so powerful.

Orochi closed Torga's profile, entered a few more commands, and began forging another.

∞∞∞∞∞∞∞∞

Name: Nidhogg

Race: Greater Hydra

Classification: God

Aliases: N/A

Possible fate lines: Savior of Yggdrasil

∞∞∞∞∞∞∞∞

Orochi shut down the tower and backtracked out of the room. He locked the door behind him and smiled. Now their fates had been merged, and Orochi had forged a new identity for himself. He could move around more freely and anything he did would be blamed on Torga.

That should keep the annoying worm busy for a while.

Orochi pulled a crystal out of his pocket and held it up to eye level. He crushed it in the palm of his hand, then vanished within a flash of golden light.

Chapter Sixteen

NIABUS, REINA, AND I WALKED THREE ABREAST through the waist high snow. Reina had started to feel more like herself now that she wasn't cooped up in the cave all day, and she was capable of keeping up with the two of us.

It was good to see her back to her old self.

"Well, looks like luck was with us after all," Niabus said, pointing off into the distance.

Reina and I glanced at each other, then back at Niabus. We clearly didn't see whatever it was that he saw. It took another five minutes of walking before I saw what had Niabus so excited; the forest of pines was coming to an end. As we approached the end of the forest, Niabus explained that this area of the forest was always moving and only stayed in one spot for about twenty-four hours before it moved to another location. Finding it at all was akin to winning the lottery; finding it in less than two weeks was practically unheard of.

The moment I stepped out of the tree line and found myself on the outskirts of a large crater, I knew this place was different. And not just because it was missing the trees I'd grown used to seeing. No, this place was actually teeming with life. At least, it was when compared with the rest of the realm.

It was different because of how alien it appeared, compared with the uniform monotony that was the rest of Helheim.

There were animals here. They looked like they were sculpted out of ice, so perhaps they were actually golems instead of living creatures, but animals were animals. I can't tell you how nice it was to see a rabbit munching on an ice-covered blade of grass after weeks of not seeing anything but the guardians.

At the center of this massive, glacial, crater stood a magnificent city, surrounded by walls that appeared to have been carved out of the very ice around us. They were taller than any of the trees outside the crater. The buildings were a mix of condensed snow, shaped to form walls, and logs from the pine trees. There weren't just one or two, either—there were hundreds, easily. And that's just what I could see from this side of the city walls.

The crater was so large it took several hours to walk from the edge to the center. Along the way, I saw races that I'd never seen before, and I wasn't sure why until Niabus noticed my interest and explained.

"Snow elves," Niabus said, pointing to a group of elves walking a dozen feet to our left. They were paler than anything I had ever seen, with bright red eyes, and hair that was so white it was basically transparent. "They have difficulty surviving outside of places with extremely low temperatures. These particular elves also appear to have made a deal with Gamos to serve as guards for the city."

"How can you tell?" I asked. I couldn't see any obvious symbols on their gear, and they certainly didn't carry themselves like trained soldiers.

"It's the weapons," he explained, pointing out that they were carrying toy-like armaments: a few swords, a spear, and one of them wielded a bow. "The only people allowed to carry weapons in Helheim are the ones that serve the lord."

"If no one is allowed to carry weapons, then why does the city need guards at all?" Reina asked, making her interest in the conversation known.

Niabus laughed, an honest to God, joy filled laugh, and motioned to the various cloaked humanoids that were also traversing the crater. "Do you think everyone here is honest? That no crime exists here?"

"Ah…" she trailed off, dropping her head, and looking at the ground.

Something about that seemed wrong, but I couldn't put my finger on what it was. Maybe I just didn't like seeing her embarrassed?

Aside from the elves, there were also large insect creatures that resembled bi-pedal ants: They were called chaurons, according to Niabus.

Humans or something close enough for the distinction not to matter.

And I spotted what I could only assume were dwarves with hormone issues. They had all the characteristics of a dwarf—short legs, stubby arms, beards that hung down to their kneecaps. They were just ten times the size of a normal dwarf.

"Those are draugur. Don't ask where they came from. It's a sensitive subject," Niabus said. The expression on his face told me that he actually wanted me to ignore his warning and ask, then suffer whatever consequences came from that decision.

"Wasn't going to, but thanks for the warning. Now that I think about it, where did they all come from? We didn't see a single person the entire trek over here, but now they're hundreds of them?"

"That's a bit complicated and even I don't understand it completely, but suffice it to say Helheim is, well massive would be an understatement. It spans millions of miles in every direction, and that number grows larger every day. Helheim— actually, the underworld in general—is constantly expanding just like the overworld. Because of this, an enchantment was placed over the crater that makes it easier for travelers to find. I don't know how it does it, but it manages to pull people from all over Helheim to a singular location."

"How does it know who to pull and who to leave alone?" I asked, now honestly interested in the answer. I don't know much about magic, but that degree of enchantment was on a completely different level from anything I'd ever heard of.

Well, almost anything. I was trapped inside a time altering enchantment for a while, and that was probably infinitely more complex than this. Either way, it was impressive to me.

"That's an easy one. The enchantment scans all living beings within a certain radius, I think. And then it takes those people and if they desire to come to the city, it does whatever it does and they're here. If they don't want to come to the city, then it leaves them alone."

"Does it call dead people too?"

"No, you have to have a certain desire to come to the city; otherwise, it won't work. And such a focused desire is very rarely found in the dead. They usually want general things like… to live again. Always heard that was a popular one."

"How do you know all of this?"

Niabus scoffed, "Did you forget who I was? I was a god of destruction; I used to visit the underworld annually to attend their many conventions... And I may have dated someone in the city for a while."

"Wait— the underworld has conventions?" Reina asked skeptically.

"That's what you're hung up on? Not the part about him being a god of destruction and dating someone in the city of the dead?" I asked incredulously.

"That God thing is old news. But the city of the dead holding a convention—that sounds interesting."

"Oh yeah, I'm sure Deathcon is one hell of a good time," I said sarcastically.

"Actually, it is. It's one of the highlights of being a god. It's just a shame they can't hold it in the underworld anymore."

"Why?" she asked.

I clamped my hand over her mouth and directed a glare at Niabus. "Can we stay on target, please?"

"Ah, yes, well. As I mentioned, there are only a few ways to safely contact the lord without getting our souls torn to pieces. And the safest involves fighting in the arena."

"Arena?" I asked, already not liking where this was going.

"Oh yes, anyone is allowed to challenge the arena at any time, and if you win, the lord of the city will usually grant you a wish. I was once a champion of it myself," he said, sticking his chest out. "So, how about it: Are the two of you ready to fight in the arena?" he asked with a wide smile on his face.

"If that's your way of asking if I'm ready to bash your skull in, then yes. Otherwise, no, that doesn't sound particularly fun."

"It's either that or we return to the forest and wander around until we find death's elevator. Your choice."

"I vote for the elevator," I replied immediately.

"I say we go for the arena," Reina interjected.

"Reina, I really don't think that's the safest option in your condition."

"I'll be fine. Just try not to drag me down," she scoffed.

"Reina, this is serious. If you die in the arena, it's for good. There's no coming back from this, and you'll be stuck in Helheim forever."

"And if I die in the pine forest, I'll also be stuck here forever. I'll take my chances with fighting in the arena," she said emphatically. Her intensely focused eyes locked onto mine, and I knew that there was no way I could convince her.

"Arena it is," I sighed. I had no other option than to follow her into the arena and do my best to keep her safe. Even if I knew it was a stupid idea.

~ ~ ~

As we drew closer to the wall surrounding the city, it became ever more apparent that this place had been created by someone powerful. Upon closer inspection, the wall wasn't just a wall. It appeared to be the staging area for what I could only describe as sixty-foot-tall ice giants.

And no, I wasn't referring to the Jötnar.

These things were massive humanoids that looked like they'd been cobbled together from ice Legos.

Niabus explained that they were ice golems, but as someone who'd faced down golems before, I felt confident in saying that comparing the two was an insult to the ice golems.

Having the two fight each other would be like having a pro heavyweight boxer fight a toddler.

It just wasn't fair.

Aside from the golems, the city was similar to others that I'd seen throughout Yggdrasil. The gate was manned by a pair of snow elves that checked the identities of everyone entering and exiting the city.

We got through the gate easily, which I found slightly suspicious, seeing as I was a wanted person in the overworld. But Niabus assured me it was fine.

Yeah, I didn't believe him either.

The buildings were neatly constructed in single file lines that allowed ample room for people to walk down the wood lined paths that were the streets.

I had a brief thought, and wondered if they tried to make the roads out of ice, and if so, why couldn't I have been here to see the repercussions of that?

"What are you smiling about?" Reina asked, suspicion clear in her voice.

"Just had a funny thought, that's all."

"Anything you would like to share with the rest of the class?"

"No."

"Fine," she huffed. She folded her arms under her chest and ignored me until we arrived at the arena.

Now, I didn't know what the other two were expecting, but when I thought of the word "arena," I pictured grand pillars, an open skyline, and seat after seat of spectators waiting for bloodshed. I didn't picture a building just large enough to house a family of five semi comfortably, but that's what I got. I may not have been expecting, but I was relieved that this was the arena we got. I wanted nothing to do with the arena idea as it was, so I certainly wasn't looking forward to fighting on behalf of the masses.

Niabus led us through the basic wooden door of a nondescript snow-covered house that wouldn't have looked out of place in any of the human controlled cities throughout Yggdrasil. Then we walked down a set of stairs and across a hallway to a pair of double doors that ripped away my hopes like a nightmare demon. These doors were black and were covered from top to bottom in glowing graffiti that was the sole reason this hallway had any light at all. He grabbed the oversized handle on one of the doors and pulled. The door swung open silently, and the stench of rot slammed into my nose and mouth.

"I knew it," I sighed.

"You knew what?" Reina asked, looking at me from beneath the hood of her fur blanket.

"I knew it was too good to be true. Should have banked on the possibility that it was just hidden underground," I explained, disappointed in myself for my naivete.

"I think it's pretty cool," she said in a half tired / half eager tone. Her eyes were sparkling with excitement over the prospect of fighting in an underground arena.

"And for the most part it is," I agreed. "But this just seems like someone put in a lot of effort to make this place appear more mysterious than it actually is. I'm betting once we get inside, there's dirt floors, bloodstained walls, and a mass of faceless audience members just waiting for one of us to die."

"You'd be wrong," Niabus interrupted. "Only one person will see us once we enter the arena proper, and that's the city lord. Though I should warn you now, there's a chance you won't be fighting living beings."

"Oh, thank the gods," I exclaimed.

"Why does that relieve you?" Reina asked. "You should be used to killing by now."

I stopped walking and stared at her back. *Is this what my marriage has come down to?* I let out a derisive snort and resumed walking. What else could I expect? I wanted to be offended. I wanted to spin her around and demand that she show me the respect she used to. But the reason she was acting like this was that I'd lost her respect. I— was a monster. And it's much harder to respect a monster than it is to respect a man, especially if you don't understand the monster's point of view.

We soon arrived at the end of the hallway and stepped into an open courtyard complete with a small fountain in one corner. The smell of rot was heavy here, and I wasn't sure if that was from the red smears covering the grass or the undead lining the walls, moaning as if in pain, when I knew that clearly wasn't the case. Standing in the center of the courtyard was a tall young woman with her back to us; she had waist length, straight black hair that was parted down the middle to hang over her shoulders and down her back. She wore a sleek black dress that hugged her figure nicely, while remaining modest enough for her to maintain a sense of regal dignity. Her skin was pale like a corpse, and I found myself wondering if it was because she never saw sunlight or if that was her natural complexion.

"Hello, Niabus. I thought I asked you to never darken my door with your presence again?" As if my eyes were playing tricks on me, the woman smiled at us; it was a kind smile, like one a mother might show to her child.

"I could never stay away from you, Gamos," Niabus said with such conviction, even I almost believed him.

"True. You always did come back begging for more."

Hearing the woman's sultry voice was like getting smacked over the head with a sledgehammer—in the sense that my head felt like it would split open if she kept talking. That seemed to have caught her attention, as she turned her face and looked at me. Her eyes moved up and down, taking in my appearance with her lifeless, obsidian-colored eyes.

"Who are you?" She moved around Niabus and stepped up to me. She slowly circled me while making quiet comments to herself about my appearance.

"Torga, my name is Torga." I responded before I could stop myself.

"Torga…" My name came out of her lips in a breathy sigh, almost as if she were tasting it. Then, as quickly as it came, her interest waned, and she moved her focus onto Reina. She circled Reina as she had done me. "Who are you?" she asked her in the same tone of voice.

"R-Reina," Reina answered quietly. The woman smirked at her. Her dainty white hand wagged a finger in Reina's direction, and she made a tsking sound.

After inspecting the both of us for another minute, the woman moved back to Niabus' side and sidled up against him. She pinned his arm against her bosom and led him away.

"I'll return shortly," Niabus called over his shoulder.

"Hopefully not too soon," I heard the woman say. "Wouldn't you rather stay for dinner?"

"What's on the menu?"

"Baked lizard."

I didn't hear his response, but I really wish I had. From the way his body tensed at her words, I had a feeling that whatever she'd planned to do to my "friend" wasn't going to be pleasant.

"Did... Were you expecting the goddess of death to be—well, that?" Reina asked me.

"Nope," I answered. "I was expecting a skeleton, to be honest with you."

"Why a skeleton?"

"I'm kind of friends with a death god named Amaar. He's a skeleton with a fondness for tuxedos and top hats."

"Really? That's a bit weird, isn't it?"

"The fact that he's a skeleton or his clothing choices?"

"Both?"

"I guess," I sighed. I looked down at Reina and noticed that she wasn't looking at me. I hesitated for a moment, but then found my courage and asked, "Would you like to go get something to eat?"

"Depends; are you going to shove it down my throat again?"

"Only if you ask me to." I received a slap on the arm for that remark, which I was all too happy to receive. It was nice to know that I could still joke with her like this. I'd almost thought— well, I'd thought I'd lost her.

Maybe I still had.

The two of us retraced our steps and left the arena in the same way we'd arrived. Once we were outside, we decided it would probably be a good idea if we explored the city a bit, you know, to get a feel for the place we would call home for at least a few days.

Right away, it became obvious that this city was much like any other city. There were houses, stores, taverns, etc. Everything that a semi medieval city needed to thrive. Honestly, I was just surprised they managed to feed everyone I was seeing, considering there were at least a few thousand people living inside the city, judging by the sheer size and scale of it.

After wandering around for about twenty minutes, we arrived at a place I can only describe as the "entertainment" district: large, flashy buildings designed to grab and keep your attention. Inside the windows of one of the buildings, I saw scantily clad snow elves gyrating their bodies in clothing that could not be comfortable to wear in this weather.

"Is that a tavern?" Reina asked after we'd been walking for a while.

I looked up and saw a sign written in a language I'd never seen before. "I suppose."

"Want to check it out?"

"I'm just following you. If you would like to check out the mysterious building with the weird sign, I'm right behind you."

She nodded her head and made a beeline for the front door. The "tavern" was a fairly average building. Obviously, it had been designed to make you feel comfortable about approaching it. Two stories tall, with windows that used ice in place of glass in strategic locations throughout the building, creating a unique, but well-lit space.

We stepped through the door and were greeted by the smell of cooked food. Were it not for the other patrons, I was almost certain that Reina would have made a mad dash for the bar in order to get some food. Instead, she power walked over to the bar and sat down on one of the few empty stools.

The barkeep, a seven-foot-tall insect that resembled a cross between an ant and a beetle, looked up from where it was wiping down the bar and spotted Reina. It spoke in a tongue I'd never heard before, and I had no idea what it was saying.

"Um—"

I'd begun to explain that we couldn't understand its language, but Reina beat me to it: "I'll have the stew," she said happily. She looked up at me. "He says it's pork stew," she said, almost giddy with excitement.

"When did you learn to speak giant ant?" I asked, still astonished that she'd managed to talk with the thing.

"Oh, um… It's kind of one of my traits? Something to do with me being hero and needing to understand all of the races."

"Interesting," I muttered. I didn't realize the humanoid races had traits like that. If she'd been a monster, sure. It would have made sense. But I'd never known Ayla or any of the other elves to have "traits" like that.

"What is?" she asked, without taking her eyes off the bowl of stew that had just been placed in front of her.

"I didn't realize elves had traits like that."

"Not normally, but I'm a reincarnator, remember. I have traits. I mean, think about it, Torga, would it make sense for me to not have a trait that allowed me to understand all of the races if it was supposed to be my job to save them? I'm sure you got such a trait as well, right?"

"Well, I suppose," I allowed. Though, I didn't get the skill through normal means, I was still given something of an "unlisted" trait to help me understand the people around me.

Of course, I had to eat one of them in order to understand their language, but that was a minor detail at the time considering I was eating almost everything.

"Would you mind ordering a bowl for me?"

"Oh, right!" She made a few weird sounds with her mouth, and the ant nodded its head in response. A few moments later, I had my own bowl of "pork" stew. I didn't think about where they got pork in Helheim because regardless of what the meat actually was, it wouldn't affect me.

Although, it did concern me that Reina didn't seem to be the least bit suspicious about where they'd acquired this so-called pork. In fact, if I didn't know any better I'd say she didn't have a care in the world, just sitting there, slurping up her stew with a large fur pelt still wrapped around her tiny body.

"You do know this probably isn't pork, right?" I asked, just to be sure.

Reina stopped eating immediately and turned to stare at me. "What do you mean?"

"Have you seen any pigs since you arrived on Yggdrasil?"

"Yes?"

"Have you seen any pigs since we came to Helheim?"

"… No?"

"So, if you haven't seen any pigs—"

"Oh." Reina sounded disgusted. She used her spoon to scoop up a portion of the stew and look at it. Then she dropped it back into the bowl and stood up. "Can we leave? I think I'm going to be sick."

"Sure. I'm fairly certain we're supposed to pay the man- woman- thing though."

"I don't have any money," she admitted.

"I thought you still had a few gold coins left?"

She shook her head. "I lost those when the gods grabbed me."

"Ah, I see the problem. Well then, in this situation there's only one thing we can do."

"What's that?"

I spun away from the bar, lifted Reina by her waist, and sprinted out the door. I accidentally hit someone with the door as I raced through it, but I didn't have time to apologize. I could already hear the patrons of the tavern getting irate at our blatant attempt to dine and dash.

I heard what I can only describe as nails on a chalkboard and assumed the giant ant had become slightly peeved at us.

"You know that elevator idea is looking better and better by the second."

"Oh, shut up. How was I supposed to know that neither of us had money?"

"Didn't I tell you I didn't have money?"

"I don't know, maybe? I've been a little too preoccupied with trying not to die to remember piddly little details like that."

I could give her that. She was in an incredibly difficult situation. In fact, I was genuinely surprised that she was holding up as well as she was. I could forgive a few discrepancies in her memory… *But why is it that I keep finding more the longer we talk*? I wondered while running through the semi-abandoned streets of this giant city with Reina thrown over my shoulder.

~ ~ ~

Reina and I were hiding out in an alley a few blocks over from the tavern. We'd run about half the distance back to the arena before I got tired of running and decided to hide. So, we ducked behind a tailor shop of some kind and waited for the heat to die down.

Reina was sitting down in an old wooden chair that had been placed against the wall of the alley.

Knowing that I needed to keep an eye out for anybody still hunting for us, I stood at the end of the alley; periodically, I would peek around the corner and judge how safe it was based on what I heard and what I could see.

"Did we lose 'em?" Reina asked. She was gasping for breath as if she just finished running a marathon, when in reality I'd carried her the entire time.

This place has really done a number on her. Before coming to Helheim, Reina was an accomplished Monster Hunter. She could run for hours without pause. Now, even the slightest bit of exercise exhausted her.

It was odd to see my independent wife so vulnerable.

"Yeah, I think so." I left my post and walked over to her. "Are you doing okay? You seem—"

"Sick?" she asked, perhaps a little more aggressively than she intended to. "Yeah, I am sick. This place is killing me, and every second I'm here I get even worse."

"I was going to say tired, but sick works too."

"Right," she scoffed.

"Why are you acting like this?" I asked, honestly annoyed with her attitude. I was trying my best to get her out of here as safely and quickly as possible. But that didn't seem to be good enough for her.

It was like she was hell bent on making me as miserable as possible.

"Why? I'm in hell!" she yelled. "I was literally dragged to hell because of you. And you have the nerve to ask me why I'm acting like this? Why don't you take a look in the mirror, Torga; then you'll know why I'm acting like this."

I sucked in a long breath and let it out as a sigh.

"You know what. You're absolutely right, it's my fault you're here. Why don't I just go and get that wish, so you can get out of here and never have to see me again— that sound good to you?"

"Sounds fantastic."

"Yeah, I figured it might." I threw her over my shoulder and then started walking in the vague direction of the arena.

Reina threw a bit of a fit because I was carrying her, but I really couldn't care less at this point. I tried— God did I try to make it up to her—but nothing I did was ever good enough.

I gave her a swift smack on the ass because her voice was starting to grate on my nerves— which both amused me and had the benefit of shutting her up.

I raised three children on my own— actually, four if you count Ayla. If Reina wanted to act like a child, I knew just how to treat her to make her behave.

"You spanked me?"

"Yep. Keep running your mouth and I'll do it again."

"You wouldn't dare."

Oh, but I did dare.

Multiple times.

And you know what? It was about the most fun I'd had since we came to Helheim.

CHAPTER SEVENTEEN

So, as it turns out, the person Niabus said he dated inside the city... It turned out to be Gamos. Yeah, surprised the hell out of me too.

I found myself back in the arena and surrounded on all sides by the lord's personal guard. I wasn't exactly worried that they would do something, so much as I worried about my response offending her if I happened to turn a few of these elves into paste.

Gamos stood across from me. Her straight black hair hung freely over her breasts and down her back. She wore a skintight black leather dress with a deep cut down the front that showed off her ample bosom, and a cut down each side, revealing the creamy white skin of her legs. A long shawl made of see-through lace was draped over her shoulders. A purple corset that clung tightly to her waist and dark shoes completed the look and added a bit of "class" to an otherwise seductive outfit.

She still looked like a corpse to me, but I couldn't deny that she was attractive.

On her left stood Niabus. It appeared that I was wrong earlier when I said that he would have an unpleasant time. He stood there in a suit of dark purple finery with not a hair out of place, and a huge grin on his face.

On her right stood a draugur and he was a big one: somewhere between twelve and fifteen feet tall. He had obsidian hair pulled into a bun on the top of his head and a curly beard that hung down to his stomach. He was bedecked in silver armor that reflected light so well, I almost went blind looking at it.

If it was just that garish armor, I wouldn't have minded it a bit. But that tacky armor combined with the "I'm better than you and I know it" stare just made me want to rip the guy's head off.

I settled for smiling and looking him in the eyes. That pissed him off and cheered me up.

After the row I'd had with Reina earlier, I wasn't in the best of moods. It didn't help that after we'd returned to the arena Reina had vanished and I hadn't heard from her in hours. I'd gone looking for her a few times, but she was nowhere to be found.

Probably off ranting to someone about how awful I was.

"If I didn't know any better, I'd think you were ignoring me."

That God-awful voice pierced through my distracted brain and brought me back to the present.

"Are you?" she asked with a hint of danger in her tone.

"Couldn't even if I tried," I told her honestly. Her voice was worse than nails on a chalkboard. The only way I could ignore that was if I destroyed my own eardrums.

"Oh, you're such a sweet talker."

"I'm really not."

"But you are. Women love a straightforward man, at least I do."

"That's… great. Look, I'm not trying to be rude, but—" I looked to Niabus for help and got a smirk in return.

Alright, so I'm on my own here.

"I'm here to challenge the arena, not socialize."

"Are you now? Well, I suppose if that's what you truly desire, I'll just have to accommodate you." She said with a kind smile on her face. "But first, we feast. We so rarely get contestants for the arena, that is cause for celebration."

"I really don't—"

She made a tsking sound and wagged her finger at me. "Surely you won't be so rude as to deny my request. After all, is that not why you're here? You would like me to gift you something, yes?"

I was hesitant to agree to anything because I didn't know how seriously she would take what I said. So, I settled for, "In a manner of speaking."

"Then indulge me, darling. Surely you can spare a few hours for some good food, and better company?"

At the moment, the only company I had any desire to keep wasn't in Helheim. Memories of Ayla, Findral, Hali, Solon, Talia, Lena, and Fenris swam through my mind and for the first time in weeks… I was speechless.

I missed them, far more than I ever thought I would. I found myself wondering if they'd made it out of the city. "If that's what it takes," I said, after taking a moment to compose myself.

Niabus gave me a weird look, but I ignored him. I doubted he would understand anyway.

"Wonderful." She clasped her hands together in front of her which did… something to her chest that I dutifully ignored like the well-trained husband that I was. "I shall have the servants start preparing the food imminently."

"You do that," I sighed. I waited for her to leave, and for her two escorts to follow her before I made to leave as well. I hadn't paid much attention to the draugur during the conversation, but now that I thought about it, he seemed familiar, somehow.

Who am I kidding? I'm probably just losing it again.

I shook the thought away and left the arena the same way I'd come in. I'd briefly entertained the idea of finding somewhere to take a nap and leaving Reina on her own, but I knew I couldn't do that. In her condition, anyone who wanted to take advantage of her or overpower her, could—without effort.

I spent the next five and a half hours looking for Reina, but I couldn't find her anywhere. I looked in every tavern, weapon shop, blacksmith, and bakery I could find—side note, why there was a bakery in a place where heat cannot exist, I'll never know. But there is at least one inside the city, because I found it. And from what I could tell, it was fairly popular with the younger, female crowd.

But enough about the bakery.

I returned to the arena for lack of a better place to go. After all, I still didn't have any money, so sleeping at an inn was out, and I had no intention of sleeping out on the street somewhere.

The arena was the safest place I knew.

Okay, that sounds bad.

I found a comfortable looking spot in the spectator seats and sat down. The arena was arranged in such a way that no matter where you were sitting, you never missed a single second of the action. There were no obstructions to block a spectator's view, so for better or worse, if you were sitting in the seats you saw everything.

Sure, the undead got slightly annoying after a while—what with their constant moaning—but that faded away and became background noise pretty quickly.

I closed my eyes and drifted off to sleep…

I felt something kick my leg. I opened my eyes to find a group of snow elves staring down at me. Judging by the looks they were giving me, they were quite annoyed. I don't know why. I'm fairly certain I hadn't done anything to them yet.

"Yes?" I asked, dragging out the word far longer than necessary.

One of the elves shoved a rolled-up scroll at me. I accepted it with a halfhearted thank you, and then unrolled it and began to read.

Torga, you're a tough man to find for someone so interested in getting out of here.

Gamos has requested your presence in her home. It would be wise not to keep her waiting.

—Niabus

I rolled the scroll up and tossed it away.

"Guess you're here to take me to your leader, huh?" The elves just gave me a confused look. "That joke was wasted on you," I sighed. "Alright." I stood up and motioned for them to move. "Let's get this crap over with."

I followed the trio down the same path Niabus had led us down originally; however, instead of going back out onto the street, we took an extra turn and headed down a set of stairs. From there, we traveled through a twisted set of tunnels that ran beneath the town proper. I was impressed they could memorize the path, because I saw no landmarks or signs denoting where we were. If I were to ever be left alone down here, I'd probably have to just start smashing my way out and trust in my durability and regeneration to keep me alive.

After about fifteen minutes of walking, we came to a stop at a ladder leaning against the wall. I looked at the top of the ladder, and saw a hole leading to the outside world.

Escape tunnel or smuggling hole? I wondered. It didn't matter either way. Truth be told, it was more of an idle curiosity than anything, but I amused myself with the idea of Gamos smuggling in lovers or whatever else rich and powerful women did in their spare time.

They directed me to the front door of an opulently decorated mansion. The outside was all twisted spires, corpses hanging from the roof, and icicles.

How very macabre of her, I thought, unable to tear my eyes away from the insane decoration style.

The door swung open before I could knock and I was greeted by Gamos in a lacy black dress with a tail that was so long, when she walked it would drag across the floor. It was the first truly "high class" dress I'd seen her wear. That's not to say the other dresses weren't nice, because they were. It's just that this dress was something I could see a queen wearing. And… come to think of it, I guess that's what she was.

"Yes, it is a nice dress."

I drug my eyes up from the floor to look at her face. She was showing me the same kind smile I'd seen earlier in the arena. I couldn't tell if that meant she was amused or annoyed.

"How do you not trip over that thing?" I asked, referring to the tail.

She looked over her shoulder at the long tail, then her smile grew wider.

"Oh, I have people take care of that for me." She said it as if it was the most obvious thing ever. She clapped her hands together and within moments a trio of female elves formed a line behind her, each picking up an armful of lace. "See?"

"I do indeed. So, why am I here?"

"You—" she stepped to my side and wrapped her arm around my own, "my tall, dark, and horrible visitor, are here as the guest of honor. Tonight, we feast in your name, so that tomorrow you may fight at your best in the arena."

"What's on the menu?"

"Baked lizard," she replied immediately.

"Is that code for eating Niabus? Because if so then I'm not sure why we're still standing out here when we could be inside eating."

"No," she laughed. And for the first time, I didn't want to burst my own eardrums just from hearing the sound of her voice. "As entertaining as it would be to boil the little dragon alive and serve him up to you on a silver platter, we're not eating him. I had a shipment of wyvern meat imported from the outer world for just such an occasion, and it shan't go to waste. Did you know the flesh of a wyvern is supposed to give you courage and make you fleet on your feet? Most of that is superstition, but it certainly tastes good, so I doubt you'll be disappointed."

"I'm looking forward to it."

"As am I." She smiled, and I'm not ashamed to admit that my heart fluttered a bit. "On the other hand, if the meal doesn't turn out as well as I had hoped, maybe I will boil Niabus after all. It's been a long time since I tasted dragon."

"You know what, same here. It's been years."

A tinkling laugh filled my ears. She patted my arm and looked up at me, revealing a set of razor-sharp fangs that wouldn't have looked out of place on a wolf. "Torga, you're a man after my blackened heart." She sighed, then stepped away. "And if I wasn't married, I'd keep you."

Somehow, that last sentence scared me more than the sudden appearance of her fangs.

Chapter Eighteen

S HE LED THE WAY THROUGH A SET OF DOUBLE
doors, where we were waylaid by a group of snow elf maids.

I noticed they were each holding articles of clothing but I chose not to speak of it in case my suspicions turned out to be correct.

"Ah, good. Your suit is ready." Gamos eyed me up and down for a minute, then she grabbed a dark green jacket from one of the maids and tossed it at me. Following the jacket was a white button up shirt, black slacks, and black leather shoes. She shoved them all at me and then motioned for the maids to take me away.

"That's really not necessary—"

"Silence," she said. For just a moment, her voice flooded with power and my vision went hazy. "I'll not have our guest of honor show up looking like a wastrel. Get him cleaned up and dressed, then bring him back."

I didn't move.

"Look, I'm not a child. You want me to go clean up, I understand. I will go clean up. But you're not just going to shove me around because I'm a guest in your house."

Gamos cupped her chin with her hand, then tilted her head to the side.

The two of us stood there for several seconds, neither willing to give in, until she finally nodded her head.

"Fine. Show him to the washroom."

The maids nodded their heads and through some unspoken conversation between them, three of them walked away while one motioned for me to come with her.

I followed her as I said I would. She led me to a room that was sparsely decorated, save for a large square tub sitting in the middle and a floor to ceiling mirror attached to the far-left wall.

The tub itself was also rather plain looking, and was clearly meant for utility, rather than decoration. Which led me to assume that this room wasn't used very often.

Upon closer inspection, I noticed small holes around the base of the tub, presumably for the firewood or whatever else they used to heat up the water. Aside from that, it was really just a large hunk of metal with pipes wrapped around it.

"I'll be right here if you need anything."

I looked over my shoulder at the maid. She was standing in the doorway with her arms behind her back. Though she had a blank expression on her face, I had a feeling that she was rather amused at the whole situation.

I put one finger on her shoulder and lightly pushed her backwards, until she was standing outside the door. Then I shut the door and twisted the little lock on the handle.

Let's get this over with. I let out a sigh as I eyed the tub and the suit I was expected to wear. I tugged off the guardian pelt I'd been using to hide my pelvis, allowing it to fall to the floor.

I made my way over to the tub and inspected the nozzles on either side. Neither one was labeled, but I could guess what they were for. I reached over and twisted the nob on the left-hand side of the tub. Boiling hot water came out in a rush.

I climbed inside and started scrubbing. I didn't see any soap, but I had already expected that. Soap was a rare commodity on Yggdrasil since most of the planets were stuck at a level of technology akin to Earth's medieval ages.

I had to admit, it was nice to soak in a tub of hot water.

Very relaxing.

But I was still set on finishing up this feast as quickly as possible and going to look for Reina, so I hurried through my bath and climbed out after only five minutes or so. I quickly got dressed and was surprised at how well the suit fit considering they didn't have my measurements. It only took a few minor applications of shapeshift for the suit to fit like a glove.

I hesitated when it came time to put the shoes on. I hadn't worn shoes for the better part of two centuries, and to be honest I couldn't remember if I ever liked wearing shoes to begin with.

I stepped out of the room, making sure to shut the door behind me, and greeted the maid with what I hoped was a pleasant smile.

"You didn't like the shoes?" she asked, a coy smile playing on her lips.

"Never been a big fan of shoes," I answered honestly.

"Oh, that's completely understandable. Many of the lord's *male* friends are not in the habit of wearing shoes. They were only given so you would have the option."

I had the feeling that she had misunderstood our relationship, but honestly it was just too much of a hassle to bother correcting her. I'd never see this elf again after tomorrow anyway, so what was the point?

"Very well, if you're ready I'll escort you to the ballroom."

"I've been ready since I entered the building but, sure, lead the way." The maid gave me an exasperated look and shook her head at my tone.

Hey, don't give me that look, lady. I didn't even want to be here.

I followed the maid back the way we had come and met up with Gamos outside a set of large double doors not too far from where we'd left her.

"I knew you would clean up well," she practically cooed. Her voice was back to being a sledgehammer against my skull. I fought off a wince and tried to smile at her, but it didn't work out like I thought it would.

"Well, that makes one of us."

Gamos scoffed. "Oh please, fake humbleness does not suit you."

"Whatever you say. Can we get this over with? I have places to be and people to find."

Gamos nodded her head and stepped to the side. The maid shuffled past and opened the door without needing to be told.

The door opened to reveal a grand ballroom. The ceilings were over thirty feet high, and the room itself was about five-hundred feet across, and seven-hundred feet long. The room was decorated in dark colors and the furniture looked remarkably uncomfortable.

Which is probably why no one was sitting down, even though the room was filled with a diverse group composed of every race I'd seen inside Soulsden, and a few I hadn't.

Upon seeing the city lord standing amongst them, a line of people formed within seconds.

"Lady Gamos, can I have a moment of your time?"

"Likewise, Madam. I require only a moment."

Several others shouted similar requests and I took that as my cue to leave.

"Excuse me," I said and beat a hasty retreat to the opposite side of the room. I had told her I had no interest in socializing, and I meant it. I only showed up to avoid ruining any goodwill I may have had, and to incentivize her into granting my wish.

I found a quiet spot near one of the windows and hid there for about an hour. It honestly wasn't that bad; everyone left me alone for the most part. I got a bit annoyed when Niabus came over and tried to strike up a conversation, but I was used to dealing with him already.

I also noticed some hostility directed at me from the draugur I'd seen standing next to Gamos in the arena. He didn't say anything to me, and he didn't make any moves to interact with me, but he never once took his eyes off of me the entire time I was standing over by the window.

Finally, I got sick of it and decided to leave. There really was no purpose for me to be here, and I'd stayed long enough that Gamos wouldn't be able to say anything about me leaving. Well, she could complain about it, I guess. But I did my bit, I showed up and let them have a party in my honor.

Now it was time for me and my honor to get the hell outta here.

Instead of making my way across the room to the door I'd entered from, I decided to leave via a side door near where I was already standing.

That was a bad idea.

Gamos' home was a freaking maze of hallways and empty rooms, and I spent the better part of half an hour trying to find the exit. It'd come to the point where I was debating whether to make a hole in the wall and leave that way.

However, somehow after getting lost I managed to stumble my way into the servants' quarters. I wasn't sure how I found my way here, and I thought about asking one of the elves to show me the way out, but truth be told I was committed to finding the exit on my own at this point.

"Look, you don't have to keep up the act much longer. I'm sure the judges are doing their best to expedite the process. All you have to do is keep pretending to be the elf bitch for a little while longer and you're home free."

My brain stopped functioning the moment I recognized the voice—how could I not—I had been traveling with him for the last few weeks. What I couldn't comprehend were the words that were coming out of his mouth. I sidled up to the wall nearest where the voice was coming from: It appeared to be a dorm room meant for the snow elf servants. I waited—for what, I didn't know, but I was waiting for something.

"No, you don't understand. He suspects something." I heard my wife's whispered voice, and any rational thought was thrown out the window as my senses became hyper focused on their conversation. "Her memories weren't enough. I don't know if she had some tells or some quirks that I was unaware of. But he knows—or rather he suspects that something has changed."

"He knows nothing," Niabus assured her. "Trust me, if he did, you'd be dead."

"He's right." I spoke before I could stop myself. I heard an intake of breath as Reina—or rather, the woman pretending to be her—gasped.

I stepped around through the doorway and quickly took in the room. It was your standard dormitory style room with two bunk beds against each wall, a table in the center with six chairs surrounding it, and a row of wooden chests near the door.

I took in the entire room in less than three seconds, and then my perception came to a needle's point as I laid eyes on Niabus and a young snow elf woman who bore a striking resemblance to my wife. They were even wearing the same clothes.

In her hand she held a necklace. I didn't know if the necklace was important or not, but I could practically taste the magic oozing off of it from here.

"Of course, never say never, right?" I asked, eyeing the both of them.

The snow elf backpedaled, placing Niabus between her and me. "It wasn't my idea. None of it."

"Where is she?" I asked, my voice little more than a whisper.

"Now, Torga, stay calm. I swear there's a good explanation for this, and if you'll just give me a minute, I'll explain," Niabus said placatingly.

"Well, you certainly have my attention." I stepped closer to him. I somehow wasn't angry, in fact I was strangely happy… no, wait—I was furious to the point of wanting to murder both of them. I was happy that it was a stranger I was about to murder, and not my wife.

That would have been awkward.

"Niabus, I don't think he's going to listen to you," the snow elf whispered. I didn't understand the point of the whispering; it was quite obvious that I could hear her from across the room.

"You're absolutely right. I'm not going to listen to him. I'm going to kill him, and then I'm going to kill you. I'm going to kill every person in this city until someone tells me where—the fuck—My-Wife-Is."

~ ~ ~

Somewhere near the lowest levels of Yggdrasil.
Reina floated inside a glass orb. Her body was still clothed in the skintight bodysuit she'd been wearing when she was first taken by Ruknar. However, both of her weapons and her bag were missing.

Outside the orb, five multicolored beings stood atop raised daises, overlooking her unconscious form.

"Are you sure about this?" a blue being asked his fellows. "This is not the way we usually do things."

"This is far from a usual case," a golden being interjected. "Were it anyone else, they would have been faded ages ago. Unfortunately, Orochi is necessary to the greater state of Yggdrasil. Without him, it could not live up to its true purpose."

"That's garbage and you know it," a green being harrumphed. "Orochi is no more necessary than anyone else. If he died, Yggdrasil would just assign his fate line to someone else and no one would be the wiser. We should have forced him to fade eons ago. To think, I'm missing my favorite show because of this pathetic waste of time."

"You don't know that, Shazai." The orange being who had spoken let out a loud yawn, only covering his mouth to be polite and not bothering to quiet himself. "For all we know that could be an entirely unique fate line. Who knows what would have happened if we had tried to interfere with it."

"There's no point in us arguing about it now. What's done is done. All we can do now is just get this over with as quickly and painlessly as possible, so we can send her to where she belongs," the lone female said. Her body was a striking shade of crimson and her body was less than half the size of her peers.

"Let's vote on it then," the blue being proclaimed. "All in favor of waking her up, say yes."

The decision was unanimous. Everyone voted to wake up the mortal so they could get this farce over with.

Chapter Nineteen

"Now, Torga. Remember what we talked about? You said you'd listen to me—"
I grabbed a chair from beside the table and whipped it across the room at Niabus' head. The slippery bastard ducked out of the way at the last second, taking the elf with him. The chair smashed against the wall and shattered into splinters.

"Torga, I'm not joking with you. Stop!"

"Neither am I!" I roared. "You were lying to me this entire time. Watching as she drove the idea that my wife hated me into my head, and you said nothing." I grabbed another chair and hurled it across the room. Niabus knocked it aside and stepped even closer to the elf.

"I couldn't tell you even if I wanted to. There are powers at work here that you just don't understand. If I told you, they would kill me. And I don't mean what landed me here, I mean true death. The one way that you can completely kill a god."

"I can think of a few ways to kill a god. Let me show you." I placed my foot on the edge of the table and shoved—it skid across the floor and forced Niabus to deflect it or risk the elf getting hit by it. I took the opportunity presented to me and followed the table, waiting for that one moment where I could strike.

The moment Niabus knocked the table aside, I was waiting there with a haymaker that smashed into his nose. His head rocked back, and I followed through with another punch aimed at his chest.

He managed to get his arm up in time to block. However, that only served to piss me off even more.

I shoved him across the floor with nothing but the strength in my arm. Then I grabbed his suit and yanked. A well-placed uppercut caught him square in the stomach and sent him crashing through the rear wall. The heavy pine logs that made up the wall splintered and cracked and began to fall apart as Niabus' body passed through them.

I turned my attention to the elf. She was shaking like a leaf in a hurricane, and before I would've felt bad. But suddenly any sympathy I may have had for her… wasn't there anymore. I reached out and grabbed her face.

"What did you get out of it?" I whispered into her ear. "Did you enjoy tormenting me? Did you enjoy making me think my wife hated me?"

"I—I was told to keep you here, that's it."

"How did you know all of those things?"

She made an odd squeaking sound, which I interpreted as "huh?," so I repeated my statement.

"About me and Reina. How did you know all of those things?"

"One of the judges has the ability to transplant memories. They said they'd give me everything I needed to keep you distracted."

Still holding her by her face, I lifted her off the ground and pressed her against the wall behind her. She showed signs of wanted to squirm, so I put one finger over her lips and made a shushing sound.

"Answer my questions and I promise you won't die."

"Um… O—okay."

"Where is Reina?"

"I don't know."

I slammed my fist into the wall next to her head. The logs ripped like tissue paper as my fist went straight through the wall. I bent my elbow and pulled myself forward, crowding her and forcing her to look in my eyes.

"I don't know," she cried. "I was just told to keep you here, and to work with him." She looked at the hole in the wall to emphasize just who *he* was. "That's it. That's all I know. Please don't kill me," she sobbed. Tears streamed down her face and her eyes grew red.

"Kill you? No, I gave you my word that I wouldn't kill you," I said quietly. "But you're not getting off scot-free either. You said they told you to keep me here… But you never said anything about them telling you to make my life a living hell while you did it. That was all you."

"No, wait—"

I twisted my body and hurled her across the room. She bounced off the table and then the wall before falling to the ground. She didn't move after that, and I didn't bother going to check if she was dead. If she survived that she could live; if she didn't… Oh well.

"What have you done?"

I turned towards the big hole in the wall and saw a tattered looking Niabus climbing back inside. His shirt was torn in several places, his pants were practically nonexistent, and he had some blood dripping from his mouth and a few other superficial wounds.

"What have I done?" I turned to face him. I moved closer to him until we were standing nose to nose. "The real question here, is what am I about to do?"

"I don't want to hurt you, Torga."

"Don't worry. You won't."

He ripped what was left of his clothes off and tossed them aside. His body began to bulge out at odd angles as his scales and muscles receded until his bones were visible on the outside, and he grew taller with every second that passed.

Within moments, Niabus had almost doubled in size. His horns scraped across the ceiling and the wings protruding from his back could touch either wall if he so much as twitched them. But he didn't stop there. He continued to increase in size until the room could no longer contain him. His head and shoulders burst through the ceiling and the walls gave way as his thick tail whipped around involuntarily. Purple flames erupted from within his body and quickly moved to cover his bones. It appeared to act as a layer of translucent skin to protect his true form from the frigid wastes of Helheim.

It was interesting enough to see his true form. After all, I'd never seen a skeletal dragon before. But I just couldn't find it in me to inspect his body closely, since the only thing on my mind was how much I wanted to rip his head off but couldn't. He had information I needed, so I couldn't kill him, not yet.

By the time Niabus stopped growing, he was over a hundred feet tall, with a wingspan that was almost four times that.

I felt his power bearing down on me as our eyes locked together, the rage in his was almost a match for my own.

A deep purple flame grew within his mouth and I knew what was coming.

Heat so intense it reduced the surrounding area to ashes in less than the time it took me to blink. I felt the pain of the heat as it burned my skin and seared my bones.

It was refreshing to finally feel something—anything—after the ice bath my brain took upon finding out the truth. My emotions were still dead, but at least my body was alive. If I wanted to keep it that way, I needed to act fast.

I shifted amongst the flames, my body breaking down into atoms and then rearranging themselves into a form far more suited for combat than my weak human body.

I transformed much faster than Niabus had, and within moments the human had been replaced by the Naga. My body expanded several dozen times as the flames washed over me; each second was accompanied by an indescribable agony. It was enough to clear my mind, enough for me to remember that purposefully taking dragon fire wasn't the smartest idea I'd had that day.

I used my two left arms to cover my face, then twisted my body and threw my right arm forward.

I felt my palm hit something, and the flames died off a moment later. The instant I got my vision back I looked around for Niabus, finding him holding the side of his head while leaning against the roof of Gamos' home.

"You slapped me? No one slaps me!"

He pushed off the roof and leapt at me, both arms extended forward with the meat hooks he called fingers aimed directly at my chest.

I brought my arms up, knocked his arms out to either side, and caught his hands and shoulders in mine. His momentum was stopped the moment I pushed off the ground with my tail, twisted to the side, and then tossed him through the top of Gamos' home.

He, of course, went straight through the building and left little more than splinters in his wake. However, the destruction didn't stop there. As he slid across the ground, his massive body tore apart any homes and businesses that happened to be in his way.

I imagined the lord of Helheim wouldn't be too pleased with either of us after that.

I grabbed Niabus by the throat and drug him into the air.

"Let's take this outside," I said as I got ready to toss him over the wall, so we wouldn't damage anymore of the city than we already had.

"Yes—let's." He put his foot on my chest and shoved me off balance. I lost my grip on his throat and collapsed to the ground, crushing a few buildings beneath my body. I felt him grab the tip of my tail and looked down.

He rotated his body to get me off the ground, and then he started to spin in place. Each rotation sent me whipping through the air faster and faster.

And then he let go.

I flew over the city, over the wall, and over half of the crater before I finally fell to the ground. I tried to stop myself from sliding, but I doubted I would've been able to accomplish that feat on rock, let alone on ice. Despite my best efforts I slid the rest of the way across the crater, only stopping when I hit the forest and took out several rows of trees.

I felt several of my bones break, including one of my arms. I pushed myself up and brushed myself off. I grabbed hold of the broken arm and pushed it back into place so my regeneration would kick in and heal the damn thing.

I heard a loud crash as something heavy landed behind me. I turned around just in time to catch some claws to the face. Though my scales deflected most of the blow, a line of fire erupted down my face from wherever his claws touched.

I knocked his hand away as quickly as I could and backpedaled to put some distance between us.

I gave Niabus a once over while scooping up a handful of snow to put on the burn. The dragon was pissed. Though he had no lungs, and therefore no reason to breathe, his body still moved up and down as if he was panting for air. His eyes glowed the same purple as the fire that covered him, and the air around us seemed to have increased in temperature by a factor of ten. A thick mist started drifting up from the ground as the snow evaporated from the sheer heat Niabus exuded with each breath.

"So arrogant," Niabus hissed. "You dare stand before *me*? Kneel, and perhaps I can still forgive you."

"Aren't you embarrassed saying that?" I rotated my newly healed shoulder and opened and closed my fist a few times to make sure it worked properly. With my self-assessment complete, I moved forward.

As if he were waiting for that exact moment, Niabus leapt off the ground and brought his right arm down like he was an executioner, and his arm was the axe ready to lop off my head.

I caught his arm easily and bared my fangs at him. "Probably should have mentioned this earlier, but I'm a bit stronger than most gods."

Niabus had time to widen his eyes before I yanked him off of his feet, over my head, and slammed him into the ground on the opposite side. I wrapped a hand around his throat, and then used my other three arms to rain down blows upon him.

I got five punches in before Niabus reacted by swinging one of his wings towards my face. At first, I didn't think anything of it. I would just take the blow and move on. But a little voice inside my head told me to dodge, so I did.

Good thing too. I looked at his wing as it passed my face and saw a wicked looking barb on the tip. He may not have been able to cut with it, but he could certainly do some damage if he decided to jam it into my vitals.

I couldn't let myself get distracted by the wing, because the next thing I knew I was upside down with my head being driven into the ice.

Pain flooded my senses as my face was crushed.

I felt myself being pulled backwards a moment later and tried to prevent whatever he was doing by digging my claws into the ice. It proved useless; I was lifted off the ground and thrown through the air. I crashed through trees as if they weren't there, and only stopped because I'd managed to get my arms down and slow my momentum enough to ride it out.

I was honestly surprised he could lift me, let alone throw me. That was a testament to how powerful Niabus truly was because I wasn't suppressing my weight anymore.

Which raised a question: If he was this powerful after dying, how powerful was he in his prime?

I rose to my full height and looked around, desperate to spot him before I could be ambushed again. I noticed two things, neither of which was Niabus: the city was gone, and I was back in the forest surrounded by trees and massive pillars of ice.

An odd sound drew my attention upwards; Niabus was floating high above my head, a ball of purple flame growing within his mouth. He threw his head forward and sent the flames flying at me.

I coiled my tail beneath me and used it as a spring to launch myself out of the way. I'd aimed at one of the ice pillars, but I was off by about fifteen degrees. I sailed past the pillar and landed in a heavily forested area on the other side.

I quickly realized that in order to avoid being bombarded by flame, I would have to bring him down to my level.

I eyed the ice pillar and a plan formed in my mind.

Using the trees as cover, I circled around to the rear of the pillar while trying not to let Niabus out of my sight. He was floating in the air, using those massive wings of his to hover in place and bombard the ground beneath him with heavy gusts of wind. He appeared to be looking for me as well, but it didn't seem like he'd found me yet.

I arrived at the base of the pillar and coiled my body as much as possible. I jammed all four hands into the base of the pillar and then used my tail to push off the ground. My muscles bulged, and my blood rushed to my head as I tried to lift even just a corner of the pillar.

My efforts paid off as a huge crack appeared around the base and the top began to sway in the direction I was pushing.

"Ahhh!" I screamed. With one final hard yank, the ice holding the base of the pillar cracked and it leaned heavily to one side. It tipped over and fell like the world's tallest tree.

I had to resist the urge to yell "timber!" as I watched it fall towards Niabus—then something slammed into my back and drove me into the base of the pillar.

Niabus had circled around, presumably after hearing the ice break.

Our bodies crashing into it did nothing to stop the pillar's descent. It fell to the ground and all hell broke loose. The ground shook so bad I thought the world had been torn asunder, trees were uprooted for miles in every direction, and once the first pillar had fallen a chain reaction began. The ice holding up the other pillars snapped due to the force of the ground shaking, causing the other pillars to come crashing down as well.

Niabus and I rolled around on the ground, each trying to gain the upper hand on the other while simultaneously trying to avoid being crushed by falling ice pillars.

I managed to get my tail wrapped around his waist and climb on top of him for an instant before his fist slammed into the side of my face, igniting it and knocking me off of him.

I hit the ground and scrambled to get to some snow to put out the fire on the side of my face. However, before I could make it to a pile of snow deep enough to sink my face in, I was suddenly hauled backwards. I looked back and saw Niabus crawling in the opposite direction, and since my tail was still wrapped around him, where he went, I was sure to follow.

I dug my fist into the ice just long enough to search for a weapon. I found one and grabbed it—a glacial stalagmite that had presumably been brought to the surface due to the ground shaking—but I didn't have time to check that thoroughly. I just grabbed it and broke it off at the base, turning it into an obscenely long needle.

I rolled onto my back and then wrenched Niabus into the air with nothing but my tail. I pulled him back and slammed him into the ground next to me. I grabbed his left horn and used it as leverage to press his face into the ground and climb on top of him. Niabus thrashed and yelled, desperate to throw me off. I wrapped my tail further around him, making sure to tie up both of his arms so he could not retaliate as easily.

His body was generating so much heat that my eyes began to burn from the steam rising from the ground. I wanted to close my eyes and just jam the needle home, but I knew if I did I might lose my one chance of finding out where they'd taken Reina.

So I raised my needle into the air and positioned the tip of it over his chest.

"I'm only going to ask you this one last time. Where is she?" I yelled.

In lieu of an answer, Niabus opened his mouth and created a massive ball of fire in between his jaws. I pressed the tip of my needle into his chest— "Try it. It'll be the last thing you ever do."

"Then I'll take you with me!" He roared around the flames.

"You don't have the guts."

"That's where you're wrong. I've already lost everything, dying here means nothing to me."

"What are you waiting for then, huh? Do it!"

"As entertaining as that would be, I'm afraid I must stop you there." At the sound of the feminine voice that made me want to burst my own eardrums, my body locked up. The power I felt emanating from just a few feet to my left was enough to send shivers down my spine.

Gamos. What the hell is she doing here?

"Now, boys. You're going to explain to me what this little spat of yours is all about, and if I don't like your explanation, I'm going to kill you. Am I clear?"

I stared down into Niabus' eyes. I was ready to drive my needle into his chest at the first opportunity, and I could tell he was waiting for the same opportunity to burn me alive.

"Crystal," I said without taking my eyes off of Niabus.

"Of course," he replied while doing the same to me.

"Perfect."

The power vanished as quickly as it had appeared, and my body slumped as whatever had been holding me vanished without a trace. My head was thrown to the side as a large black fist slammed into my cheek.

I grabbed his wrist and hissed.

"You deserved that."

"Oh yeah?" I slammed the spike into the joint connecting his wing to his torso. He opened his mouth, presumably to yell, but I backhanded him across the face and pulled his wing a second later. The wing detached at the joint and I raised it above my head.

"You deserved that." I put the tip of the wing in my mouth and bit down. The bone was tough; it was actually harder than anything I'd ever tried to eat before. But I wasn't going to let that stop me.

I bit down harder and was rewarded by crunching as the thin bones of the wing gave way to my teeth.

"What part of 'this is over,' didn't you understand?"

I winced at the sound of Gamos' voice.

With the wing still in my mouth, I turned my head to see Gamos standing on the very tip of a pine tree that had somehow managed not to fall over amidst the chaos caused by our fight.

Gone was the elegant dresses. Gamos appeared in a suit of pitch-black armor that covered her from the neck down. The armor had wicked looking spikes on her pauldrons, gauntlets, and two six-inch-long spikes on each knee. Her hair had been pulled into a bun that sat behind her head, and her skin appeared more blue than white. With a large battle axe slung over one shoulder and a tower shield held in her left hand, the dark seductress had become a grizzled warrior ready to take my head off at the slightest hint of treachery.

I took her fingers tightening around the handle of her axe as my cue to start talking, so I laid everything out: Why I was in Helheim and what I'd caught Niabus and the elf doing, before ending my explanation with why we'd come to Soulsden in the first place.

Gamos listened to my explanation without saying a word or showing any emotion on her face. Once I was finished, however, that changed *immediately.*

"You were carrying out the machinations of the judges in my kingdom!" she screamed, and a wave of power flooded out from her. It was so condensed and heavy, it drove Niabus and me to the ground, unable to move so much as a single muscle fiber, and reduced everything for miles around to ashes.

I thought about running away, but that idea came to a screeching halt as exhaustion hit me.

I guess discovering the truth about Reina and then fighting Niabus took more out of me than I'd originally thought... Unable to hold up my own weight any longer, I relaxed my arms and fell to the ground.

Several heavy objects landed nearby, and since I didn't want to be hit with a surprise attack, I forced my tired body to roll over so I could see what it was. A group of twelve draugur surrounded us, each looking like they had just stepped out of a war zone.

"Hey, Torga?" I winced at the sound of her voice and debated whether or not to play dead.

"Yes?" I asked, twisting my head around to see the rather striking form of Gamos standing next to my head. She was many times smaller than I was. But the sheer level of power she possessed made me feel insignificant by comparison.

She wasn't the type of person I could fight, and I knew it, the only reason I did as well as I did against Niabus was that he'd lost most of his power after his death. Had I challenged him at the peak of his power, I would've lost and there was no doubt in my mind about that.

Gamos didn't have that problem.

"I have a proposition for you, Torga. And please feel free to say no." I had the impression that I wouldn't actually be allowed to say no and she was only saying this to give me the illusion of choice.

I nodded my head anyway.

"You're going to come back to Soulsden and fight in the arena. If you win, I'll let you go under the condition that you never return to Helheim again."

"And if I lose?"

"Take my advice; if you ever want to see your dear wife again; don't lose."

"...Roger that."

"Perfect, I'm glad you understand." She turned her back on me and began to walk away. "I'll be expecting you in the arena by no later than tomorrow. Don't be late."

Niabus, Gamos, and the draugur vanished simultaneously in a flash of dark purple light, leaving me alone in the wilderness with no idea of how exactly I was supposed to get back to Soulsden.

I'd been lying there; eating the wing I'd rightly won, when—

Ding

∞∞∞∞∞∞∞∞

You have eaten the following race for the first "???????" Time: Dragon God of Fire & Destruction.

Because of this, your affinity with dragons has decreased by 1,000 points (Current affinity -1,000/1,000; Status: Loathed Entirely)

For reaching -1,000 affinity with dragons, you have unlocked a new Title! The one who is hated by Dragons. +100 to all stats when facing draconic opponents.

For turning on your summoner and consuming part of their essence, you have unlocked a new Title! The Anti-Summoner. Explanation Unavailable.

Name: Torga

Race: Quasar Serpent/Gluttonous Dark God of Hunger and Gravity (Minor)

Classification: Tier 10(+1)

Level: 100(?)

Experience: N/A

Titles: Destroyer of Asgard, The Dark Serpent, The Unwavering One, Royal Serpent, Free, The Devourer of Worlds, God of Hunger, God of Gravity, The One Who Is Hated by Dragons, Anti-Summoner

Stats:

Physical

Strength: ∞/85

Endurance: ∞/85

Dexterity: 1,051/51

Speed: 1,583/83

Mental

Intelligence: 74

Wisdom: 51

Charisma: 31

Resistances

Elements: 90%

Divinity: 90%

Mental: 60%

Immunities

Mind Control

Illusions

Disease

Skills: Major Stealth, Heat Detection, Absolute Gluttony, Absolute Growth, Greater Petrifying Gaze, Superior Acid Venom, Detect Concealment, Energy

Breath, Fly, Magic Enhancement, Elemental Manipulation, Omnipotent Control over Hunger and Gravity, Shapeshift, Aethereal Form, Size Control

Traits: Dark Gluttonous Aura ∞, Growth +1,000, Forever Growing, Indomitable, Absolute Regeneration, Ageless, Oxygen Independent, Self-Sustaining, God of Hunger, God of Gravity

∞∞∞∞∞∞∞∞

I let out a long sigh as I read through the pop ups. *It just doesn't end, does it?*

CHAPTER TWENTY

WHEN REINA OPENED HER EYES, SHE FOUND herself floating inside an endless abyss with only a few faint lights to serve as her guide. She looked around for Torga, Donna, or Leon, but no matter where she looked, she was completely alone—

"Finally, she's awake! Can we get this over with now?" A crotchety old voice spoke up from the abyss.

Reina whipped around and saw five multicolored beings floating in a line in front of her. She tried to back away from them, but without the ability to grab or push against the floor, she just flailed in place for a few seconds before giving up and glaring at them.

"Calm yourself, Jorthim. You're scaring the mortal," a being composed of dark blue light, so dark it barely stood out from the abyss, said in an authoritative tone.

"Don't try that high and mighty tone with me, Shazai. You're as annoyed with this situation as I am," a huge dark green being spoke up in the same crotchety old voice she'd heard earlier.

"Guys," a light red being said in a placative voice. This one sounded distinctly female to Reina. The female raised her arms towards the two others. "Is all this fighting really necessary? We're all unhappy with this situation, but we *do* have a job to do."

The three beings that until now had been talking amongst themselves and the two, as of now, silent beings turned their heads to face her. She could feel their scrutinizing gaze as they silently stared at her... Finally, after what felt like an eternity, but was probably only a few minutes, the extremely tall and thin golden being at the center of the group spoke up.

"Mortal," it began in a soothing tone. "Forgive us for this sudden meeting. But, with things being as they are, we do not have much choice in the matter."

"Where am I? Why am I here? What happened to my husband!?" Reina fired off her questions one after the other and would have continued asking questions had the orange being at the far left of the group not snapped its fingers and erected a barrier around Reina that prevented her voice from reaching their ears.

"Please... Keep your voice down," the being mumbled in a sleepy tone.

The tall golden being sighed in annoyance and destroyed the barrier with a snap of its fingers. Then it looked down at the orange being and groaned in frustration as it began snoring. "I know you're tired, Pthelios, but please refrain from sleeping or silencing the mortal while we're trying to question her."

"No promises," it replied sleepily.

"Anyway, Mortal?"

"What?" Reina snapped.

"We would just like to reiterate a few things before we begin, so I would like to ask that you listen carefully to our questions and answer them as honestly as possible. Should you not understand something, you must speak up and ask us to repeat the question. Is that clear?"

"Doesn't seem like I have much of a choice, do I?"

"Unfortunately, not." The golden being turned to the dark blue being on the end and nodded its head.

"You are the chosen of Forna, Ex-goddess of Life. Are you not?"

"What does that have to do with anyth—" Reina was startled out of her response when the large green being slammed what appeared to be a pole of some kind into the "ground" and sent vibrations throughout the space.

"Answer the question, Mortal. Some of us might not die of old age, but I had to miss my favorite show to be here."

"Oh!" the red being exclaimed. "How's he doing, by the way?"

"Ha! He killed Magni. Just as I thought he would—"

"Please, not in front of the Mortal." At the golden being's reminder of where they were, the green and red beings cleared their throats and floated in silence.

Magni? Reina thought she recognized the name, but for whatever reason, her memories were jumbled and out of place. The last thing she remembered was Ruknar confiscating her dagger, then nothing but darkness.

"Are you or are you not, the chosen of Forna, Ex-goddess of Life?" the blue being repeated.

"I am, or I was."

"Explain."

"After our initial conversation where she reincarnated me, I haven't spoken to her."

The other four beings collectively looked to the orange being and waited for it to notice. "Truth," Pthelios mumbled.

The other beings whispered amongst themselves for several moments, then the green being spoke up. "Are you aware of what the being known as 'Torga' truly is?"

"He's my husband."

"Yes, but do you know *what* he is?"

Reina remained silent for a moment, then she snorted and said, "Yeah, he's an inconsiderate jackass. But he's *my* inconsiderate jackass. I don't care what else he is."

The green being burst into a fit of laughter, the other three turned to look at Orange.

"She speaks the truth."

Again, the beings whispered amongst themselves for several minutes before the red being seemingly "stepped" forward and waved at her. "Before I start, I just wanted to say how great it is to finally meet you. I'm a *huge* fan of your husband."

"There she goes," the blue being groaned. "Typical fangirl." He spoke with a tone that was absolutely dripping with disdain.

My husband? Suddenly the image of a dying Torga ran through Reina's mind and her eyes widened in realization. "No!" she screamed. "I have to get back to him!"

The green being burst into another fit of laughter and slammed his "pole" into the ground several times in his amusement.

Reina's eyes narrowed dangerously at the green being and she growled under her breath.

"What's so funny!? He's dying right now and you're laughing about it!?"

"Ahem..." The red being cleared its throat to get Reina's attention. "What Shazai is *trying* to say in his own *unique* way, is that your husband is fine. It will take a lot more than a few weeks in Helheim to take down Torga. I can assure you with full confidence, if you just believe in him, he'll get through this just fine."

Reina narrowed her eyes in suspicion and stared directly at the red being.

"Can we get back to the topic at hand?" the blue being interrupted.

"No." Reina growled. The beings stared at Reina in surprise for several moments.

"Care to repeat that?" the blue being replied in a dangerous tone.

"I said, *No*." She swallowed down her nerves and pressed on. "I refuse to answer any more questions until I know he's safe."

The five beings looked to each other, then back to Reina.

"You do realize that with a snap of my finger I could end you, right? And I don't just mean your life. I snap my fingers, and any trace of your existence in this world is gone." The blue being snapped his fingers for emphasis. "Like that."

"I don't care. Until I know he's safe, I'm not giving you the satisfaction."

The four other beings turned to the blue being and waited. "Fine," it sighed. "Just show her the video."

"Yahoo!!" a high-pitched voice screamed from the abyss.

Suddenly, a two-foot-tall bird-like creature flew out of the abyss with a black book almost as large as it was dangling from its talons. Its bright yellow feathers stood in stark contrast to the book it carried, its red eyes glowed in the darkness, and the razor-sharp teeth within its beak sent a chill racing up Reina's spine... At least they did until the bird slammed into the ground and slid to a stop a few feet from her.

The multi-colored beings and Reina stared in shock at the bird for several seconds, then the silence was broken by an annoyed sigh from the blue being. "Damnit, Mob."

The bird-thing hopped to its feet with a wide smile on its face. "I'm okay!"

"A terribly sad outcome for us all. What are you even doing here?" the blue being asked in that same annoyed tone.

"Well, for your information, Mr. Grumpy-no pants, I'm here to offer my legal services to the Mortal."

"That's really not necessary—"

The bird-thing ignored the blue being and practically skipped over to Reina. It reached out and took her hand between its wings and rapidly shook her hand up and down. "Hey, how's it going!? I'm Nyarlathotep, Esquire. But my friends call me Mob!" The bird seemed to remember something and quickly released her hand. He walked over to the massive book and snatched it off the ground and showed it to her. "And this is my book!"

"Um, it's nice to meet you? And that's a nice book, I guess—"

"Hehe, thanks." The bird's eyes turned pitch black, and its face twisted into a parody of itself; its cheeks grew gaunt, its eyes sunk in, its feathers blackened at the roots. "You *can't have it*," it said in a demonically low voice.

Reina swallowed nervously and looked to the multi-colored beings for help. Luckily, the red being took pity on her and cleared her throat to get Mob's attention. "We were just about to check in on her husband—If you'd like to join us?"

The bird's face returned to normal and it innocently smiled at Red. "I thought you'd never ask!"

Gold snapped its fingers and a massive television screen materialized in the air in front of them.

"Popcorn! Get your popcorn here!" the bird yelled as it pushed a popcorn stall from somewhere within the shadows, over to the group.

"I'll take three."

"Three for Shazai, coming up!"

"Oh, two over here please!"

"Jorthim, my dude! How're the chicklings?"

"They're great!"

The bird continued to chat with the multicolored beings for a few more minutes while Reina and Blue stood off to the side. "Where did—"

"Don't ask," Blue interrupted her.

"But how did he—"

"Look, you want to keep your sanity? Then don't ask how Mob does *anything*. It's better for everyone's long-term health if you just don't think about it."

"This is *normal* for you?" Reina asked; she was completely flabbergasted at the absurdity of what she was seeing play out in front of her.

"Unfortunately," Blue groaned.

The two looked away from each other and suddenly the bird was wearing a Santa hat and had a Big Gulp held tightly in its right wing.

"Where did—"

"Ignore it. It'll go away if we don't acknowledge it."

"Would you two shut up!? The movie's starting!" Mob yelled.

Sure enough, the screen lit up and a massive Naga was waiting with his four arms folded across his chest. Reina assumed this was meant to be Torga and if so it didn't match up with a description Ayla had given her of his Naga form. However, she had never seen this form herself and Torga had never really spoken of his other forms. She knew this could be a trick the beings were playing on her.

She stepped closer to the screen and inspected the Naga for any signs that he was who they claimed him to be.

He had a look of what Reina could only assume to be annoyance on his face, but otherwise, Reina couldn't see anything wrong with him.

"Is that meant to be Torga?" she asked, feeling unsure of herself. "Where is he?"

"Yes. That's your hubby alright. As for where he is, I think he's in Helheim," Mob confirmed around a mouthful of popcorn. "Did you never get to see this one?" he asked, possibly referring to the Naga form or possibly the snow covered, undead-filled arena he was standing in. Reina wasn't sure which.

Truth be told, she wasn't sure *he* knew which he was referring to either.

"No—I mean I heard about it, but I never actually saw it."

"Well, you're in for a treat. Watch. I love this part." He shoveled more popcorn in his mouth and made some type of vague cheering noise as the screen panned around to Torga's back and Reina saw the reason for his expression.

Four people were standing in front of him. As she watched, more and more people were landing behind the original group with each passing second, before maxing out at fifteen people. There were humans, some odd looking elves with pale skin and bleached blond hair, and insect beast folk the likes of which Reina had never seen before. She even saw a minotaur and a cockatrice amongst the group.

What is happening over there? Reina was horrified at the thought of him facing them alone.

"Woo!" Mob cheered. He leaped on top of the screen and his Santa hat changed to a black headset with a microphone attached.

"In this corner!" The bird's voice echoed throughout the void as he did a, rather bad, impression of a famous announcer. **"He is currently twenty-one feet and three quarters of an inch long, and weighing in at the ungodly weight of two-pounds heavier than Shazai's mother-"**

"Watch it!" Shazai snarled.

"Yeesh, tough crowd. **We have the reigning champion: Torga: The devourer of worlds!"**

Red cheered while the others stood in silence.

Worlds? As in... Plural? Reina's brain was hung up on that little tidbit for far longer than she'd like to admit.

"And in this corner! They currently stand at... Well, somewhere between five and fifteen feet tall and weighs—Does anyone actually care? No? I didn't think so. **I present to you, the vict**—I mean, **the gods of Yggdrasil!"** Mob took in a deep breath. **"Let's get ready to rum**—" A popcorn container came flying from out of nowhere and smacked into Mob's face, causing him to fall off the screen and crash into the 'ground.'

"Jorthim, you ruined my intro!"

"And you're annoying everyone!"

"Tch." Mob folded its wings over its chest and started sulking. However, it still pulled a small boombox from behind it and pressed the big red button on the front that said "play." A heavy percussion ripped from the boombox, loud enough to cause Reina's eardrums to vibrate and the battle began.

～ ～ ～

"You're my opponents?" I asked while eying them. It seemed Gamos had gone above and beyond to find opponents for me.

Speaking of the goddess, I peeked into the audience section and spotted a large throne floating above the arena. Gamos had forsaken the armor in favor of a lacy black dress that was cut off above her knees, revealing a dangerous amount of creamy white skin.

By her side was the massive draugur in silver armor. I still hadn't gotten his name yet, and to be honest, I didn't think I would either. I'd die here in the arena or I'd get kicked out almost immediately after. Either way, I didn't see a pleasant conversation in our future.

I returned my gaze back to my opponents. I towered over most of them. Even after reducing my length to a much more manageable twenty feet, the difference was obvious.

"So, you're the great devourer. I expected you to be bigger," someone said from my crowd of opponents.

The phrase hit a sore spot. I let out a low hiss and felt my stomach churn as my anger skyrocketed.

"Alright, who said that?" I looked around but no one stepped forward. "Come on, who just volunteered to get eaten first?"

The twelve-foot-tall minotaur stepped forward and with a mild huff, it spat flames out of its nose. The thing was built like an Olympic bodybuilder who *ate* other bodybuilders. The bull half of its body was covered in dirty brown fur thick enough to sink my fingers into, while its human half was covered by a black fur vest, leaving only its arms exposed to the icy winds. "Don't try to intimidate us, Devourer. We know you can't access your powers down here," the minotaur rumbled.

"Bold of you to assume I *need* them to rip you apart." I moved closer to the group. "So, this is what's about to happen." I pointed to an overweight bird god. "I'm going to eat Chicken Little over there first as an appetizer." Then I pointed to the minotaur. "And you, since you got such a big mouth, are gonna be the entree."

The bird beastman looked around at the gods surrounding it and gulped. "You know what. I—I think I left the oven on." It flapped its wings as if it were getting ready to fly away but was grabbed by the minotaur at the last second.

"Coward! What about our revenge!?" the minotaur roared.

Revenge? What did I do to these guys?

"That's easy for you to say! You died instantly last time, so you don't know what that psychopath is capable of!" the birdman yelled.

"Hey, I understand this might not be the right time, but do I know you? Because I've been over here racking my brain and trying to figure out what I've done that would warrant you wanting to get revenge, but I got nothing."

"Lies!" the minotaur roared. "Fight with everything you have, devourer and I'll prove that it isn't enough.

Who's with me!?" The rest of my opponents cheered alongside the minotaur; its words were all they needed to hear to forget any fear they had of me.

The minotaur took a few steps forward, then leaped forward to land on all fours, where it charged like the enraged bull that it was.

I felt myself tense as my anticipation ramped skywards. I had high hopes for him. I could only hope he wouldn't let me down.

The minotaur crashed into me horns first and I met his charge by shifting my body to the side and throwing a right hook aimed at the center of his head, directly in between his horns.

My fist hit the minotaur with enough force to crack a mountain. A shockwave passed throughout his body. Bones were reduced to ash, muscles ruptured, veins exploded, and the minotaur's body burst into a cloud of red mist covering my scales and dyeing me crimson.

"Next," I muttered, annoyed by the blood covering my body. I reached up and wiped some of the gore off of my face then licked it off my palm.

It didn't taste as good as I was hoping, but it wasn't bad. Unfortunately, I'd have to take a shower after this was done; otherwise, I was going to be sticky for the rest of the day.

"We—we still have him surrounded and outnumbered! Stick together and don't get separated. That's how that idiot died!"

"Yes. You're right. I am surrounded." A grinding sound filled the air as the black hole within my stomach began to slowly spin, "I'm surrounded by dead morons." I smacked away a hammer aimed for my head and snarled, "Now move, you're hindering my ability to find. my. wife!" My fist slammed into the chauron's stomach, cleaving it in two.

And my attack didn't stop there. I followed through with the blow and spun into a backhand that knocked the head off of a snow elf. I continued to spin, grabbing the headless snow elf's right arm as I moved around it, then I lifted the body and used it to smack another giant bug into the ground. The bug twitched, so I knocked away a human with a flick of my tail aimed at his pelvis, then I brought the elf corpse down on the bug a few more times for good measure. By the time I was done, the corpse was useless to me. The bones had been reduced to dust, and the flesh was falling apart so I discarded it.

The brutality I'd shown was causing some of the less experienced gods to hesitate, which was annoying because it meant I had to go to them instead of waiting for them to come to me.

I looked up at Gamos again and noticed that she was watching me with a smile on her face.

I shook my head and returned my focus to the fight. I had my doubts that any of these people could so much as scratch my scales, but that didn't mean I was going to give them the opportunity to prove me wrong.

~ ~ ~

"And—that means it's time for a break!" The bird clapped its wings together and headed away from the group. Reina looked away from the screen, almost missing Torga lifting the cockatrice off the ground by its throat, tossing it into the air, then grabbing its legs and driving it straight into the ground. Its neck was unable to support the pressure and the creature collapsed into a puddle of blood and bone dust.

Reina fell to the ground around the time Torga decapitated an elf with a back hand and was simply staring at the television in silence. "I—I get the feeling I need to take a step back and re-evaluate how dangerous I thought Torga was."

"Probably a good idea," the blue being replied.

Suddenly, a loud gasp filled the room as the Orange being stopped floating and he fell to the ground with a *thump*. He lifted his head and stared in the direction of the group for a few seconds. "What'd I miss?" he asked lamely.

"We really need to work on that sleeping habit of yours, Pthelios," Red sighed.

Almost in spite of herself, Reina started giggling at the absurdity of her situation.

It took her several minutes to calm down enough to climb to her feet and stand beside the floating Nyarlathotep.

"I still don't understand what all this is about, but I'm a woman of my word. Ask away."

"Thank you," Blue said, its voice seemingly radiating gratitude. "Now, we've discussed it, and we've concluded that this would be much easier if I asked the questions and my fellow judges only speak in the event they need something clarified. Do you accept these terms?" Reina nodded for lack of anything else to do. "Good. First question: When did you first meet your husband?"

"Before I was reincarnated."

"Yes, but when specifically—What was your solar date?" Blue pressed.

"I'm not sure about a solar date, but we met in 2071, when we were both five years old."

"Did you ever meet his parents?"

"I met his father. His mother passed when he was three due to cervical cancer."

"Did he have any siblings? A brother or perhaps a sister?"

"He had two brothers. Both died before we started dating."

"Did he have anyone else that he was particularly close to?"

"Not to my knowledge. But I died when he was in his thirties, so that may have changed later on."

"What about after his appearance on Yggdrasil; who does he care for?" the green one interrupted.

Reina didn't answer immediately. Instead, she asked something that'd been bothering her for a while. "What's this all about? Why are you so interested in him?"

Blue looked around at the other judges. Something seemed to pass between them, as he returned her question with another of his own. "Would you still love him if he wasn't the man you thought he was?"

"What are you implying?"

"It is our belief, and the belief of the one who brought this case to our attention, that Torga is not who he claims to be and is, in fact, one of the oldest dark gods: a being known as Orochi."

"… Pardon me, but—What the hell are you talking about?"

"We believe Orochi has been systematically erasing his presence and knowledge of his existence across Yggdrasil. We know not his purpose, nor what dark powers he's used to pull this feat off, but we have both eyewitness accounts from trusted sources and physical evidence that both claims are true."

"Ooo—Ooo Can I explain it!? Can I!?"

"If it'll shut you up."

Mob rubbed his wings together in front of his body, then turned to face Reina and somehow made his wing look as if he were holding one finger in the air. "As you may or may not know, Torga is an incredibly powerful being, easily ranking within the top ten percent of all gods. However, by all verified accounts, Torga is only a few centuries old. If this is true, then he has broken all records of measurement used to keep track of the gods, with the next fastest taking around 3000 years. Most gods find it hard to stomach the idea that a 'child' such as Torga was able to pass them so easily. Envy is an ugly thing, but in this case it's what brought to light some… irregularities with Torga's life. And after reviewing his fate stream myself, I'm inclined to agree with them. There are massive irregularities in Torga's life that need to be addressed, if not for the sake of truth, then for his own sake, because someone is messing with his destiny.

"He's fought beings that should have killed him multiple times over and killed them instead. Sometimes so easily as to make it look effortless. Normally I would say this was just dumb luck, but it's happened so many times that even I began to suspect that he was using fate altering spells or curses. And if Torga's as young as he appears to be, then he should have no knowledge or ability to use such things.

"He's traveled branches that, for all intents and purposes, he should have had no way to access, as they'd been decommissioned millennia ago. There's only a handful of ways to do this, most of which involve divine intervention or ancient spells that he should have no access to.

"There's also the fact that Torga was reincarnated by Niabus: a known associate of Orochi. Granted, it's well known that Niabus has despised Orochi for what he did to the Lady Forna. But that means very little in this case, as it is no secret that Niabus would do almost anything for his precious sister, including working with his greatest enemy.

"And let's not forget the fact that he is a dark serpent. That alone would cast doubt over any evidence of his innocence, as the last dark serpent was…" He trailed off.

"Orochi," Reina sighed.

"There are other minor details, but in order for you to understand them, I would have to explain hundreds of years of 'divine' legal mumbo jumbo. Instead, I'm just gonna gloss over them and say this: It doesn't look good. They have all the evidence they need to force Torga to fade."

"Then why am I here? Why take the time to interview me like this if you were going to execute him anyway?"

"Because that is not the way we handle cases," Blue declared. "We see a lot and know even more. However, we have brought you here to act as a character witness for Torga, to tell us of things we cannot see. What he's like as a person, and if that changes when he believes himself to be alone. By all accounts, Torga is not a 'good' person. However, throughout the interviews we conducted, one thing has been made abundantly clear.

"If this is Orochi, then he is not the same one we locked away eons ago.

"Gods do not change easily; we are far too long lived and stubborn for that. So, if this is Orochi and he has undergone such a drastic change, we want to know why."

Reina watched the five beings for over a minute without saying a word, then she turned her head to look down at Nyarlathotep. He seemed calm, all things considered, far calmer than she was.

"It's OK," he told her, for once looking both sane and competent.

"Alright, where do I start?"

"Start from the beginning. Tell us about the man known as Torga, and maybe we can help him."

Reina nodded her head and resigned herself to answering their questions. If they were right—no, even if they were wrong—then someone was messing with Torga's life. And Reina vowed to be cold in the ground long before she allowed that to continue.

INTERLUDE: SURVIVOR STORIES

AYLA: ASGARD

Ayla awoke to the sound of someone moving around inside her tent. She opened her eyes and spotted her fiancé, Thor, trying to quietly leave.

"Where do you think you're going?" she asked around a yawn.

Thor's body tensed with his hand on the flap. He sighed like a child who had been caught doing something they knew they weren't supposed to do. He turned to face her, revealing that he was wearing a full suit of leather armor and had his trusty sword in a scabbard across his back.

"I was going to go hunting, you know, get out of camp for a while."

"Want me to come with you?"

"If it's all right with you, I'd rather go alone. It's not that I don't want to be with you. It's just—"

"No, I get it," she said with a smile on her face. She did understand where he was coming from. He'd been under a lot of stress lately and he deserved to get out and just have a day to himself every once in a while.

Thor crossed the tent in two steps, bent down, placed a soft kiss on Ayla's lips. "You're the best," he whispered. He kissed her on the forehead, then once on either cheek before pulling away and leaving the tent. She heard the rustling of the leather straps they used to keep the tent flaps closed in the middle of the night being put into position and smiled at his thoughtfulness.

She returned to bed with the smile still on her face; however, it faded as the reality of their situation settled in once again.

Even though they weren't married yet, she and Thor had the duties of king and queen of Asgard foisted upon them. Thor's parents, the real king and queen, had disappeared when Taranis was taken, and no one had seen or heard from them since.

This left Ayla, Thor, Thor's brother Loki, and Findral as the sole protectors of over three hundred civilians.

There would've been a few more, but Hali, Solon, Talia, and Uriel had taken their elves with them when they left.

Ayla couldn't blame them. If Thor wasn't the de facto king of the Asgardians, Ayla would've begged him to leave with them. But she knew he wouldn't. Thor was many things, but he'd never been one to shirk his duty to his people.

Thor had been trying to train some of the civilians how to wield weapons and how to defend themselves, but the main problem came from a lack of motivation. People had lost hope. Losing Taranis was the last straw for the Asgardians after what happened with their capital city.

Now they were just… existing. Barely surviving day to day on what little food Thor and the other hunters could collect. And even that meager amount was growing more scarce by the day as winter set in and the animals went into hiding.

Ayla had been trying to supplement their food supply by growing vegetables and fruits, but there was only so much she could do as things stood.

Winter had well and truly arrived, and from the looks of things, it was going to be here for a while. The soil had frozen over, preventing most crops from ever taking hold. As it was, Ayla struggled to get a few baskets of fruit and vegetables a week. Even using her druidic magic around-the-clock only slightly improved what they got at the end of the week.

She'd never felt so useless.

After tossing and turning for another forty-five minutes, Ayla had enough and got up. She quietly slipped on her clothes and got ready for the day.

Judging by the light peeking through the tent flaps, she knew that it was still early in the morning. Most people wouldn't be up for another few hours, so she had the camp to herself.

She stepped out into the moonlight and breathed in the chilly air, allowing it to fill her lungs and finish lifting the haze of sleep from her mind. She looked up at the waxing moon hanging overhead and sighed.

"Time to get to work," she muttered to herself.

She headed towards the center of camp, passing row after row of tents in various states of disrepair. A few times she saw tents in such bad shape that she knew if left alone, the people inside would get sick. So, she would stop and chant quietly under her breath for a few seconds.

The material the tent was made out of would respond to her request and repair itself. It was never perfect, as you could always tell that it had been repaired, but it would hold, and it would keep out the cold.

Ayla couldn't ask for more.

This was something of an everyday thing for Ayla. She may not have been able to grow food, but she could keep their equipment in shape, and she could repair their clothes and tents to make them last far longer than they normally would have.

Ayla arrived at the tent they'd designated as the headquarters or "throne room" as Findral liked to joke.

Aside from being larger than the other tents by half, headquarters wasn't much different: Inside there was a table with four chairs surrounding it, where the main group took their breakfast and other meals. There was also a high-backed chair, which Findral lovingly referred to as the throne of Thor, in the center of the tent. Finally, there was a large map hung up on the leftmost wall.

Ayla was here for none of that. She'd come here for one thing, and one thing alone.

Findral liked to hide snacks inside their headquarters in case she got hungry during one of their daily meetings.

Ayla still had a few hours before breakfast, so she wanted to steal a cake she knew Findral had squirreled away before Findral woke up.

Now, if I was Findral, where would I hide my precious cakes?

~ ~ ~

Hali: Two planets south of Asgard; Rastapsa; the Silent Sea

A massive ship made of material that looked like stone, but was much lighter, was slowly moving forward across a motionless ocean. The ship was over 350 feet long, a hundred feet wide, and seventy-five feet tall. It moved via three small propellers at the rear of the ship that pushed the vessel along without making a sound.

Onboard, a number of elves scurried around, trying to complete today's tasks before they were forced to return below deck. Amongst those elves, Hali and Solon stood by the railings with their younger sister, Talia, standing between them.

They were staring over the rails at the water below: It was an odd emerald color. It was one of the strangest aspects of the ocean, and also why it had received its name. Thanks to a twenty-foot gel layer that covered the surface, the water didn't move unless something beneath it was passing through it.

Even their ship, as large as it was, only made small ripples as it passed through the gel layer. Which was good because there were things in this ocean that they didn't want to disturb.

"Do you think they made it out of the city okay?" Hali muttered to Solon.

Solon knew who she meant even without her specifying. He nodded his head. "Yeah, I'm sure they did. You know how stubborn Ayla and Findral can be."

"Right," Hali chuckled. "It would take more than a few Jötnar to take her out, especially with those two by her side."

"Do you think Dad made it out okay?" Talia asked. She was too short to see over the railing, so she'd settled for poking her head through the gaps in the railing so she could see the water like her siblings.

Hali turned her head away from Talia and Solon. "Yeah, of course, he did. It's Dad. I bet he's going to show up on our doorstep one day with that big, stupid smile on his face."

"You really think so?" Talia asked quietly.

"Why do you ask, Talia?" Solon said, wrapping his arm around her shoulders, and pulling her against him. "Huh?"

He felt Talia shrug into his arm.

"Hey, what is it?"

Solon's question drew Hali's attention and they both looked down at Talia. She still had her head through the gaps in the railings, so they couldn't see her face.

"It's just… I heard someone talking about it. They say Dad died."

"Don't listen to them, Talia," Hali told her. "They don't know what they're talking about."

"How can you be so sure? We had to evacuate before he came to find us. What if he died fighting the Jötnar? What if he needed our help—"

"Hey." Hali grabbed Talia's shoulder and pulled her around so she could look at her. She saw tears running down Talia's face and Hali's heart broke. She wanted to go find whoever did this to her sister and throw them overboard, but she knew it wasn't totally their fault.

Truth was, there was little chance that their father had survived the attack on Taranis. Even if he had survived, Hali knew what awaited him had he returned with them. He would've been forced into another partnership, one where he would've had to wait a minimum of ten years before he could contact them, and then only with his bonded's permission. Or he would've been summarily executed to avoid the withdrawal symptoms.

Their father died, whether his body still lived, the moment their mother died and there was nothing they could do about it.

A bell rang from somewhere high overhead, drawing Hali and Solon's attention away from their sister into the commotion going on around them. That bell only meant one thing: It was time to go back inside.

Hali took Talia's hand and the three of them joined the line of people waiting to head below deck.

There were two ways to get below deck, and which path you took depended on which cabin you were in.

As the grandchildren of Uriel, the tribe elder, the three of them were heading to the rear of the ship to enter through the door there. That door would lead them into the first-class cabin area, where only the elders of the tribe were welcome.

They passed by the line that headed into the common area and once again were grateful that they were able to stay with their grandfather. There were over fifty people in that line, with more arriving every second.

To get to the common area, you had to go down one of four ladders arranged in a square at the center of the ship. Each ladder could be closed off via a heavy metal cap that was slid into place once everyone was inside, or in case of emergencies.

The three siblings continued walking towards the rear of the ship without stopping. Along the way they ran into their grandfather Uriel, who joined them. Aside from Talia, who was too young to understand exactly what happened, Uriel was the one who kept Hali and Solon sane with his dry humor and weird antics.

It helped that Uriel was truly ancient, being well over a thousand years old, and was incredibly difficult to surprise. It was he who led their tribe away from Asgard after the attack, and it was he who had taken on the responsibility of protecting them.

Hali didn't know where they would be without him.

But… There was always that little voice in her head that reminded her of someone who should be here but wasn't.

And no, she wasn't referring to her father. She missed him terribly, of course. But the person she was deeply missing was Torga. He'd been something of an uncle to the three of them for so long they were having trouble picturing their lives without him… Okay, *she* was having trouble picturing her life without him in it.

She knew he was married, and quite happily too, but she'd always hoped he'd come to her one day and—

"Hey, Hali," a deep voice said from behind her.

Hali let out a small gasp of surprise, which quickly turned into anger. She whipped around and pointed her finger at the much larger boy standing behind her.

"Damn it, Drannor I told you to stop doing that!" she yelled.

Drannor was an older boy of the warrior caste. For some reason, he'd made it his personal mission to talk to her every single day. It didn't help that he usually started those conversations by scaring the crap out of her. Honestly, more than once she'd thought about putting a bell around his neck so that he'd stop sneaking up on her.

It was maddening.

Drannor just laughed and smiled at her. "Just wanted to say 'hey' before we turned in for the night. Did you miss me?"

"Like an irritating gnat," she said, narrowing her eyes at him and smirking.

"Hello, Drannor." Uriel greeted the boy with a wide smile and dip of his pipe. "I haven't seen your uncle today. Is he inside?"

"Yes, elder. Uncle Daxus was feeling a bit under the weather today, so he stayed in the room."

"Ah, that explains it. Mind if I pay him a visit?"

"Please," Drannor agreed with a nod of his head. "I'm sure he'd enjoy the company."

Uriel nodded back. He took a few steps towards the common area before stopping and turning around to look at them. "Actually, I think I'm going to stay over at your place tonight. Daxus still owes me for that chess game he ran away from. Now that he's bedridden, he can't get away," Uriel told them in a conspiratorial whisper. "Say, Drannor. Why don't you take my room tonight?"

Hali rolled her eyes because she knew were this was going.

"If that is the elder's request, I won't say no."

"Excellent. Have fun you four."

Hali sighed as she watched her grandfather walk away. Now she was stuck with Drannor for the whole night.

"Hey, Hali," Drannor whispered. "I think Uriel likes me. Isn't that great?"

Hali rolled her eyes again and didn't answer him.

"Hey, Solon. I think Uriel likes me!"

Solon smirked at Hali, before giving Drannor a thumbs up—which Drannor enthusiastically returned.

Talia looked up at her big sister and pointed at Drannor. "Why is he so happy?"

"Because he's an idiot," Hali sighed, not noticing that her mood had improved significantly since Drannor had first spoken to her.

˜ ˜ ˜

Fenris: Location Unknown

Far, far away from civilization in a land no civilized being had ever seen, a gargantuan black wolf ran free.

It was taller than the volcanoes that were so common on this planet. It moved faster than the wind, its paws creating gusts of wind every time it ran. And its eyes: Crimson red with flecks of gold shone brightly under the light of the moon.

Though the land around him was cold, and flakes of white fell from the sky, the wolf remained unfazed.

The cold was an annoyance, nothing more.

Currently, the wolf was hunting down its next meal. He knew not why it so craved the meat of the blue-skins, but it knew it must have them. Their tough hides and blisteringly cold blood sent shivers of pleasure down the wolf's spine when it ingested them. It was an addiction; one the wolf had no qualms about enabling.

So, when it caught the scent of this particular blue skin, the wolf knew what it must do.

The wolf hunkered down in the snow, its onyx black fur helping it blend into the shadows of the night. It didn't need to hide, the wolf's strong jaws and deadly claws ensured that it would win any altercations with the blue skin.

But he enjoyed these hunts, enjoyed the smell of fear that wafted from the blue skins when they realized he was following them. Oh, how he enjoyed their screams as he pursued them.

Their cries as he ate them.

But for now, the wolf would wait. The blue skin it was tracking was not alone.

Pesky blue skins. They thought they were safe in groups, but all the wolf had to do was wait; they would separate eventually. And when they did, he would pick them off one by one as he had done so many times before.

The wolf would feast this night, and the next. The wolf was sure he would not be satisfied until every last blue skin was wiped out, and it didn't bother him that he did not know why he harbored such hatred for them.

The wolf's ear twitched as movement in the forest caught his attention. His big head swiveled in the direction of the sound and he instinctively knew to hold his breath.

There was a blue skin, a big blue skin. It lumbered through the forest while carrying a big stick in its hand.

The wolf lifted its hindquarters off the ground and leaned forward, putting its weight onto its front paws. It tucked its neck in, folded its ears back, and bared its teeth.

The wolf would feast this night, and it would start with this blue skin.

Ding

ꝏꝏꝏꝏꝏꝏ

You have completed the requirements for the *Vánagandr* evolution to begin. Would you like to evolve?

ꝏꝏꝏꝏꝏꝏ

The wolf ripped the leg off of the blue skin and swallowed it in one go. It huffed at the window that blocked its vision. It cared not for the words on the screen, all it cared about was the meal before it.

∞∞∞∞∞∞∞∞

Evolution has commenced. Time until evolution is complete: 1 Year, 11 Months, 31 Days, 23 Hours, 59 Minutes, 59 Seconds.

∞∞∞∞∞∞∞∞

A transparent white dome grew around the wolf's body. It howled as its meal was torn away from it and shoved outside of the shell. Its howl traveled for miles around, sending shivers down the spine of all who heard it.

Chapter Twenty-One

I THOUGHT MY FIGHT IN THE ARENA WENT PRETTY well. I killed some people, entertained the crowd with my witty banter, and even got a few laughs out of some of my opponents.

Okay, those last two things were not true. Which is probably why I found myself standing in my human form before a rather annoyed Gamos, with a small army of guards surrounding me.

She was sitting on her throne, which, as I'd previously expected, was about as creepy looking as she could possibly make it; I mean, it had several moaning heads impaled on a trident above her seat. It also looked incredibly uncomfortable, with plenty of sharp edges to cut yourself on and no armrests.

None of that seemed to bother Gamos though. She sat with her back straight and one leg crossed over the other, looking for all the world like she was ready to appear on the cover of some magazine.

"Do you know why you are here?" she asked, and I could tell from her tone that this wasn't the seducer. This was Gamos the warrior, and there was every chance my response could get me killed.

"Nope, not a clue," I told her honestly. "I did as you asked. I showed up, killed my opponents, and was ready to leave until you had the goon squad here drag me back."

Gamos' face remained blank and I took that to mean she didn't find my joke very funny.

"Then let me explain so there's no misunderstandings between us. You were brought here because the judges wanted you to be… I don't like it, in fact, it infuriates me. The judges are in charge of the overworld. Once someone comes to the underworld, they fall under the purview of the lords, not the judges.

"With that being said, Niabus has informed me that should I help you leave, I am likely to have an inquisition at my border.

"And I can't have that."

"Did he offer any proof of this, or are you just taking him at his word?"

"The judges, and by proxy; their armies, are not something you can just lie about. If it got back to the judges that Niabus had been using their armies to threaten me, he'd spend an eternity wishing they had made him fade. That's how serious his situation is."

"Okay—does that mean you're going to stop me from leaving?" I asked, not quite understanding why she was telling me this. I hadn't been expecting her to help me leave to begin with. I was just hoping she would point me in the right direction and be done with me.

"No," she snorted. "It just means I cannot help you leave. In fact, I'm duty-bound to alert them of the fact that you have left my territory and are heading towards death's elevator, which is a thousand miles due south of here, where it will remain for a few cycles because of an unscheduled maintenance request."

"You don't say?" I wanted to smile, but since she remained completely expressionless throughout her little spiel, I felt it only fair that I played along. "And just how would I have come across this information?"

"Niabus told you," she replied immediately.

"I—I see. I should thank him," I replied while struggling not to laugh.

"You'll have all the time in the universe to thank him. He's going with you."

Any humor I found in the situation evaporated immediately upon hearing that Niabus, the guy who was almost solely responsible for my worst days since coming to Yggdrasil, was going to be traveling with me once again.

As if she'd called his name, a door opened on the side of the throne room and Niabus, back in his quasi-lizard man form, stepped through. He looked about as uncomfortable as I felt, maybe even more so since he was still missing that wing…

"Can't you just kill him?" I swear, I was not whining. My voice just got a little high at the thought of traveling with this backstabbing asshole again.

"No, she can't." Niabus said, shattering my hopes and killing my dreams. "As part of my work for the judges, I am considered to be one of their agents. I can't be tried, and I can't be killed, by any god lower in rank than a judge, so long as I am doing my job. Like it or not, that's what I'm doing."

"What would've happened if I drove that icicle through your chest?" I asked suddenly. The question had been haunting me since our fight. I wasn't even sure if it would've killed him, but at the time it seemed like a good idea.

"You would've been marked for death by the judges," he replied. His eyes had narrowed at the question and while he wasn't glaring at me, it was close.

"Interesting," I mumbled. Judging by his answer, I can only assume that it would've killed him and that's why I would've been marked for death… I think it would've been worth it though.

"While that is a gross exaggeration of his importance, Niabus is correct in one thing. If you had killed him, the judges would not have been lenient with you. Death would've been unlikely, but imprisonment for the rest of your life or torture for a thousand years are both likely outcomes to killing one of their agents. That's partially why I stopped you."

"Partially?"

"Despite his many mistakes… His *very* many mistakes, Niabus does not deserve to die here, in a place so far from his homeland," she said somberly.

Her words seemed to make everyone in the throne room uncomfortable. None more so than Niabus himself, who looked like he wanted to be anywhere but here.

"You're not just saying that because you don't want to be stuck with him forever, are you?" I asked, and I was only half joking.

Gamos smiled and shook her head at me. "I think it's time for you two to be on your way."

"No need to tell me twice. Just tell me which door to take and you'll never see me again."

"I know the way," Niabus sighed. "Follow me—"

"There is a greater chance of Helheim turning into a tropical paradise, than there is of me following you of my own free will," I said without moving to follow him. I looked at Gamos and crossed my arms over my chest.

"You don't even have to speak," I told her. "Just point towards a door and that's where I'll go."

"Don't be like this, Torga," Niabus said. "It's childish."

"No, it's common sense. You lied to me from the day we first met. If you think I'm just going to blindly follow you now, you're even stupider than I thought you were."

"Hey, you followed me before," he sneered.

"Yes, I did. And because I followed you, you lost a wing. Maybe I will follow you again. Who knows what I'll get the next time."

"Enough."

I flinched at the sound of Gamos' voice.

"If the two of you aren't outside of my city within the next two minutes, the judges be damned, I'll kill you myself." I didn't bother sticking around past that point, because I was fairly sure she would do it, and I was almost positive that I wouldn't enjoy the experience.

Without pausing to say a word to one another, Niabus and I just started running. A couple of unfortunate guards got in our way as we were heading out the door, so we ran them over. I made sure not the step on the guy's head. I didn't want to kill him, after all. But I didn't have time to stick around to make sure that he was okay. We had two minutes to travel from the center of the city to the wall— that was a three-mile trip.

As soon as open sky was above me, I wasted no time in putting all of my strength into my legs and jumping as high as I could.

I may not have regained my ability to fly yet, but I could certainly fall with style.

The ground beneath me exploded in a shower of ice chunks and rubble as I lifted into the air. Within seconds

I was hundreds of feet in the air and traveling at speeds far higher than the mortal can survive without the assistance of some type of vehicle.

"Are you insane?!"

I thought Niabus' voice sounded too close. I looked behind me, but he wasn't there, so I looked to both sides and in front of me. He was nowhere to be found. And then I looked down— Niabus was hanging onto my leg with both of his eyes shut.

"What are you doing? Let go!" I yelled. I kicked him a few times with my free leg, but because he was on the outside of my left leg, I was having trouble getting a decent kick in with my right.

"You ripped off my wing, remember? I can't fly."

"That sounds like a whole lotta not my problem. You can jump, can't you?"

"Oh, but it is your problem. She said if *we* weren't out of her city in two minutes, she would kill *us*. And if I die, who do you think she's gonna blame it on? You, she's gonna blame it on you."

"And?"

"And, if the judges think that you killed me…"

"Right, torture and/or punishment for the rest of my life. Gotcha." I reached down and grabbed him by the back of the neck, then lifted him up until we were nose to nose.

"Guess what, we're out of the city now." I twisted his head so that he could see the crater beneath us. "So, get the fuck off." I drew back my arm and tossed him straight down. The motion encouraged me to start heading towards the ground too, but I was fine because I didn't want to fly too far in my current direction.

Gamos' mansion wasn't facing south, so during my hasty retreat, I had jumped east. Traveling too far in this direction would just make this trip even longer.

Niabus hit the ice first, of course, and I landed about 2000 feet away from him. I wish I could say my landing was graceful, but the truth was I landed on my head and bounced about six times before I came to a stop with half my body in the ice.

I broke myself loose, then used what I could see of the city to find out which direction I was facing. I knew the city faced east from the direction Gamos had indicated when she was telling me which way to go. Since I was now facing the front of her house, that meant I was facing west… I hoped.

I turned my body to the south and started running. I only had a few days to travel a thousand miles. That was going to be more than a little annoying since I couldn't fly. Actually, maybe I'd get lucky and run into a few guardians along the way.

I crossed my fingers, prayed for luck, and then jumped again. The ice beneath my feet shattered with the force of my jump and ice soared through the air faster than any bird, and most planes.

As it turned out, Niabus could also replicate this feat. In fact, I did not realize until I'd already jumped twice more. I could tell that Niabus wasn't as used to jumping as I was, most likely because he'd been able to fly for most of his life. Whereas I'd learn to use my tail as a spring and throw myself across the horizon long before I gained the ability to fly.

An idea struck me, and I felt like an idiot for not thinking of it sooner. Since there was no reason to continue hiding my true form from Niabus, I simply transformed back into my Naga form.

My bones broke, my legs fused together, and my entire body shifted into that of a completely different species. In the time it took me to jump and then land, I'd shifted into my Naga form and used my much stronger tail as a spring to increase the length of my jumps.

I sprung off the ground with all the force a seventy-foot-long tail of solid muscle could muster.

Much better. I smiled as the ground beneath me imploded, and I was thrown through the air. My speed had effectively doubled due to the massive increase of muscle fibers working to get me moving.

Sure, each jump took slightly longer to perform, but the sheer distance that I traveled between jumps now made it worth a few extra seconds.

Plus, traveling further per jump meant that I left Niabus behind even faster.

What was that old saying about killing two dragons with one stone?

I began to fall out of the sky after my tenth or eleventh jump. There was no purpose in keeping track of how many times I jumped, so I didn't bother. Instead I focused on the more important things, like scanning the forest below for guardians and thinking of ways to lose Niabus in the forest.

Unfortunately, I hadn't seen any guardians yet, and I could still see Niabus leaping through the air after me, but I was hopeful on both counts.

Maybe if I was really lucky, one of the guardians would kill him for me.

Who am I kidding? I'm never that lucky. I shook my head and sighed. Knowing my luck, I was probably going to be stuck with that bastard for the rest of my life…

~ ∴ ~

Because I was able to regenerate faster than my muscles could exhaust themselves, I was able to consistently jump for hours on end, and if Gamos was right, then I should be nearing the elevator anytime now.

Except, I didn't see anything. For miles and miles around, the only thing that I saw were trees, snow, and ice pillars.

Had I missed my window and not realized it? It was certainly possible; time was basically meaningless without something to base it off of, and as far as I could tell, the only thing you could possibly base it off of was the time it took a single fireball to travel across the sky. However, it seemed to take only a few seconds for each fireball to dissipate.

Was that considered a cycle?

I hoped not.

I briefly entertained the thought of waiting for Niabus to catch up so I could ask him, but I decided against it. If I found the elevator and it wasn't there, then I would ask him. Until then, I had no desire to speak to Niabus more than absolutely necessary.

Call me petty and I'll wear that title with honor.

I mistimed my landing roll and ended up on my back. My weight caused the ground to shake, which shook the trees, causing more snow to fall on top of me. *Guess that's what I get for letting myself get distracted.*

I dug myself out of the snow and prepared to jump again. Then the ground shook for a second time, only it wasn't my doing. I paused just before extending my tail and listened to my surroundings…

Boom

Is someone fighting? I could hear a series of steady crashes and loud thumps off in the distance. Either someone was fighting or there was a rock concert a few miles to my left.

To hell with it. I turned in the direction of the noise and jumped. At this point, anything would be better than staying lost. Maybe I'd get lucky and whatever was over there would be able to point me in the right direction. Or maybe they wouldn't, and this deviation would cost me my chance at getting out of here.

I flew through the air, and excitement filled me as I spotted a structure I'd never seen before: a seventy-foot-tall, cylindrical building stood surrounded on all sides by trees that would've hidden it from me, were it not for the sounds I'd heard.

Aside from the general shape, and the odd blue-and-white stones it was constructed out of, I couldn't see much of it.

I landed about a thousand feet from the building and cautiously moved to get a better look at it. More details became clear the closer I came. The building was even shorter than I'd originally thought and was closer to fifty feet in height. It had a diameter of about twenty-five feet, and that was true from the base of the building to its roof. From what I could see, it was a perfect cylinder.

Another thing I noticed was how much care and effort someone put into the construction of this building. Each brick fit so perfectly with the others that were it not for the lines where it was clear ice had formed, it would've looked as if the entire thing were carved out of a single large stone.

As I walked around to the front of the building, I got a sinking feeling at the bottom of my stomach. At first, I didn't know why… And then I realized why.

I hadn't heard any more loud noises coming from the building.

Almost as if the first one had been a lure designed to get my attention.

I felt a sharp pain stab into the side of my neck and then everything was suddenly spinning. I felt myself tumbling through the air, with no idea how or why it happened.

My question was answered as I finished my rotation and I noticed two things: Ruknar standing behind me with a one-handed axe in his outstretched hand. And a bloodied stump where the upper half of my skull used to be.

CHAPTER TWENTY-TWO

I CAME TO, TO THE SOUND OF TWO PEOPLE ARGUING. The first was a voice I recognized all too well. I couldn't understand half of what Niabus was saying, mostly due to a weird humming noise inside my head, but it was clear that he was pissed. The other voice I didn't recognize as much, but if my fuzzy memory of the last few minutes was correct, then it was most likely Ruknar who was on the receiving end of Niabus' anger.

I tried moving my body around, but no matter what I tried to move, it was as if I was completely paralyzed.

The haze surrounding my brain vanished suddenly, and my memories rushed back in a wave of agony and confusion.

I'd been decapitated. In fact, I could see my headless body lying on the ground not five feet away.

How the hell am I still alive?

I looked around and noticed that while I had indeed been decapitated, my body had regrown most of its skull. The only part still missing were my eyes, the very top of my skull, and judging by the empty cavity were my brain should be, my brain.

Watching my body regenerate from a decapitation was truly fascinating. I had no idea how it worked. I always thought getting decapitated would've killed me. I guess I was wrong.

"What are we supposed to do now?" Niabus' voice was coming through clearer now, almost as if he were radio and I had found the right frequency.

Wait a second... Am I regenerating too? I looked down—or rather, I looked towards my nose and noticed that it was beginning to regenerate as well.

Both halves of my body were regenerating; at different speeds to be sure, but both halves were slowly regenerating.

A few moments passed, and my "other body" had regrown its eyes and its skull had closed up.

Its eyes rotated to look at me and I felt a jolt of electricity pass between us. We were connected. I knew what it was going to do as it planned to do it, and what it was planning to do was take that axe and shove it straight up Ruknar's ass.

~ ~ ~

"Fine, fine, fine, you can blame it on me if you want. It doesn't change the fact that he's dead." Ruknar shook his head out of exasperation. So, he'd killed the slimy worm, who cares? With its rap sheet, it was bound to be executed anyway.

"Of course, I'm going to blame it on you. You're the one who decided to kill him, when you knew we were only supposed to delay him until the judges were finished interrogating the elf.

"They've had weeks to do that. They're so backlogged as it is, they'll never get around to actually interrogating her. All I did was expedite the end result."

Niabus slapped Ruknar across the face hard enough to make the much larger god stagger backwards. "Those weren't your orders. Your orders were to pretend to be a loyal soldier until they made the determination that Torga was Orochi. With him dead, anything Orochi does to further our plans will be blamed solely on him and not Torga." Niabus slapped Ruknar across the other cheek, twisting his head around so quickly that he was almost knocked off his feet. "If he'd wanted him dead, don't you think he would've told me to kill him?" Niabus growled.

Ruknar rubbed his cheeks and stretched out his jaw. For a second there, he thought Niabus had knocked out a tooth.

"I suppose he would."

"You suppose?" Niabus sneered. "And what do you *suppose* Orochi will do to you when he finds out you wasted five hundred years of planning on a whim?"

"If he finds out," Ruknar corrected.

Niabus stepped forward, putting him and the much larger man chest to chest. "He will find out because I'm going to tell him… Unless you plan on stopping me."

Ruknar smirked and stared down into Niabus' eyes. "No, I'm not going to stop you. If you want to tell him go right ahead. Just remember that you're not the top dog anymore, Niabus."

Niabus put one hand on Ruknar's chest and *shoved*. Ruknar was thrown backwards, his feet flailed in a desperate attempt to maintain some level of balance.

The only thing that finally stopped him from sliding into the forest was a thick pine tree that he was able to grab hold of to halt his momentum.

By the time Ruknar had finally stopped sliding, Niabus was standing in front of the building with his hand wrapped around a golden bar that was seemingly attached to a flat piece of the building.

Niabus tugged on the bar, and a door frame appeared from within the stone. Niabus tugged again, and the door slid open silently. Before stepping over the threshold, he directed one final glance at Torga's body, smiled, then stepped inside and pulled the door shut behind him.

The door vanished within moments, leaving Ruknar to stare impotently at the building.

"Fucking dragons," Ruknar grumbled. He climbed to his feet and began walking towards the building.

Let's see if that jackass can maintain that level of cockiness after I chop his head off, he sniffed. He scooped up his axe from where he'd dropped it and continued walking towards the building.

Something wrapped around Ruknar's leg, and he had just enough time to widen his eyes before he was yanked off his feet and slammed face first into the snow. He was lifted again and slammed onto his back.

Torga stood over him; the violence he intended to inflict upon Ruknar was clear to see within his malevolent orange eyes.

Without saying anything, Torga picked up Ruknar's axe and did a cursory inspection on it.

"You can't use it against me. It's been enchanted," Ruknar said. He was feeling confident in spite of his situation. He'd taken out Torga once before in a straight up fight, and he knew he could do it again.

Torga, lifted the axe up and gripped it with all four of his hands.

Crack!

The axe snapped in half; the magic within it exploded outwards in a maelstrom of dark blue energy, buffeting Torga from all sides as it washed over him. Once the maelstrom had subsided, it revealed Torga standing in place with both halves of the axe held in a single hand. He tossed them aside like they were garbage.

"Do you think that intimidates me?" Ruknar laughed. He clearly wasn't taking the situation seriously. "So, you broke my axe. I'll just buy another."

Torga still refused to say anything. He turned around and brought Ruknar close to him. Ruknar did not struggle. He allowed himself to be brought within arm's reach, and still did not struggle.

"I am curious. I killed you—cut your bloody head off—so how are you still standing here?"

"Fuck you, that's how."

"Fair enough."

Torga twisted his body and threw Ruknar as hard as he could. Ruknar's body slammed into the ground and carved a hundred-foot trench into the snow.

He shook off the blow, then climbed out of the hole and turned to face Torga.

"Was that—" His neck popped as he rolled it around, then his eyes glowed with unrestrained power "—supposed to hurt?"

"No." Torga's eyes shined brightly in response to his anger rising. He moved closer to the god and held his hand out. Power swirled inside his body as the black hole picked up speed. Faster and faster it spun, each revolution multiplying Torga's weight—and as his weight grew with each passing second, so too did his strength rise to match it.

This fight wouldn't go like the last one.

"I don't know what you're planning, but it's not gonna work." Ruknar vanished in a burst of speed and reappeared a foot away from Torga. A shot to Torga's stomach nearly doubled him over, and a right cross to Torga's temple sent him reeling backwards.

Ruknar grabbed Torga's arm and hammer-threw him with such strength that Torga briefly broke the sound barrier.

He destroyed over three dozen trees as he flew through the air, only stopping once he'd struck an ice pillar and was buried deep inside it

Ruknar reappeared above the ice pillar and slammed his boot down. It fractured down the center, falling off into two equal pieces that shook the ground upon impact.

However, Torga was nowhere to be found.

"You know you can't hide from me." Ruknar proclaimed. "I'll find you."

Torga appeared at the end of one half of the ice pillar. He dug the claws of his right arms into the ice and lifted it above his head. Without a word, Torga drew back and threw the oversized block of ice like it was a javelin.

Ruknar jumped over it, kicked the tip towards the ground, then used the momentum from that kick to run over the top of the pillar. He reached the end and jumped off, aiming a double overhanded smash at Torga's head.

Torga dashed forwards and grabbed Ruknar's boot, then yanked him off balance. Before Ruknar's face could hit the ground, Torga coiled his tail beneath him and used it to spring into the air.

Torga rotated his body around and around, each rotation driving Ruknar faster. At the apex of Torga's jump, he let out a roar of effort and threw Ruknar towards the ground as hard as he could.

Ruknar hit with enough force to create a tidal wave of snow as it exploded outwards. The blackened ground beneath the snow swayed up and down as whatever was beneath it became destabilized.

But Torga wasn't done yet. Eight black objects burst free from his back, revealing themselves to be eight serpents with mouths so wide they almost wrapped around their own heads.

The serpents opened their mouths, each presenting Ruknar with over a dozen rows of dagger-like teeth.

The eight heads shot forward, each head sinking its teeth into the ground and using its body to pull Torga towards Ruknar's body.

Torga "fell" three times faster than he otherwise would have and threw all four fists into simultaneous punches that slammed into Ruknar's body with enough force to crack a planet. Then, for good measure, Torga put all of his weight into a haymaker that crashed into Ruknar's face, causing it to twist to the side. Torga swung twice more and sent Ruknar's head swinging with each blow.

"I must say, I'm disappointed," Ruknar began, each word coming out between a punch that spun his head to one side or the other. "I can't believe I thought you were stronger than this—"

Torga's hand covered Ruknar's face, and the next thing Ruknar knew he was tumbling through the air.

Momentarily losing his wits, Ruknar was unable to react when a *massive* blow slammed into the god's jaw and sent him flying. In less than a second, he'd traveled over two miles into the air, completely leaving Helheim and entering the borderland in between it and Tartarus.

"How's that for strength, you arrogant shit!"

Ruknar smiled as he plummeted towards Helheim. "Now that's what I'm talking about! I knew you had it in ya!" he laughed.

He vanished in a burst of speed and was on Torga in the blink of an eye. Torga managed to dodge the first swing and block the second, but the third strike—a kick to his right side—surprised him enough to throw him off balance. Torga barely managed to get his guard up before Ruknar returned the favor and slammed his fist into Torga's arms, sending him skidding for several feet across the ground.

"C'mon, worm! Don't disappoint me now!" Ruknar appeared behind Torga and wrapped his arms around him. He lifted Torga off the ground, then quickly bent at the waist, suplexing Torga onto the ground.

Torga felt several organs and bones inside his body rupture simultaneously. He was paralyzed for a moment before his regeneration kicked in and his spine healed enough for him to move.

Torga felt himself being lifted off the ground again; however, this time he twisted out of Ruknar's hold and wrapped his body around the god's legs. Torga coiled around him like the constrictor he used to be and started squeezing with all his might.

Ruknar managed to wiggle one arm free from Torga's grasp. He swung that arm with the intention of taking Torga's head clean off.

Torga ducked the punch, grabbed his arm, and locked it down. He put Ruknar into an arm bar; however, he was not using the bar as a deterrent. Torga slammed his elbow into the back of Ruknar's arm, enjoying the satisfaction he felt when Ruknar's elbow let out a sickening crack and snapped backwards.

Torga didn't have the words to describe it.

Ruknar wailed after his arm snapped. He whipped his broken arm forward, dragging Torga along with it, then came back with his other arm and punched Torga in the stomach.

As Torga was forced backwards, the eight serpents shot forward and latched onto Ruknar's body. Two grabbed each limb and one bit down on his pelvis.

Ruknar wailed once again.

Torga grunted, and the eight serpents yanked Ruknar off his feet and pulled him after Torga.

Torga pivoted, grabbed Ruknar by the head, and then thrust him into the ground. The two of them slid through the snow for several feet before coming to a stop. Ruknar tried to throw Torga off, but the eight serpents had a hold on Ruknar's body, and they had no intention of letting go.

"Where is Reina?" Torga hissed through clenched teeth.

"Wouldn't you like to know?" Ruknar spat a globule of golden blood into Torga's eye.

Torga flinched at the sudden blindness in that eye. Ruknar used that moment to pry his right arm free from the two serpents holding it and wrapped his meaty fist around Torga's throat.

He pulled Torga's head down and headbutted him. Then he shoved off the ground with his right foot and rolled Torga over, so he was pinned to the ground and Ruknar was sitting on his chest.

Ruknar shoved Torga's face into the snow and began digging his fingers into Torga's scales.

The eight serpents tried to come to Torga's rescue. However, they could no longer overpower Ruknar as he had seemed to be growing in strength as the fight dragged on.

Ruknar began punching Torga in the stomach. Every blow buried Torga a little deeper into the blackened soil beneath and slowly wore through his guard. Until Torga's tail joined the eight serpents and wrapped around Ruknar's midsection. With Torga's tail to assist them, the eight serpents were able to pull Ruknar off of Torga and shove him onto the ground.

Torga came up swinging. He threw a punch while falling on top of Ruknar and knocked out one of Ruknar's teeth.

Torga punched Ruknar in the stomach as hard as he could from this position. Even though he didn't get the full range of motion, Ruknar felt his ribs break.

"Ooo... Well, tickle a wolf's testicles and call him Betsy. That's gonna hurt in the morning," Ruknar groaned. He used his uninjured arm to push Torga back enough to get his leg in between them, then he *shoved*.

Torga was tossed bodily into the air, only to come crashing down six feet away. He groaned as pain ballooned within his body. Everything hurt, and he did mean *everything*.

Torga rolled over and tried to stand. But before he could, a massive foot slammed into his ribs and Torga was knocked onto his back again.

Ruknar stomped on Torga's chest and pressed down until he could hear Torga's spine popping under the pressure.

"That sounded painful; did that hurt?" Ruknar asked, a cruel smile spreading across his face.

"Not as much as this will..." Torga mumbled.

"Hah? What is that supposed to mean—"

A second Torga, this one in his human form, tackled Ruknar with everything he had and carried the two of them high into the sky. At the apex of his jump, the second Torga started raining down blows on Ruknar: three to the face, six to the body, two to the groin. Then he grabbed the god's arms and began rotating at high speeds. After six full rotations, Torga flung Ruknar back towards the ground; to his eyes, Ruknar flashed red for an instant before he slammed into the ground and caused a tidal wave of snow and debris to explode out in every direction.

For good measure, Torga landed on the god's face when he descended, forcing Ruknar's head to sink even deeper into the dark soil.

Torga stayed in his position until he heard groaning, then he hopped off and landed on the edge of the forty-foot hole they'd created.

He sat down on the ledge and stared down at the god. "Where'd you take Reina?"

Ruknar let out a low moan, then sat up. He pressed one side of his nose in and blew out a globule of blood, then cracked his neck and back. "You might as well kill me. I'll never tell you anything."

Torga shrugged. "Okay, I tried."

Ruknar turned his head as he heard movement behind him. The first Torga— second Torga? Either way, there were now two Torga's, one on either side of him.

Ruknar sighed. "That's just not fair. What, you can clone yourself now?"

Torga shrugged again. "I'm a Hydra," he said, as if that explained everything. Which, in a way, it did.

"And I cut off your head, right. So, it's my fault there are two of you. I guess you're going to kill me now?"

"The thought has crossed my mind, yes."

"All right—get it over with. I'm tired of this fight."

"How about you just tell me where Reina is and we'll call it even?"

"You just don't quit, do ya?" Ruknar laughed.

"No."

"Yeah, well, even if I did tell you where she was, you couldn't do anything about it."

"Want to place a bet on that?"

"Sure." The god grinned ferally and leaped out of the hole. He landed with a heavy *thud* beside Torga and walked past him.

"Reina should be with the judges at the heart of Yggdrasil. And no one gets in there without the judges knowing about it. Besides, if you could get to her, with your rap sheet, you'd never make it out alive."

"Not even if I told them about Orochi's plan to frame me?"

"You were listening," Ruknar laughed. "Go ahead and tell them; they're not gonna believe you."

"Maybe not. But I've got to try."

Ruknar shrugged his shoulders. "You're gonna die," he said after a moment.

"Isn't that what you want—isn't that what you've been trying to do?"

"Well, yeah. But it's not personal, never was. If it were up to me, I'd buy you a tall glass of mead and the two of us would duke it out to see who got to be the older brother."

"You decapitated me ten minutes ago."

"And then we fought, and you earned my respect. It's not easy to find someone who can go blow for blow with me, but you did, and I respect that."

"Bullshit. Look at you. You could go another ten rounds if you wanted to."

"So could you," he pointed out.

"Yes, because I regenerate. You never even got to that point."

Ruknar shrugged. "At the end of the day, it doesn't matter. Just kill me and leave."

"I'd rather you help me. You said it yourself, I can't get to her without them knowing I'm there. If you help me, maybe—"

"No, I can't help you. The only help I can give you is to let you go. Whether you kill me or not, I will die here today. I don't have a choice about that."

"What do you mean? You always have a choice."

"Not always. A word to the wise, Torga. Not everyone working for Orochi does so of their own free will. Sometimes, they're just doing what they have to."

Torga was silent for a long moment. "It wasn't a whim, was it?"

"Hmm?"

"What Niabus said—he said you killed me on a whim, but I don't think that's true. You killed me for a reason."

Ruknar slowly turned to face Torga. He had a genuine smile on his face, one that reached his eyes. "It was nice meeting you, Torga. I only wish we could've met under different circumstances."

Ruknar reached up, grabbed his own jaw and the back of his head, and then broke his own neck.

His body collapsed to the ground, but Torga couldn't move.

He found himself staring at Ruknar's unmoving body; Ruknar's eyes were open and he was looking towards the sky.

Torga continued to stare for a long time, so long that at some point he regained the ability to move and collapsed to the ground, yet he hadn't realized it.

When he could finally walk, Torga, and his clone, stood over the body of the target that had fueled so much of his anger with only one thing on their minds.

They needed to bury him.

~ ∻ ~

Torga brushed the snow off of his hands and the two of them headed towards the building. The grave wasn't pretty, and anyone who found it would most likely not know who was buried there. But Torga would know.

Suddenly, they stopped walking and looked at each other. They were both thinking the same thing: There had to be a way to rejoin, right? They weren't just stuck like this.

They thought it over for several minutes, then decided to just go for it. They tried running into each other, they tried hugging, the clone slapped the original across the face… It wasn't an attempt to rejoin with the main body; he did it because he wanted to.

Finally, the two Torgas decided to use Shapeshift, and merge their bodies together that way.

~ ∻ ~

Surprisingly, that worked.

With that done, I stepped up to the building and repeated the actions I'd seen Niabus do earlier. I grabbed the golden handle and pulled.

∞∞∞∞∞∞∞∞

Thank you for using the underworld instant transmission system. For your safety, please keep all arms, legs, and extra appendages by your side at all times. The underworld instant transmission system is not responsible for the loss of life or limb during the process of your journey.

Warning: you do not have permission to be using the underworld transmission system.

An alert has been sent to an underworld maintenance specialist and you will now be expelled from the underworld.

Transmission has begun.

∞∞∞∞∞∞∞∞

God damn it. Why hadn't Niabus told me about the alert—oh, right. Niabus was a backstabbing traitor.

It all made sense now.

The door appeared in the wall and I pulled it open. Inside was a black tube that seemed to suck in light.

I stepped inside.

Instantly, my body felt like someone was sucking me up through a straw. I didn't even have time to close the door before my feet were yanked off the ground and I was sent hurtling towards oblivion.

CHAPTER TWENTY-THREE

REINA WALKED ALONGSIDE THE FLOATING Nyarlathotep as he guided her down a darkened hallway towards what he called the "cafeteria."

"Do they normally call for breaks like this?" Reina asked. She thought it was a bit sudden; during a rather long series of questions about Torga's past military service, the orange being had suddenly declared that they needed to take a recess. They didn't explain why, but Reina had a feeling that Nyarlathotep would know.

"Oh no, they never take a break. Something happened," Nyarlathotep told her. The insane grin on his face told her that he had an idea what that something was.

"Any idea what?"

"Nope, but it's safe to say that if Pthelios thought it was serious enough to suspend their questioning, something serious has happened. Possibly involving Torga or Orochi."

"Can we do something—*should* we do something?" Reina asked. Her first instinct upon finding out that it was possibly related to Torga, was to turn around and run back into the courtroom and demand that they tell her what they knew. However, she wasn't stupid enough to believe that plan would work.

"There isn't much *we* can do… Though there is quite a bit that *I* can do." Nyarlathotep stopped walking and looked back the way they'd come. "If you keep following this hallway, you'll eventually find the cafeteria." He held his wing out to show her several jangling coins." Take these and get yourself some food. I recommend the eyeballs of Ghalesta; they're particular spicy this millennium."

Reina took the proffered coins and inspected them. She thought they seemed normal enough. Each one was about the size of a thumbnail and they were all forged out of a transparent silver metal. Though they were little more than an outline of a coin, they had real heft to them and felt like they weighed about the same as a gold coin.

Nyarlathotep's words finally registered in her mind and she looked up— "Wait, whose eyes?" But he was gone, and she was left standing alone, in a pitch-black hallway.

"Great, I'll just stand here and talk to myself, shall I?" Reina sighed. Deciding that she may as well grab something to eat while she could, Reina continued walking down the hallway as Mob had shown her. She walked for about five minutes or so, before the hallway opened up into an expansive room of bright colors and chrome—lots and lots of chrome.

For some reason, the cafeteria in a building at the center of the known universe, owned and operated by beings who could bend the laws of reality to their whim, reminded Reina of the inside of a burger joint.

She'd never felt so out of place.

"Not bad, eh?"

"The hell!?" Reina yelled. She spun around and found Mob standing behind her with his ever-present book clutched within his wing.

"You scared the hell out of me. Warn a girl next time."

"Warn you about what?"

"Before you just pop up out of nowhere."

"Ah, I see. Will this suffice?" Mob reached behind his back and pulled out a little dinner bell, which he then proceeded to ring—it somehow sounded like a foghorn.

Reina blocked her ears with her palms and screamed for him to stop. Which he did, but only after he had already done significant damage to her hearing, or so Reina believed.

"So, what did you find out?" Reina asked after making sure that her ears weren't bleeding.

"The boring stuff can wait until after we grab food. I'm starving."

"You ate twenty-seven bags of popcorn less than fifteen minutes ago. How are you hungry?"

"Dunno, just am." He led her through the line of people to the register, where a 12-foot-tall gelatinous blob stood. It was wearing a colorful apron around its midsection, and a colorful hat that said "Shazai's burgers and other novelties." across the front in bold black letters.

The blob made a weird gurgling sound and Mob responded by saying, "Two rare double burgers with cheese, and four baskets of fried pickles."

"Oh, no thanks I don't want any—"

"What're you talking about? These are mine. If you want some food, you get your own."

Reina watched in horrified fascination as the blob reached into a cooler next to where it was standing and pulled out two meat patties. It shoved them into its mouth for a few seconds, and when it pulled them out, the burgers were steaming hot.

"You know what… I think I'm okay."

"You sure?" Mob asked. "The food here is delicious."

"Yeah, I'm really not hungry anymore."

"Suit yourself. Just go find us somewhere to sit. I'll be over there soon as my food is ready."

Reina took one last look at the blob who was in the process of shoving four dozen pickles into its mouth at the same time. She shook her head and walked away. She'd seen some weird things since reincarnating on Yggdrasill, but that… That was a bit too much.

~ ~ ~

Reina found a booth near the entrance and sat down to wait on Mob. While waiting, she found herself looking around at the sights and sounds of the cafeteria.

Of the many different races currently eating inside the establishment, Reina only recognized three: There were high elves, which she was also a member of. And there were pixies, the thumb sized members of the fey who thrived in forests and hidden grottoes across Yggdrasil. They looked like humans, but they were usually between three and five inches tall and had insect-like wings on their back.

Then there were Tivali. If you think of the word demon, and the first thing that pops into your mind are red-skinned people with pointed tails and horns, those are the Tivali. In Reina's experience, they were some of the friendliest people you could ever meet. Of course, there was another name for them: Incubus and Succubus… Yeah, they were sex demons—okay, they weren't really demons. They just happened to evolve to look that way. They did feed on the sexual energy of other races, though. Kind of like vampires, but with a different bodily fluid.

"Sorry I'm late," Mob said as he took the seat across from her. "They had to remake my pickles twice, can you believe that?"

Reina could believe it, but she was too busy staring at the propeller hat on Mob's head to answer him.

"Anyway, apparently there's something big going down and the trueborns are having a fit about it. And, since they're throwing a fit, all the ascended gods are going along with it. The entire thing is a mess."

"Sorry, but I don't understand what you mean by trueborns or ascended gods. Aren't gods, you know, gods?"

"Oh, right." Nyarlathotep somehow made his wing look as if he were holding one finger in the air. "Much like monsters, beasts, and classes, gods possess 'tiers' and 'ranks' in accordance with their power levels. This is fairly common knowledge and anyone who devotes themselves to serving gods is aware of this fact. However, what most mortals don't believe, or refuse to believe, is that a class system is also prevalent amongst the gods."

"Class system? Are we talking about 'job' classes or hierarchy classes?"

"A bit of both, actually. Gods can be divided into three main classes and each class has ten 'tiers' just like a beast or monster would." He showed her a frightening grin and held up a second "finger."

"The 'ascended' gods are the lowest class of god. They are the class of the reincarnated and reborn heroes that, through their own deeds and blessings from a patron, have ascended to godhood. Of course, they are usually the weakest of the lot and are little more than peasants/civilians in the eyes of the other two classes. Torga happens to be an ascended god, a minor one with no followers, but he is still a god.

"The second class is that of the 'trueborn' gods. They are the class of gods that were born with their powers and domains. They are the 'Kings' and 'Queens' of the gods and rule the ascended gods just as their mortal counterparts rule their subjects. Also, they are usually the direct descendants of the first class of god."

Nyarlathotep made an uncomfortable face and cleared his throat before speaking. "The originals are called such because they've been around since the beginning. There may only be five of them, but they are the gods *of* gods. Each one is the very incarnation of their domain and all other gods 'borrow' their power from the originals. Take Amaar, the original God of Death, for example. If he wanted to, he could wipe out all life in the universe with just a snap of his fingers and, well, there's not a damned thing any of us could do to stop him."

"Okay, so if Amaar is death, then who are the other four?"

"There's the twins Uoas and Sorus: Gods of Creation and Destruction, respectively; Dryna: Goddess of Time; and Axaas: the Life Bringer. These four, plus Amaar, are the original gods and they alone are responsible for the protection and maintenance of Yggdrasil."

"Um... Protection from *what* exactly?"

"What do you mean?"

"You said they were responsible for the 'protection and maintenance' of Yggdrasil so, what are they protecting it *from*? It's not like there's anything powerful enough to destroy or seriously harm a supposedly multiversal being, so why is 'protection' even a part of their title?"

"Oh, my sweet girl... But there *is* something powerful enough to destroy her. The Father, or as some have taken to calling it, the source, is a multiversal being that lives near the base of Yggdrasil. And not only *could* it destroy Yggdrasil anytime it wanted to, but it could also recreate it in a single breath. And here's the best part. Rumor has it, the Father is a—"

"Enough."

"Tsk..."

Reina jumped at the sudden appearance of the blue judge. He was standing beside their table with his arms behind his back. She guessed that he would've been frowning at Nyarlathotep.

Fortunately, he took a deep breath and let out a sigh. "Nyarlathotep, would you mind escorting Reina out of the building? I believe we have asked all the questions we need, and we have no further use of her services. Besides, there are some people waiting to see her."

"Yeah, whatever. C'mon," Nyarlathotep grumbled. He grabbed his basket of food and got up.

Reina hesitated for a brief moment considering what to do, but she eventually got up and followed Nyarlathotep's back as he led her into the darkened hallway. After several minutes of walking with only the faint glow from Nyarlathotep's body to guide her, Reina spotted a large wooden door with opulent golden depictions of a tree in its center. Nyarlathotep used his talons to grab the heavy golden ring the door used as a handle and easily pulled the door open. A sudden explosion of white light blinded Reina for a moment, but once her eyes adjusted, she noticed they were now standing in a well-lit courtyard with massive oak trees surrounding them.

"Welcome to the silver city." Nyarlathotep announced. "This is the home of the gods— most of them anyway."

Reina stepped past him and found herself once again mesmerized by her surroundings. The courtyard was beautiful. She'd even go so far as to call it perfect. She sucked in a breath of fresh air, then let it out. The air here was crisp, and clean. Exactly how paradise should be.

Off to the side of the courtyard, Reina saw Donna and an unfamiliar dark-haired man with huge snow-white wings standing beneath an open, dark wooden gazebo. Before she could open her mouth to announce her presence, the dark-haired man reached out and cupped Donna's jaw with his left hand and said, **"I missed you, Donna."**

Donna? Reina motioned for Nyarlathotep to get down and the two of them hid behind a group of trees. They watched as Donna slapped the man's hand away from her face and glared defiantly into his eyes.

"Don't touch me," she hissed. "You have no right to touch me after what you did."

"What I did? I'm the reason you and your friend are still alive, and this is the thanks I get?"

"Oh, thank you ever so much for saving us," Donna sarcastically replied. "But need I remind you that I wouldn't have needed your help if you hadn't turned me in to the elders. It's *your* fault I'm like this. Never forget that." She pushed past him and began walking toward the large white-stone building connected to the courtyard. The man grabbed Donna's hand and forcefully turned her to look at him.

"Damnit, Donna! It's not like I knew they would banish you!"

"I'm curious what you thought would happen after you told them that I fell into a supposed *sin.* Did you think they'd give me a medal? A slap on the wrist with a stern 'don't do it again?'"

The dark-haired man looked decidedly uncomfortable with this line of questioning, as he just stared at Donna's face with a grim frown.

"Yeah." She jerked free from his grasp. "That's what I thought."

"A fair warning, Donna. I have to report to the higher-ups that you're back."

"I'm not 'back.' As soon as my friend is released, I'm heading to the mortal world."

"Even so, I—"

"I know, I know. You have to wag your tail for the boss, right? As I said, I won't be here long."

Donna left the man standing there as she turned on her heel and walked away.

A few seconds after she left, the dark-haired man disappeared in a flash of silver light. Reina sighed in relief.

"Your friend is rather interesting."

"Hmm?"

Nyarlathotep looked up from the page he'd been silently reading from his book and nodded in the direction of the gazebo.

"Angels don't often associate with those outside of their race." His voice went down an octave. "Mostly because they're a group of self-entitled brats with a daddy complex." His voice returned to normal and he smiled at her. "But that's really just my opinion. No need to go spreading it around and causing a stir..."

"That guy was an angel? Like the kind from the bible?"

"I don't know." He shrugged. "Was that some form of holy text where you're from?"

"Yeah, it was. It started to decline in popularity by the time I was born, but it was still a fairly common religious item."

"Eh, it's certainly possible. Angels are a fairly new race in the grand scheme of things, so I don't know all the details. The oldest amongst them is only a few millennia old, barely more than a child by our standards."

"Erm—That reminds me. What were you saying earlier? About the Father of creation and Yggdrasil?"

"Sorry, but orders are orders. I'm all for annoying them at every available opportunity, but even I know not to cross *that* particular line. Besides, you remember the orange guy?"

"The sleeper?"

"Yeah," he chuckled. "Well, he's watching us, so even if I wanted to, I couldn't tell you."

Reina glanced around the courtyard for any sign of someone spying on them but failed to notice anything right away.

"You won't find anything. Pthelios is the judge of fate, so he's basically forced to perceive all of reality: Past, Present, and Future simultaneously. Okay, so maybe he's not watching *us* per se and more like he's watching *everything*."

"Is that why he was so sleepy?"

"Ha! If only. He's just a lazy bastard that likes to sleep more than anything else."

Nyarlathotep's book suddenly started to vibrate, startling both of them. "Oh crap, I gotta go! Hey, just head inside that building and ask the lady sitting behind the counter to take you to see your friends. See ya!"

"Hey, wait!"

Nyarlathotep vanished in a flash of red light, causing Reina to grumble in annoyance. The least he could've done was tell her why they were here to begin with and how the hell they were supposed to leave.

~ ~ ~

Reina entered the building and found herself in a place she'd never thought she'd see again. The walls were painted purple, with simple designs and images of winged humans healing people along the base of the wall. The floors reminded her of an asymmetrical checkers board, though the colors were purple and white instead of red and black.

The scent of antiseptic cleaner filled Reina's nostrils and she smiled in spite of herself.

She never thought she'd set foot in a hospital again.

To her left and right, rows upon rows of chairs were laid out, awaiting patients to fill them. And against the far wall, behind a wide desk, sat a young blonde woman. The woman appeared to be working her way through a stack of papers that was easily two and a half feet tall.

She looked up as Reina approached and put on her best customer service smile.

"Hello." The woman's voice had a two-tone effect, almost as if multiple women were speaking at the same time, and their voices perfectly overlapped with one another. **"May I help you?"**

"I was told my friends were here? Their names are—"

"Ah, you're with the mortals. They are in room 706. Take the left hallway out of the lobby and follow it until you reach the stairs, then take them to the seventh floor. Their room will be the fourth door on the right after you leave the stairs." After saying all of this without giving Reina a chance to interrupt, the woman went back to working through her stack of papers.

Reina knew she wouldn't get anywhere by trying to speak with the woman anymore. Judging by that stack of papers, she would likely be at it for hours, so Reina couldn't blame her for her curtness.

Reina followed the receptionist's instructions, finding her way to the stairwell within a few minutes, then to the seventh floor and to room 706.

Reina lifted her hand to knock but froze. Would they be happy to see her? Would they be angry with her for dragging them into this mess?

Could she blame either of those reactions? The answer was no, she couldn't.

She summoned her courage and knocked on the door.

"Coming." Reina recognized Donna's voice immediately and let out a breath she hadn't realized she'd been holding.

The door opened to reveal a haggard looking Donna. Their eyes met over the threshold, neither saying anything as they took in the state of the other.

"You look awful. Leon's been keeping you awake that much, huh?" Reina joked.

Donna let out a quiet sob, then nodded her head. "Yeah, something like that."

~ ∴ ~

Reina and Donna sat across from each other in a surprisingly normal looking hospital room in complete silence. They'd talked a short while after Reina had first entered the room, Donna telling her everything that'd happened since she'd disappeared, and Reina explaining what she'd seen and heard from the judges. But it quickly turned awkward after that as both women struggled to ask what was on their minds.

It didn't help that their other friend was currently unconscious in the hospital bed in front of them.

Donna said every mortal handled being exposed to an angel's power differently. Some woke up immediately, but the vast majority usually took a few days to recover from the shock of the angel's power affecting them.

Leon had been in a coma for over a week.

His body had been cleaned after he was admitted, and any superficial wounds were healed. But for the most part, they'd shoved him into a room and left Donna to deal with the multiple lacerations across his torso, two cracked ribs, and minor head wound he'd gained in the battle for Taranis.

"You saw, didn't you?" Donna asked without raising her eyes from the floor.

"Hmm?"

"In the courtyard... You saw us, didn't you?"

"Yeah. I saw," Reina admitted.

Donna laughed self-depreciatingly and shook her head. "Were you ever going to say anything?"

"I hadn't planned to."

"Why not? Aren't you curious?"

"Of course."

"Then why haven't you asked yet?"

"Because you're my friend, Donna. If you wanted to talk about it, you would have told me a long time ago."

"Yeah," she scoffed. "Some friend I am."

"Why do you say that?"

Donna was silent for several seconds as she internally warred with herself. Eventually, however, she spoke. "It's my fault."

"What is?"

"This." She waved at the room around them. "Everything we've been through. It was all my fault."

"Donna, none of this is your fault. We were dragged into the mess because of one person, and one person alone: Orochi. So, don't you dare blame yourself."

"You don't understand," Donna muttered while shaking her head. "That can also be blamed on me."

"No, it can't—"

"Damnit, Reina. I'm telling you it's my fault!"

"How, Donna!? How is any of this *your* fault?"

"Because I chose you."

"You what?" Reina stammered.

"I chose you, Reina. I chose you and—and I failed to follow through. I lost sight of my duties to you and now, because of one mistake, you're stuck here instead of back on Earth with your family."

"Donna, you're not making any sense."

"You being here; from the moment of your rebirth until now, all of it can be traced back to one mistake that I made. Now, instead of living out your life on Earth with

Albert and your kids, you're stuck here, in this godforsaken shit show."

"Donna… I—I don't. What?"

"I used to be an angel," Donna admitted. She had her eyes cemented to the floor and refused to meet Reina's eyes. "Well, more specifically, I was *your* angel, back on Earth."

Reina immediately wanted to interrupt her—to ask her what the hell she was talking about, but Donna pressed on without giving her the chance.

"I was one of the seventy-seven angels in service to Uenar. My duty was to nudge people in the direction of their soulmates and to ensure they found the love they so desperately craved. But when I saw you, when I saw your soul I—I forgot all about that. You see, you humans weren't the only ones made in the image of our Father. Though most of us were little more than duty-bound machines, some of the older angels developed free will… Some of us could fall in love."

"Wait—Are you saying you love me? Like, actually, love me?"

"... I used to," she sighed. "I originally chose to be your guardian angel on a whim, which wasn't an uncommon thing for me. I'd grown bored of my duties and just wanted to have some fun; you know?"

"Being a guardian angel is fun?" Reina asked incredulously.

"Not even remotely," Donna chuckled. "But compared to what I'd been doing, it was a much-needed break. But... As you grew older, I slowly became more protective of you. I'd chase away a bad influence here, turn away a potential boyfriend there... Then Albert showed up and made my life a living hell."

Reina, despite the sudden seriousness of the situation, snorted at that.

"Yeah, it's funny now, but you should have seen me back then. I tried everything short of outright killing him to scare him off, nothing worked. Every woman I sent after him was turned down, every *man* I sent after him was either punched in the face *or* turned down. Hell, at one point I went down *myself* and tried to seduce him at the risk of falling." Donna made an uncomfortable face at the dark look she'd seen in Reina's eyes at *this* little tidbit, but she pressed on. "The bastard actually had the gall to take one look at me and say, 'No thanks, I don't think I could afford you even if I wanted to.' Can you believe that!?"

"Uh..." Reina laughed. "Surprisingly enough, I do."

"Your husband's always been a dick."

"I'm aware."

"... He's a good man, though."

"I'm also aware of that."

The two sat in comfortable silence for several minutes as Donna tried to collect herself, and Reina was merely happy her friend was talking again.

Was she surprised at this revelation? Of course, but there was nothing she could do about it now. No, all she could do was wait and let her friend share as much as she wanted to share.

Then, and only then, would Reina ask the twelve dozen questions she had swimming around inside her head.

"After Albert showed up and turned my world upside down. I split my time between protecting you and resuming my duties as an angel of love to get away from the sight of the two of you together. I attended your wedding, by the way. You were so *damn* beautiful in that white sequin dress with the see-through back."

Reina turned red in embarrassment in remembrance of just what her husband thought about *that* particular dress. Not seeing the bride before the wedding be damned, he wouldn't leave her alone until he saw her in it... And then they had to buy a second one because he ruined the first.

"After you died, and I couldn't find your soul, I—I lost myself. It got so bad that I began slacking off in my angel duties and the higher-ups noticed. They ordered me to drop the search, to forget about "one measly human soul" and focus on my duties.

"I didn't.

"Eventually, I came across a human god from one of the other pantheons at a bar here in the silver city. He'd let the honeyed wine go to his head and started bragging about a human being chosen as the next hero. I offered him everything from gold and jewels to priceless artifacts for the name of the human, but he only wanted one thing from me."

"So, you slept with him," Reina said matter-of-factly. She wasn't accusing, mocking, or making light of what Donna was telling her. It was just the conclusion she'd come to.

"Yep."

"That's when you fell?"

"No," Donna snorted. "You can only truly 'fall' if you give in to one of the cardinal sins and allow it to consume you. I never truly fell; I was cast out."

"What? Why?"

"Apparently, the god had a big mouth and bragged about nailing one of Uenar's angels. Well, as it turns out, one of the archangels had it in his head that my virginity was his, so when my *friend* decided to rat me out to the elders in the hopes of earning a promotion, the jealous bastard used his power to have me cast out of heaven. I've been having sex with as many people as I possibly can out of pure spite ever since."

"Wait, so—you're doing it out of spite and not because you enjoy it?"

"Oh no, I definitely enjoy it. But if I get to piss off the great big, perverted eye in the sky while having a good time, then I'm all for it."

"I guess some things really don't change."

Donna and Reina jumped up from their chairs and turned to the door in time to see a tall and incredibly well-built angel step into the room. He had bronze colored skin, long silver hair that swayed around his waist, golden eyes, and four massive fiery wings curled up behind him. A few seconds after he stepped into the room, the angel Reina saw with Donna earlier in the courtyard walked in behind him and shut the door.

"Speaking of perverted old men. How's it going Zuriel?"

"Do not say my name so casually, Donna."

"That's the beauty of being a fallen, Zuriel. I don't have to give a shit who you are."

"I take it this is the angel in question?" Reina asked.

"Yep. This is ol' little dick himself."

The temperature in the room climbed several dozen degrees instantly as Zuriel glowered at Donna. **"I'll not be made fun of,"** he said in an icy tone that made chills run down Reina's back.

"Bite me. Actually, scratch that. You might enjoy it a little *too* much."

A spear made of orange flames appeared in the angel's hand in less than a second and scorched the air around them, making it incredibly difficult to breathe.

"My lord, I don't believe it wise to do that here," the dark-haired angel interrupted.

"Did I ask for your opinion?"

"No sir, but—"

"Then unless I do, keep your opinions to yourself."

Zuriel walked around to Donna's side, ignoring the fact that she and Reina were struggling to breathe, and lifted a lock of her hair up to his nose and breathed in. **"Such a pity. And I'd hoped to make you my wife one day."**

"Not... a chance... in hell," Donna growled. She slapped his hand away and glared up at the much larger man.

"I would have taken care of you."

Donna spat in his face, earning her a hard slap to the face that sent her crashing into the wall beside the bed. The angel turned to face Reina and lifted her chin until he could see her eyes.

She stared back defiantly.

"Yes, you'll do nicely. Take her."

Reina smacked Zuriel's hand away, then spun and jumped, performing a spinning heel kick in the air. Her foot smacked into Zuriel's chest, but the only thing she accomplished with the maneuver was pushing herself backwards.

"I *really* don't like you."

"That kick might do something to a mortal, but you couldn't harm me, even if you attacked me for the next hundred years."

"Wanna bet?"

Unbeknownst to Zuriel, Donna had climbed to her feet, wiping the blood from her chin as she did, and crept forward. A spike of ice formed around Donna's hand and she swung it with as much force as she could muster. Without looking, Zuriel shifted his body to the side and stopped the ice with two fingers, then easily caught the kick Reina threw into his back with the other hand.

"What a pathetic display." He let go of Reina's leg, only to slap her across the face hard enough to send her head crashing into the nearby wall. Then one of his wings smacked Donna into the wall behind her. He raised his spear high into the air and just as he was about to bring it down on Reina's head, Donna screamed, "Wait!!"

The spear tip stopped a millimeter from Reina's face and Zuriel turned to look at Donna. **"What?"**

"Don't. You can't kill her."

"Why not?" he asked without moving his spear an inch.

"She's under the judges' protection. You kill her, you're liable to face punishment too."

"So?" he laughed. **"Do you really think they'll punish *me* because I killed some pathetic *mortal*? Of course, they won't."** He pressed his spear down, causing the tip to pierce her body suit and the blade to slowly sink into her chest. The pain awoke Reina, who quickly grabbed the spear with both hands and desperately tried to push it away from her.

The spear didn't move.

"Oh, that's it, is it? To think an archangel would get off on bullying mortals. At least give us a fighting chance you piece of shit!!" Donna screamed, a twinge of madness entering her voice.

"Hmm… alright, I'm a merciful angel. You want a fighting chance? You've got one," Zuriel said, a frightening smile appearing on his face. **"Just don't regret it later."**

The room was emptied in a flash of red-light seconds before a massive quake hit and shook the silver city to its very foundations.

CHAPTER TWENTY-FOUR

Y TRIP THROUGH OBLIVION DIDN'T LAST LONG. I'd been inside the dark tunnel for only a few minutes before I saw a portal of light opening in front of me.

Here's the issue with a portal suddenly appearing in front of you while you're traveling, at who knows how many times faster than light: There were no breaks. So instead of stopping and stepping out of the portal like a normal person, I left the portal like I'd been fired out of an anti-material rifle.

I only slowed down because I bounced off the ground a few times, then crashed through the wall of the building, landing in a heap of rubble inside a pitch-black room.

"Well, you were right, Pthelios. Our next appointment did show up on time." The voice sounded entirely too bored for what had just happened, presumably in front of them. Which meant one of two things: they were a god, or they'd broken into Uriel's stash of "medicinal" herbs.

Either way, I pulled myself out of the rubble and stretched out my body.

Ding

∞∞∞∞∞∞∞∞

Connection with the Yggdrasil server acquired.

All stats, skills, and traits have been returned to optimal conditions.

Name: Torga

Race: Quasar Serpent/Gluttonous Dark God of Hunger and Gravity (Minor)

Classification: Tier 10(+1)

Level: 100(?)

Experience: N/A

Titles: Destroyer of Asgard, The Dark Serpent, The Unwavering One, Royal Serpent, Free, The Devourer of Worlds, God of Hunger, God of Gravity, The One Who is Hated by Dragons, Anti-Summoner

Stats:

Physical

Strength: ∞/85

Endurance: ∞/85

Dexterity: 1,051/51

Speed: 1,583/83

Mental

Intelligence: 74

Wisdom: 51

Charisma: 31

Resistances

Elements: 90%

Divinity: 90%

Mental: 60%

Immunities

Mind Control

Illusions

Disease

Skills: Major Stealth, Heat Detection, Absolute Gluttony, Absolute Growth, Greater Petrifying Gaze, Superior Acid Venom, Detect Concealment, Energy Breath, Fly, Magic Enhancement, Elemental Manipulation, Omnipotent Control over Hunger and Gravity, Shapeshift, Aethereal Form, Size Control

Traits: Dark Gluttonous Aura ∞, Growth +1,000, Forever Growing, Indomitable, Absolute Regeneration, Ageless, Oxygen Independent, Self-Sustaining, God of Hunger, God of Gravity

∞∞∞∞∞∞∞∞

I dismissed the pop up with a wave of my hand and hissed as my body returned to normal. The bonds that made up my flesh and blood broke apart and dissipated into green lights, the cycle continuing until every atom had been replaced by green light. The black hole where my stomach used to be, and the two stars that acted as my eyes were the only organs that remained.

My body elongated; losing the features of the Naga, in favor of a pure serpent form that was more than four times the length of the Naga and several times as wide.

I heard a hissing noise near the end of my tail. I looked over and saw that a single star was floating inside it, and I immediately knew what it was. I felt the connection with it that superseded any other bond.

My clone was awake.

I became aware that my aura had come rushing back along with my body and was currently trying to devour the room around me. I wrestled it back under control and shoved it down inside my body, forming something of an aura shield around the black hole to keep it contained.

"As fascinating as this is to watch, might we get a move on? We are on a schedule after all."

"Hmm?" I stopped inspecting my body and turned towards the voice. I'd forgotten it was there in my excitement about my body returning to normal.

I saw five multicolored beings standing on raised daises at the end of the room.

I heard a whooshing sound from my left that drew my attention away from them. By the time I turned my head, the wall had been completely repaired and not even a single crack remained.

I lifted an eyebrow at the five beings and tilted my head towards the wall. "Where can I get one of those?"

"It's patented, I'm afraid," the blue being replied.

"Damn. Do you have any idea how much you could sell that for? You'd make a killing if you sold that wall to a friend of mine. Her husband's always breaking down walls."

The beings whispered to each other for several moments, then Blue spoke up again. "You're referring to Lena, yes? The elf who married the warg."

"Yeah," I confirmed.

I sighed as my memory of a time before Helheim entered my mind, and I remembered something that I'd tried to forget. Unless they'd managed to find another healer after I left, Lena was most likely dead by now.

"Do you know who we are?" The blue being asked, pulling my attention from my memories.

"No, but I could guess. You're the asshole judges who made my last few weeks a living hell. That sound about right?"

"I suppose you could say," Blue agreed. "Though, I must caution you about your language regarding us. If you would like us to continue treating you with respect, we would request that you do the same."

"Respect?" I laughed. "I don't know if I'd call it respect. Mockery with a certain amount of caution mixed in is more likely."

"I told you that you were wasting your breath," the green being chuckled. "It's not in his nature to be respectful of things he fears. He would rather hide his fear behind mockery and sarcasm."

Fear? Was I afraid of them? I didn't think so, but hey, maybe it was right. "Hey Doc, is this therapy session complimentary or are you going to charge my insurance?"

"See?" the green being chuckled.

The blue being sighed. "So, it would seem."

"All kidding aside, I know why I'm here. Can we just get this over with so I can leave?"

"You do?"

"Yeah, you guys think I'm Orochi, and you're either trying to figure out what to do with me, or you're trying to figure out if I am indeed, Orochi. I'm not an idiot. I know if I tell you I'm not Orochi, you won't believe me. And I know that if I admit to being Orochi, then you can take that as evidence that I am Orochi and run with it. But just because I find it annoying to leave things unsaid,

I am not Orochi, nor have I ever been affiliated with him."

"Duly noted," the blue being sighed. "However, we must still go through with the trial."

"Can't we just pretend that we did the trial and you found me not guilty?"

"No."

"Worth a shot," I sighed. "Alright, let's get this over with so I can go find my wife."

"Your wife is here," the blue being said offhandedly. "Now, we need you first—"

"Wait a second, timeout— what do you mean she's 'here'?"

"What I said. She is here. In fact, her partners Donna and Leon are also here. They were brought in to be character witnesses for you."

I had nothing to say to that. Everyone I'd asked had told me that they—it didn't matter. What did matter, was that if she was here, and was she safe?

"And she's okay?"

"Yeah, she's fine. Back to the question—"

I was so relieved that if I'd still had legs, I imagined that they would've given out and I would've fallen to the floor.

I bowed my head to the blue being. "Thank you for telling me. You have no idea how worried I was."

The five were quiet for a minute, then Blue cleared his throat. "Yes, well, if I could get back to the questions?"

I nodded my head.

"When did you first meet Orochi?"

"I've never met Orochi. Not really, anyway. There was this plot to have me take his place, but it failed, and

I broke out."

"Explain." The gold being spoke up for the first time.

"Okay." I described the events as I knew them. I explained how my reincarnation was solely because Niabus made a deal with someone for Forna's freedom, and the payment was a scapegoat for Orochi.

I explained how they planned to seal me into Orochi's place, so the real Orochi could move with impunity. However, since I'd broken out before they were ready, they switched tactics and instead spread the rumor that I was Orochi.

While I was telling my story, the judges were quiet. Some would say they were too quiet, but most courtrooms were meant to be quiet, so I tried not to worry about it.

Once I was finished telling my side of the story, the judges whispered amongst themselves for a few minutes. I waited patiently in hopes that they would allow me to go see Reina soon.

"We thank you for telling us your side of the story. However, it is your word against a trusted source's word. As such, we must deliberate on this before we may come to a decision."

"What does that mean for me? Can I go see my wife—can I go see Reina?"

The blue being turned around and looked at his peers for moment, then he turned his attention back to me. "We will allow this on the condition that you do not attempt to leave the silver city. You are to remain within the borders of the silver city until we say you may leave. Failure to follow this edict will be taken as an admission of guilt. Understand?"

"Absolutely," I agreed immediately.

So, I wouldn't be able to leave the city for a while, who cares? Reina was in the silver city, and as long as I could determine if Ayla and the rest were safe, I had no reason to leave.

~ ~ ~

I walked the silver coated streets of the aptly named silver city with one mission in mind: Find Reina, tell her everything, and ensure she's able to leave. I wasn't going to force her to stay here, with me, if she didn't want to.

I also wasn't stupid enough to believe that her staying was safe. If Orochi really was as bad as people made him out to be, then I was sure he was going to have enemies here. After all, this was the home of the gods, and the seat of their power in Yggdrasill.

The gods here were old, and I was positive that over the years they'd accumulated more than a few grudges; Orochi would be no exception.

As I walked, I took in the sights, sounds, and smells of the silver city. Everything was as the name described and looked as if it were all plated with silver. Even the food stalls along the side of the road had silver aura surrounding them.

The buildings were a mixed bag, depending on where you looked. Some areas had collections of more modern buildings such as skyscrapers, duplexes, and multistory apartment buildings, while others had more traditional huts, and hovels like I'd grown used to seeing across Yggdrasil.

Most of that paled in comparison to the group of castles I could see in the distance. Each one had a weird symbol hovering in the air above it, but from my current distance I couldn't make out what the symbols were.

The people were also a mixed bag. If I had ever seen a race on Yggdrasill, I can almost bet that I would see it here as well. And I could tell just from looking at them that all of the "citizens" either served gods or were gods themselves, as each and every one exuded an aura of divinity that made my mouth salivate.

I imagined what it would be like to let my aura lose, just a little bit. Just enough to get a taste of the surroundings. But I knew that if I did, I would only be giving the judges more evidence to use against me.

And I wasn't about to sabotage my ability to see Reina because I was curious what the gods would taste like.

"Hey, did you hear Zuriel brought some humans into the Coliseum?"

My head shot up and I looked in the direction of the voice. Two young men were standing outside of what I could only assume was some kind of store. They weren't dressed in finery, no; their outfits were closer to that of a peasant or farmer.

"Really? Where did he get humans in the silver city?"

"No idea, but here's the best part. There's an elf with them, and—"

Before I could stop myself, I was standing over the two men. I was doing my damnedest not to glower at them, but I could tell from the way their bodies stiffened that I'd failed.

"Where can I find this Coliseum?" I asked them as politely as I could.

Chapter Twenty-Five

Reina, Donna, and the still unconscious Leon were dragged out of their holding cells and thrown into a dome-like Coliseum made entirely of dark gray stone. Bright yellow stones that seemed to mimic the LED lights of Earth illuminated the ring in which they were expected to fight.

Separating the "gladiators" from the crowd of tens of thousands of angels and gods, was a wall of obsidian, roughly a hundred feet tall, while the wall separating the inside of the Coliseum from the outside was six or seven hundred feet high. It was clearly meant to prevent the "volunteers" from escaping once the battle had begun.

Reina couldn't tell if they were underground or not due to the lack of natural light filtering in from the outside.

"Reina, you need to focus!" Donna yelled. "Leon needs your help and we're going to need his!"

"Right!" Reina shook her head and promptly ignored the sounds coming from the stands as thousands of beings flashed into the Coliseum.

"What's happening!?" Reina yelled over the cacophony as she scanned Leon's body. She quickly cast "regenerate" on him, then began pumping as much mana into the spell as she could while simultaneously scanning for more severe injuries.

Regenerate could take care of most wounds, but the concussion and the cracked ribs would not heal in time. She needed to be a bit more proactive in healing them.

"We've been brought to Zuriel's Coliseum, the place ol' little dick likes to *show off* for his supporters. If I had to take a guess, I'd say he plans on letting his followers watch our execution."

"Why'd he bring Leon? If he wanted to punish us, then surely he could have left him at the hospital!"

"He *is* punishing us, Reina! Zuriel is, was, and always will be a megalomaniacal narcissist—and we insulted him. We're lucky he didn't just kill us in the hospital and be done with it."

Reina bit into her bottom lip as she slowly pushed Leon's ribs back into place and threw approximately fifteen percent of her total supply of magic into healing it as quickly as possible. She needed him up and moving *before* whatever Zuriel had planned for them began.

"Ladies and Gentlemen, Boys and Girls... Welcome to the show," Reina heard Zuriel say over the sound of cheering angels.

Hurry— must hurry!

"Tonight, for your viewing pleasure. An old friend has decided to pay us a visit and look, she's generously brought some snacks for our champion!" The dirt floor of the arena shook with the excitement from the crowd and their cheers made Reina's ears ring.

There, that's the ribs! Reina quickly moved onto the concussion.

Now to remove the blood from his lungs so he could breathe properly...

The entire Coliseum shook violently as a sudden earthquake sent most of the angels, Reina, and Donna sprawling. Reina protectively covered Leon's body with her own and rode out the quake by sitting on his waist.

... For once, she was *really* glad Torga wasn't around to see this.

"Now, now, calm down everyone! No need to let a little quake ruin our entertainment for the evening, eh? I've dispatched soldiers to investigate what happened. In the meantime, what say we get this party started!?"

The roars of the crowd were truly deafening and were making Reina's head throb, but she needed to *focus*. One wrong move and she could accidentally flood Leon's brain with blood.

"Donna, I don't know what's about to happen, but I need you to cover me until I can stabilize him!"

Donna didn't respond.

"Donna!?"

Still no response.

"Answer me goddamnit!" She whipped her head around and saw what had rendered Donna speechless.

From the center of the arena, a massive twenty-foot-tall, hideously disfigured demon was being raised from an area below the floor on a previously unseen platform. The demon was built like an Olympic bodybuilder with massive pectoral muscles and wide tree trunk legs, fire-red skin, bloodshot eyes, and four massive arms.

"Is that a demon!?"

"What have you done, Zuriel..." Donna trailed off, unable to believe what she was seeing.

"DONNA!"

Donna turned and stared at Reina, her eyes were wide, her pupils were dilated, and her body was shivering.

Donna was *truly* terrified.

"I know you're scared, but I *need* your help. I can't do this without you."

"R-Right," Donna nervously replied.

The platform raising the demon locked into place with a loud *thunk* and the crowd went silent as it scanned the arena with those ominous bloodshot eyes.

"Demon."

The demon's head turned to stare somewhere above Reina's head.

"You want your freedom?"

The demon slowly nodded its head.

"Then butcher them, and I'll grant you freedom from this place."

The demon's eyes shifted downwards until they landed on the forms of Reina, Donna, and Leon. Its lips drew back, revealing a mouth full of horrifyingly sharp teeth and a long-forked tongue.

"Reina?"

"You don't have to fight it alone. Just stall it!"

"I don't think I can. That's not a normal demon, Reina. That's an Arch-Demon."

"I don't care if it's a god, Donna! I refuse to die here and I'm not letting you die either, so put on your big girl panties and *focus!*"

"I don't want to die."

"Neither do I."

The demon roared. Its heavy power reverberated off the walls and sent dirt flying everywhere.

"Shield, now!!"

Donna lifted her arms and a solid dome of magic appeared around them in a fraction of a second, just barely managing to block the elephant-sized fist that slammed into it. The shield rippled under the force of the blow, but Donna was able to repel that first one.

Then came the second. The shield cracked under the force, so Donna had to reinforce and repair it.

"You should *really* hurry up! I don't know how much longer I can keep this up!"

As if to emphasize that point, a massive impact cracked the shield once again and almost made Donna's knees go out.

"I'm going as fast as I can!"

Reina finished repairing the concussion and was in the process of pulling her mana out of his body when she noticed a strange substance within his blood. *It's a damn sedative.*

She dumped as much magic as she safely could into his system and began a rapid purge of everything she considered "harmful" to him. Leon's eyes shot open a few seconds later and he greedily sucked in as much air as he could.

He quickly climbed to his feet and spun in a circle to look at the barrier protecting them.

"What—Where—What's happening!?"

"Long story short. Bastard stalker of Donna's is trying to feed us to a demon—" A sudden impact cracked the barrier and caused Leon to reflexively jump away from it.

"Seriously!? How many exes do you have!?"

"Is that really the problem, here!?"

Another impact cracked the barrier.

"Probably not, but I need something to focus on or else I'm going to start panicking!"

"Fine, then focus on this. If we make it out of this alive, then you and I are locking ourselves in a room for a month."

"Really?"

"Can we focus on the fact that a demon is trying to—" A red fist smashed through the top of the barrier, revealing the hideous face of the demon glaring down at them.

"Never mind!" Reina hurriedly ran through a spell's incantation.

She threw her arms forward and created a barrier of solid light. The demon's arm bounced off the barrier, throwing it back several steps. She followed up that spell by pointing two fingers at the demon and casting *"light beam,"* a spell that does exactly as its name suggests.

Twin beams of light shot through the barrier and incinerated the demon's eyes.

The behemoth roared in pain, cupping its head between its hands and jumping up and down.

"Yes, really. Hell, I'll even let you stick it in my ass if you want. Just. Don't. die!"

Leon's eyes grew comically large and he stared at Donna.

"Right then," he said after a moment. "It's time to get serious."

"...Really? *That's* what you're getting serious about!?" Reina exclaimed.

Leon ignored both Reina's words and her dumbfounded expression and narrowed his eyes at the demon through the hole in the shield.

He took a step forward, then another, then another, and then he *moved.*

"Juggernaut's reign," Reina heard him whisper just before a glowing suit of transparent plate armor over seven inches thick formed around his fist and flowed over the entirety of his body.

He smashed through the shield and slammed his fist into the demon's ribs.

The demon doubled over in pain, briefly forgetting about its rapidly regenerating eyes, and roared down at Leon.

Leon jumped into the air— "You're in my *way!*" and slammed his armored fist into its mouth, sending its head spinning to one side. He landed then threw a sweeping kick at its left leg.

The kick didn't knock it down, but it did make the demon yelp from the pain of having its kneecap smashed in.

A massive transparent longsword, over seven feet long and a foot wide, appeared in Leon's raised hand.

He grunted as he slashed downwards, nearly bisected the demon from skull to crotch, though it managed to jump back in time to avoid it.

The sword slammed into the ground with a heavy *clang* and cratered the ground.

"Tsk." Leon shifted his weight and spun like a top, causing the blade to whip through the air faster than the human eye could see.

When the demon attempted to block the sword with its beefy hand, it lost three fingers and would have lost its entire hand had it not jerked away at the last second.

Leon ended the swing by bringing his sword high into the air and once again slamming it into the ground mere inches away from the demon's body.

Reina leaped over Leon and kicked the demon square in the nose, then she flipped backward and threw two icicles at its eyes before landing in a crouch and diving out of the way of a wild swing of its fist.

Leon took the blow head on and shrugged it off with nary a grunt or a whimper and returned it with one of his own. He grabbed the demon's arm and swung his sword with one hand up and *through* the arm, chopping it off just above the elbow.

He stepped to the side to allow a spike of ice to pierce the demon's chest, then used the pommel of his sword like a hammer to drive the spike deeper in while Reina continued to pester the demon with an array of spells.

The ice spike was driven deep into the demon's body, then Leon swung his longsword and took its head clean off. The demon's headless body collapsed to its knees, then collapsed forward onto its stomach.

Leon's armor and sword vanished a moment later and he dropped onto his butt, panting from exhaustion.

"Why—the fuck—didn't you use that before!?" Reina rounded on Leon.

"I wanted to surprise you?" Leon asked. Even he wasn't sure himself.

"Color me surprised, Leon."

"Hey, it's not like I've always been able to do that. But you know how slow my mana regenerates. It'll take me two months before I'm able to use that skill again."

Reina let out an annoyed sigh and noticed that Donna had done the same. The two women stood protectively in front of Leon. Reina conjured a pair of ice daggers and pointed them at Zuriel's throne, which sat on a raised dais, while Donna created a towering ice nail that floated in the air behind her.

"You're going to let us go now."

Another earthquake rocked the Coliseum and faint screams could be heard coming from the nearby hallways. Reina had an idea of what was causing the screams, and if she was right, and Zuriel didn't let them go... Reina was afraid that none of the angels would survive.

"Right. Now."

"Are you giving me an order?" Zuriel snidely asked.

Yet another earthquake shook the building as the screams grew even louder.

"No, I'm trying to save your people!" she yelled.

"What could we possibly need you to save us from?"

"Me... Most likely." A power-laden voice echoed from the tunnel behind Zuriel's dais. **"A fruitless effort, but one you should thank her for, nonetheless."**

Reina's eyes widened as the angels nearest to the tunnel dissolved into a black mist that was sucked into the tunnel... Save for Zuriel who stood up and spun around with his spear in his hand to face the incoming threat.

"You think that toothpick is going to save you?"

Zuriel was driven to his knees by the malice and power in the voice. Even though she was looking at his back, Reina could see his hands shaking, his legs trembling, and his chest heaving with unneeded breath.

This was what she'd hoped to avoid.

As the sound of scales moving across stone filled the arena, more and more angels were dissolved where they stood. Even the angels that wisely tried to flee the scene soon found themselves faced with a problem. The faster they tried to escape, the more that simply flashed away, the faster they dissolved.

Torga wasn't just doing this to scare them, Reina realized.

He was set on exterminating them all.

"By all means, run, flee, tell your friends, your family of what's happening here. And pray that whatever god you worship has plenty of mercy to go around. Because you'll find none here."

Reina saw the glowing orange eyes of the man she loved appear in the tunnel behind Zuriel's throne, but... There was something different about them. They weren't filled with the love, the kindness she'd come to expect from him.

There was only anger in those eyes.

The eyes vanished from sight, only to reappear an instant later directly in front of Reina.

Torga appeared before Reina in all his glory: his body, no longer the flesh and blood she'd grown used to seeing—to touching. Torga's body was a maelstrom of emerald light. A solid mass of darkness spun wildly where his stomach should be.

Reina's ears itched at the sound caused by the black hole as it devoured the air around them. And then there were his eyes: twin pools of orange and red. Torga's eyes exuded more power than Reina had ever felt, and it was at that moment that she realized how the judges could mistake Torga for an elder god.

However, in the blink of an eye that all changed and Torga looked as he always had.

He looked human again.

He reached out and gently cupped her chin, presumably to inspect the bruise on her face. "Are you hurt anywhere else?"

"A few scrapes and bruises. Nothing to be concerned about."

"I see."

Torga held out his hand and the still motionless Zuriel was dragged towards him, as if he'd been grabbed by invisible hands, to kneel at Reina's feet. He kicked, clawed, and stuck his spear into the ground to keep from being pulled.

Torga was unmoved by his efforts.

Zuriel threw all of his weight against his spear in his attempt to stop himself from being dragged across the ground.

And it worked—for a moment.

And then the spear snapped, and he had nothing left to hold onto.

Torga caught him with one hand and held him off the ground by his robe. "Did he give you those 'scrapes and bruises'?"

"N—"

"Yes, and he would have killed all of us had you not shown up," Donna interrupted. She left the exhausted Leon's side and went to stand by Reina.

"Leon?" Torga greeted him with a nod of his head.

"Yo," Leon mumbled lamely.

"I should've known you wouldn't die. Bed bugs are a stubborn bunch."

"Y—You—You're the devourer," Zuriel whispered reverently. He refused to look at Torga, choosing instead to keep his head down and his eyes pointed towards the Coliseum's floor.

"Did I give you permission to speak?"

"N—No?"

"I didn't think so."

"It—It all makes sense now. The reason I couldn't see her—was that you were protecting her."

"Her?"

"The bitch!" Zuriel hissed through clenched teeth.

Zuriel was suddenly driven into the dirt by a *visible* wave of gravity that descended upon his body. His perfect skin sagged, his robes tore, and Reina could hear his bones break from several feet away.

"S—Sorry, I meant Donna. The fallen angel. I haven't been able to see her for some time now, so I thought the bi—Donna had finally died," Zuriel quickly explained. The pressure on his body vanished and he sighed in relief as his wounds began to stitch themselves back together.

"Donna?"

"He's an old stalker of Donna's," Reina said without taking her eyes off of Zuriel.

"Ah, I see."

Zuriel's, Reina's, Donna's, and Leon's bodies slowly floated into the air.

Reina watched as Torga waved his hand and a visible wave of pressure left his body and passed through the wall of the Coliseum.

The wall collapsed in on itself, crushed under the intense force of gravity that Torga exerted upon it.

The four of them were forced to follow Torga as he levitated out of the hole he'd created and floated high above the silver city.

They came to a stop when they were approximately a mile above it, and it was there that Reina finally got to see were she'd been. The Coliseum they'd been trapped in was inside the grounds of one of the three castles that overlooked the silver city.

Though she didn't recognize any of the symbols, the castle in question had a symbol that depicted a pair of white bird's wings on a black background. The castle and the Coliseum both followed this color scheme, with the majority of buildings built out of a kind of stone that exuded white light. The white stones were accented by lines of black metal that traced out lines and gave the buildings depth.

"This is your old home, Donna?"

"Yeah," she sighed.

"If you were given the choice between sparing it or destroying it, which would you choose?"

"Pardon?"

"If you were in my position, would you destroy it or show mercy?"

Reina's eyes widened as Donna actually *seemed* to be giving his question some thought.

"Donna, you can't seriously be considering this!? Think of all the innocent people down there!"

"You're too naive, Reina. There are no *innocent* people down there. There haven't been since Father died."

"Blasphemy—"

"Shut it." Torga grabbed Zuriel's hair and wrenched his head back so he could look Zuriel in the eye. "I use this threat a lot, but for you I might actually do it, so I would advise you to keep your mouth shut before I rip your tongue out and make you taste your own ass." He shoved Zuriel's head forward, forcing him to look straight down.

"Keep telling yourself that, Zuriel. There's a reason no one in silver city has seen him for millennia." Donna added.

"So, Nietzsche was right?" Torga asked aloud.

"Oh no, Father was very much alive while you two were still human. It's only been within the last thousand years or so that news of Father's death spread to even me."

"Oh, it doesn't matter to me whether he was or not. I lost all of my faith when Reina died. To my knowledge, Reina was still a devout follower though."

Reina felt all eyes on her as she tried to process that *that* God was dead and had been dead since before she was ever born. Logically, something like this shouldn't surprise her since—well, you know—she was kind of *married* to a living god. But it hurt to find out something she'd believed in for the whole of her human life was a lie. Then something registered in her mind.

"Wait, you said he was alive when we were human, but he's been dead for a thousand years. Then, does that mean—"

"That you were dead for over a thousand years?" Donna said. "Yeah, I thought you two knew that."

"How the hell were we supposed to know that?" Torga asked her with an incredulous look on his face.

Donna opened her mouth to reply, then hesitated. "You know what, I guess there is no way you could have known that. Sorry."

Torga let out a long sigh. "Very well, I've decided."

"On what?" Donna asked.

"Their sentence, of course."

Torga held out one hand, palm down, and grabbed Zuriel by the back of his neck with his other hand and held him in the air in front of him. "There is only one judgment that fits your crime, bird-boy." A wave of green light flowed over Torga's body, instantly transforming him back into that monstrous Naga Reina had seen earlier.

Zuriel wailed in pain as his body was destroyed atom by atom from the bottom of his feet to the hair on his head, while the castle that used to be the angel's home was crushed beneath a visible gravity fall that flattened it brick by brick.

The entire process took less than ten seconds, though it probably felt like an eternity to Zuriel, whose remains drifted through the air for a moment before being sucked into Torga's body.

"What are we going to do about them?" Reina heard Leon ask from behind her.

She looked over her shoulder and saw thousands of angels floating in their wake. She tensed her body in preparation for the fight she thought sure to come—but instead, the angels looked scared.

And Reina realized why.

Their home had been destroyed. None of these angels had a thing to do with their capture, or their torment at the hands of Zuriel, and yet their lives had been ruined.

"Ah, I almost forgot about my messengers."

Torga floated over and forced them to look at him.

"I suppose I should tell you why your castle is gone and what is about to happen. Do you see that beautiful elf over there?" he asked, pointing over his shoulder at Reina.

"That is Reina; she's my wife. Your leader, or one of your higher-ups I suppose, thought it would be a good idea to kidnap her and throw her into the arena to fight for her life.

"That wasn't very wise of him." Torga's body began to increase in size until he dwarfed all of them.

"I have a job for you, angels. It's a simple job, and I'm sure you won't turn it down. I want all of you to carry the information of what has happened here as far as your little wings will carry you. I want every god, angel, demon, titan, or whatever else exists out there to know this: Harm one hair on her head and you'll suffer the consequences.

"I clawed, I killed, and I fought to obtain my current power and now—Now I'm going to put it *all* to use. Come for her, I'll kill you. Injure her, I'll butcher everything you've ever held dear, and then kill you... And should you *somehow* manage to kill her?

"All of Yggdrasil will pay the price for your mistake."

"Now, who wants to go and tell the judges what I've done, eh?" Torga asked, a hint of amusement in his voice. "And I'd appreciate it if you'd inform them that I had no intention of running." Torga lifted his hand and snapped his fingers— Reina, Donna, Leon, and Torga himself all vanished in flashes of green light.

~ ~ ~

They reappeared outside of an inn Torga had passed earlier in the day. As soon as they landed, and he was sure that they were all safe, Torga returned to his human form and dropped to his knees.

He exhaled a shaky breath and grabbed hold of Reina's legs, burying his face in her outer thigh. "Thank God you're okay," he sighed.

"Come on, Leon. Let's give them some privacy."

"But it's just getting good—"

"Leon, I'm going to rent a room right now, and if you're not there with me, I'm going to grab the closest person and take them up there instead."

"I'm on the way," he quickly replied and dashed after her, leaving Reina and Torga alone.

"I'm sorry I wasn't there to protect you. I'm sorry you were dragged into this. I'm sorry—"

"Hey," Reyna said, interrupting Torga's string of apologies. "You can apologize to me later. Right now, how about we go get one of those rooms and get off the street?"

Torga showed her a halfhearted smile and nodded his head. "All right, whatever you want to do."

Reina took him by the hand and led him inside the inn.

~ ~ ~

The next morning, I watched as Reina zipped up her skintight black bodysuit and pulled her hair into a tight ponytail. I was lying in the same position I'd been in since before she fell asleep and I was reluctant to get up.

"Are you going to stay in bed all day?" she asked.

"Don't see why not. The view here is fantastic."

Reina smiled and rolled her eyes. "While I appreciate the compliment, we really do have to get going."

"What's the rush?"

"Aside from Donna and Leon waiting for us downstairs? I want to leave this place before the judges come for you."

"Reina… I can't leave."

"No, you couldn't leave. You can leave now, and you're going to leave with me and we're going to—"

I sat up and took her hand in mine. I brought it to my lips and placed a gentle kiss on the back of her knuckles. "I wish I could. If I leave now, they're going to use that as an excuse to come for me and possibly you too."

"Are you the same person who threatened the entire universe yesterday?" she asked, only half joking.

"No, that was Torga or Orochi. However, you want to pronounce my name. Right now, I'm Albert. Right now…" I tugged on her arm until she stood up and walked over to stand in front of me. I wrapped my arms around her hips and placed my head on her stomach. "I just want to spend time with my beautiful wife and not think about what happens when I step foot out that door."

Reina moved forward, placing her knees on either side of my waist, then sitting down on my lap. She wrapped her arms around my neck and hugged me. We both knew what would happen when we left this room, and neither of us was ready for it.

~ ~ ~

"Can I see it?"

"I mean, sure, but you can at least give me ten minutes to recuperate." Reina slapped me across the chest and laughed.

"I'm serious, I want to see what you look like—what you *really* look like."

"You sure?"

"Yeah, I'm sure."

I furrowed my eyebrows in concentration and half a second later my physical body exploded into emerald light and was replaced with light green mist.

I'd seen myself enough to know what she was seeing now: My eyes had become miniature stars that floated within the emerald light, and my stomach returned to its natural state. My body had naturally taken the form of a large serpent that floated just above the floor.

Reina jumped back in surprise and almost fell over a chair in her haste to get away from the creature standing in front of her. She backed up until she was firmly against the wall on the far side of the room and stared at me.

"You okay?"

Her body shook from the shock of seeing my body explode and then reform into a completely different creature, one that looked... well, like me.

"This is what I naturally look like."

Reina nervously glanced around the room until she spotted an empty gold and silver candlestick on a nearby table. She slowly reached over and picked it up by the base, then threw it at me.

The candlestick phased through the front of my chest but never came out the other side.

"Was that really necessary?"

"S—sorry. I'm just freaking out a little right now. Give me a minute."

"Want me to turn back?"

"No, I'm f—fine."

She slowly stepped away from the wall and nervously swallowed. Her eyes moved up and down my body several times. With each pass, she grew more confident until she was able to forcefully calm herself down.

"Does that hurt?" She motioned to the slowly rotating black hole where my stomach was supposed to be.

"No."

"Can I?" She stepped closer and reached for me.

"You should probably avoid touching my stomach. But sure, I don't mind."

She slowly extended her arm until her hand was just above my head and waited for my approval.

"I'm not going to bite you," I joked.

"You're a giant mist-snake," she said dryly.

I flicked my tongue, which was composed of slightly darker green mist. My tongue brushed against her cheek and I had to stop myself from laughing at the surprised squeak she made.

She gradually lowered her hand until it brushed against my "head," then she quickly jerked her hand back.

"Everything all right?"

"It's cold. Not unpleasant or painful, just cold. Can I—"

I nodded my head.

She slowly pushed her fingers into the mist.

"It's amazing. The outer edge of the mist feels like ice cold water, but beyond that there's an intense heat that warms my hand immediately."

She also noticed the "current" that ran throughout my body. Like the waves of an ocean, the outer edge of the mist pulled in one direction while the inside pulled in another. This caused my body to constantly undulate in a way that Reina said she found mesmerizing.

She slowly moved her hand from side to side and watched as my body rippled and moved in response to her touch.

"Having fun?"

She jerked her hand away and turned a bright shade of red.

"Sorry."

"Don't apologize. I like it when you touch me."

Her face turned a slightly darker shade of red and she stepped away from me. She turned to face the door, took a deep calming breath, and said in a slightly higher tone than normal, "Thank you for that."

All I could do was laugh. A ripple of light passed over my body and a few seconds later, I was back in my human form.

~ ~ ~

They say all things must eventually come to an end. And a knock on the door was what brought an end to our little honeymoon.

I opened the door and found myself almost nose to nose with the blue judge. He was standing in the hallway of the little inn, and a cursory glance told me that he was alone.

"I allowed you this moment because of everything that you've been through and because it was our negligence that allowed Zuriel's misdeeds to continue. But it's time for you to come with me. I trust that you will not give me a hard time?"

"Just—let me have a minute, okay?"

"I'll give you five. Don't waste them."

I nodded my head and shut the door. Turning around, I found myself almost knocked on my ass by the silver-haired missile that slammed into my chest. I wrapped my arms around her and held on as tightly as I could.

If we had five more minutes together, then I was gonna make them count.

I pulled her face up to mine and kissed her.

When she needed to breathe, I pulled her into another hug and held on.

"Promise me something," I whispered into her ear.

"Anything."

"Find Ayla and Findral. Make sure they're okay and let them help you, okay?"

"Okay."

"I need to hear the words."

"I promise."

I kissed her again and held on like she was the only thing that mattered in my world, because at that moment she was.

I was a husband.

I was a father.

I was the devourer of worlds.

But in that moment, Reina held infinitely more power than I ever would.

Another knock at the door brought my attention back to the present. I placed a kiss on her forehead and then I reluctantly stepped away from her.

At first, she clung tightly to my tunic, but as I stepped away her grip loosened until it finally came undone.

I backed towards the door, never once breaking eye contact with her because I felt that as soon as I did, she would disappear, and I'd never see her again. Just before I reached the door, I remembered something.

I smiled at her and brought my index finger to my lips.

At first, she looked confused, but then her eyes widened comically as my body flashed emerald green. When the light cleared, there was a perfect copy of me standing beside me. Our hearts and minds were perfectly in sync, and it instinctively knew what to do.

It shifted its body into a bracelet that clattered to the floor. The bracelet was solid green, the same color as my scales, and was in the shape of a snake eating its own tail.

I picked it up from the floor, and quickly walked over and fastened it around her wrist.

"This guy will let me know if you're ever in any danger and will act to protect you in case any gods or angels decide to ignore my warning. Never take it off," I cautioned her.

She nodded her head, clearly understanding that I didn't want the judge to know what I'd just given her.

Another series of knocks on the door brought our reunion to an end and I opened the door.

EPILOGUE

TORGA STOOD ON A RAISED PLATFORM IN THE middle of a darkened room. His body was translucent and tinted blue, a product of the device being used to remotely watch him. Dark metal chains hung off his body, preventing him from using any of his skills and making him feel as weak as a mortal man.

"We let you have your freedom, and what did you do?" the blue being asked.

"I did what I had to. My family had been threatened, and I cannot abide that."

"You idiot. If you'd come to us, told us of what was happening, we could have had the entire thing shut down and Zuriel imprisoned for what he'd done. But with his death, you've effectively made an enemy out of every angel. You think they won't come for her?

"I want them to try," Torga laughed. "I meant what I said, judges. If she is hurt, directly or indirectly by any god in some halfcocked revenge plan against me… I'll bring all of Yggdrasil down with me. I will die at the end; I know that much. But I will not go quietly into that abyss. I swear to you, now, that I will have company— and plenty of it."

The blue being groaned. "You're not making this easy for us. How are we supposed to believe that you're not Orochi when you go in and do crap like this?"

Torga shrugged. "Maybe you should stop worrying about if I'm Orochi and start worrying about what Orochi is up to. After all, while you've been focused on me, there's no telling what he's been doing."

The blue being waved his hand and Torga vanished, the enchantment they'd been using to watch him powering down before finally winking off and casting the room into darkness.

"He has a point," the green being mumbled. "We would've gotten a lot more done tracking down leads of Orochi's misdeeds than we would've tracking down Torga. After all, it's not like Torga knew we were looking for him."

"Be that as it may," the red being spoke up. Like the rest of them, her voice sounded tired. "It doesn't change the fact that we had to grab him when we did. You heard what Pthelios said. If we didn't grab him before he left Asgard we'd never see him again. Is that not correct?" she asked, motioning for the orange being to back her up.

"… Yes."

"See," she stated, as if that were all the evidence she'd needed.

"I don't know," the gold being sighed. "Maybe we should go back and review the evidence, call in that witness again, and go over their testimony one more time."

"I like that idea," the green being said, nodding his head emphatically. "Bring them back in here and let's go through what we know one more time."

A round of murmured yeses and nods of agreement traveled through the room. The blue being nodded his head and motioned for one of their court assistants to find the witness.

Twenty minutes later, the door to the courtroom opened and the assistant led someone in. The woman that entered was clearly an elf of some kind. She had skin tanned from many years in the sun, and her short silver hair swayed with each step she took.

She looked at each judge in turn, before bowing her head.

"This one greets the judges."

"Let's skip the pleasantries and get down to why you're here, Freja. Tell us of what you know about the being known as Torga one more time."

Freja bowed her head, her hair splaying to either side of her neck to reveal a nearly transparent tattoo in the shape of a serpent with eight heads and eight tails.

"Gladly," she said, and then began recounting her meeting with Torga.

A Snake's Rise

Books, Mailing List, and Reviews

If you enjoyed reading about Torga and the rest of the gang in *A Snake's Rise* and want to stay in the loop about the latest book releases, awesome promotional deals, and upcoming book giveaways be sure to subscribe to our email list at:

www.ShadowAlleyPress.com

Word-of-mouth and book reviews are crazy helpful for the success of any writer. If you *really* enjoyed reading *A Snake's Rise*, please consider leaving a short, honest review—just a couple of lines about your overall reading experience. Thank you in advance!

About the Author

Hello, everyone. My name is Kenneth Arant and I like to pretend I'm a writer in my spare time. A bit about myself: I'm a retired martial artist with fourteen years' experience, six of which I used to teach others how to not knock themselves out with a pair of nunchucks.

Currently, I'm a full-time night owl with a minor caffeine addiction and a penchant for letting my imagination run wild. My dream is to write awesome books that people will enjoy for years to come.

BOOKS FROM SHADOW ALLEY PRESS

If you enjoyed *A Snake's Rise*, you might also enjoy other awesome stories from Shadow Alley Press, such as Viridian Gate Online, Rogue Dungeon, the Yancy Lazarus Series, School of Swords and Serpents, or the Jubal Van Zandt Series. You can find all of our books listed at www.ShadowAlleyPress.com.

James A. Hunter

Viridian Gate Online: Cataclysm (Book 1)
Viridian Gate Online: Crimson Alliance (Book 2)
Viridian Gate Online: The Jade Lord (Book 3)
Viridian Gate Online: The Imperial Legion (Book 4)
Viridian Gate Online: The Lich Priest (Book 5)
Viridian Gate Online: Doom Forge (Book 6)
Viridian Gate Online: Darkling Siege (Book 7)

VGO: The Artificer (Imperial Initiative)

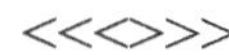

Kenneth Arant

VGO: Nomad Soul (Illusionist 1)
VGO: Dead Man's Tide (Illusionist 2)
VGO: Inquisitor's Foil (The Illusionist 3)

VGO: Firebrand (Firebrand Series 1)
VGO: Embers of Rebellion (Firebrand Series 2)
VGO: Path of the Blood Phoenix (Firebrand Series 3)

VGO: Vindication (The Alchemic Weaponeer 1)
VGO: Absolution (The Alchemic Weaponeer 2)
VGO: Insurrection (The Alchemic Weaponeer 3)

Strange Magic: Yancy Lazarus Episode One
Cold Hearted: Yancy Lazarus Episode Two
Flashback: Siren Song (Episode 2.5)
Wendigo Rising: Yancy Lazarus Episode Three
Flashback: The Morrigan (Episode 3.5)
Savage Prophet: Yancy Lazarus Episode Four
Brimstone Blues: Yancy Lazarus Episode Five
Red Reckoning: Yancy Lazarus Episode Six

MudMan: A Lazarus World Novel

Two Faced: Legend of the Treesinger Book 1
Soul Game: Legend of the Treesinger Book 2

Rogue Dungeon: Rogue Dungeon Series Book 1
Civil War: Rogue Dungeon Series Book 2

A Snake's Rise

Troll Nation: Rogue Dungeon Series Book 3
Rogue Evolution: Rogue Dungeon Series Book 4
Dungeon Duel: Rogue Dungeon Series Book 5

eden Hudson

Revenge of the Bloodslinger: A Jubal Van Zandt Novel
Beautiful Corpse: A Jubal Van Zandt Novel
Soul Jar: A Jubal Van Zandt Novel
Garden of Time: A Jubal Van Zandt Novel
Wasteside: A Jubal Van Zandt Novel

Darkening Skies: Path of the Thunderbird 1
Stone Soul: Path of the Thunderbird 2
Demon Beast: Path of the Thunderbird 3

Death Cultivator Book 1
Death Cultivator Book 2

Aaron Ritchey

Armageddon Girls: The Juniper Wars 1
Machine-Gun Girls: The Juniper Wars 2
Inferno Girls: The Juniper Wars 3
Storm Girls: The Juniper Wars 4
War Girls: The Juniper Wars 5

Sages of the Underpass: Battle Artists Book 1

Kenneth Arant

Gage Lee

Hollow Core: School of Swords and Serpents 1
Eclipse Core: School of Swords and Serpents 2
Chaos Core: School of Swords and Serpents 3
Burning Core: School of Swords and Serpents 4
Infinite Core: Schools of Swords and Serpents 5
Eternal Core: Schools of Swords and Serpents 6

Shadowbound: Ghostlight Academy Book 1

J.D. Astra

Zero.Hero Book 1
Zero.Hero Book 2

Foundations: Bastion Academy Book 1
Malware: Bastion Academy Book 2

Morgan Cole

Inheritance: The Last Enclave Book 1
Redemption: The Last Enclave Book 2

Kenneth Arant

A Snake's Life: A Snake's Life Book 1
A Snake's Path: A Snake's Life Book 2
A Snake's Rise: A Snake's Life Book 3

A Snake's Rise

Mark Stallings

The Elements: Silver Coin Saga Book 1

Travis Heermann

Tokyo Blood Magic: Shinjuku Shadows Book 1
Tokyo Monster Mash: Shinjuku Shadows Book 2

David Sanchez-Ponton

Dungeon Heart: The Singing Mountain

Nathan Ameye

Black Dawn: Fae Nexus Book 1

D.J. Bodden

The Starborn Heir: Zack Lancestrom Book 1

BOOKS FROM BLACK FORGE

Aaron Crash

War God's Mantle: Ascension (Book 1)
War God's Mantle: Descent (Book 2)
War God's Mantle: Underworld (Book 3)

Denver Fury: American Dragons Book 1
Cheyenne Magic: American Dragons Book 2
Montana Firestorm: American Dragons Book 3
Texas Showdown: American Dragons Book 4
California Imperium: American Dragons Book 5
Dodge City Knights: American Dragons Book 6
Leadville Crucible: American Dragons Book 7
Alamosa Arena: American Dragons Book 8
Alaska Kingdom: American Dragons Book 9
Wyoming Dynasty: American Dragons Book 10

Barbarian Outcast: Princesses of the Ironbound 1
Barbarian Assassin: Princesses of the Ironbound 2
Barbarian Alchemist: Princesses of the Ironbound 3
Barbarian Gladiator: Princesses of the Ironbound 4

A Snake's Rise

Raider Annihilation: Son of Fire Book 1
Kraken Killjoy: Son of Fire Book 2

Boss Build: Creature Girl Creations Book 1
Master Build: Creature Girl Creations Book 2
God Build: Creature Girl Creations Book 3

Time Jacker Book 1

Robot Bangarang: Full Frontal Galaxy 1
Space Dragon Boogaloo: Full Frontal Galaxy 2

Nick Harrow

Dungeon Bringer 1
Dungeon Bringer 2
Dungeon Bringer 3

Witch King 1
Witch King 2
Witch King 3

Valhalla Virus: Ragnarok Rebels Book 1

* 9 7 8 1 9 5 6 5 8 3 1 4 4 *